# A Cool Billion

# A Cool Billion

Michael C. Perkins

Co-author of the bestselling *The Internet Bubble*

and Celia Núñez

iUniverse.com, Inc.

San Jose New York Lincoln Shanghai

# A Cool Billion



Published by iUniverse.com, Inc.

For information address:
iUniverse.com, Inc.
620 North 48th Street, Suite 201
Lincoln, NE 68504-3467
www.iUniverse.com

ISBN: 0-595-09734-0

Printed in the United States of America

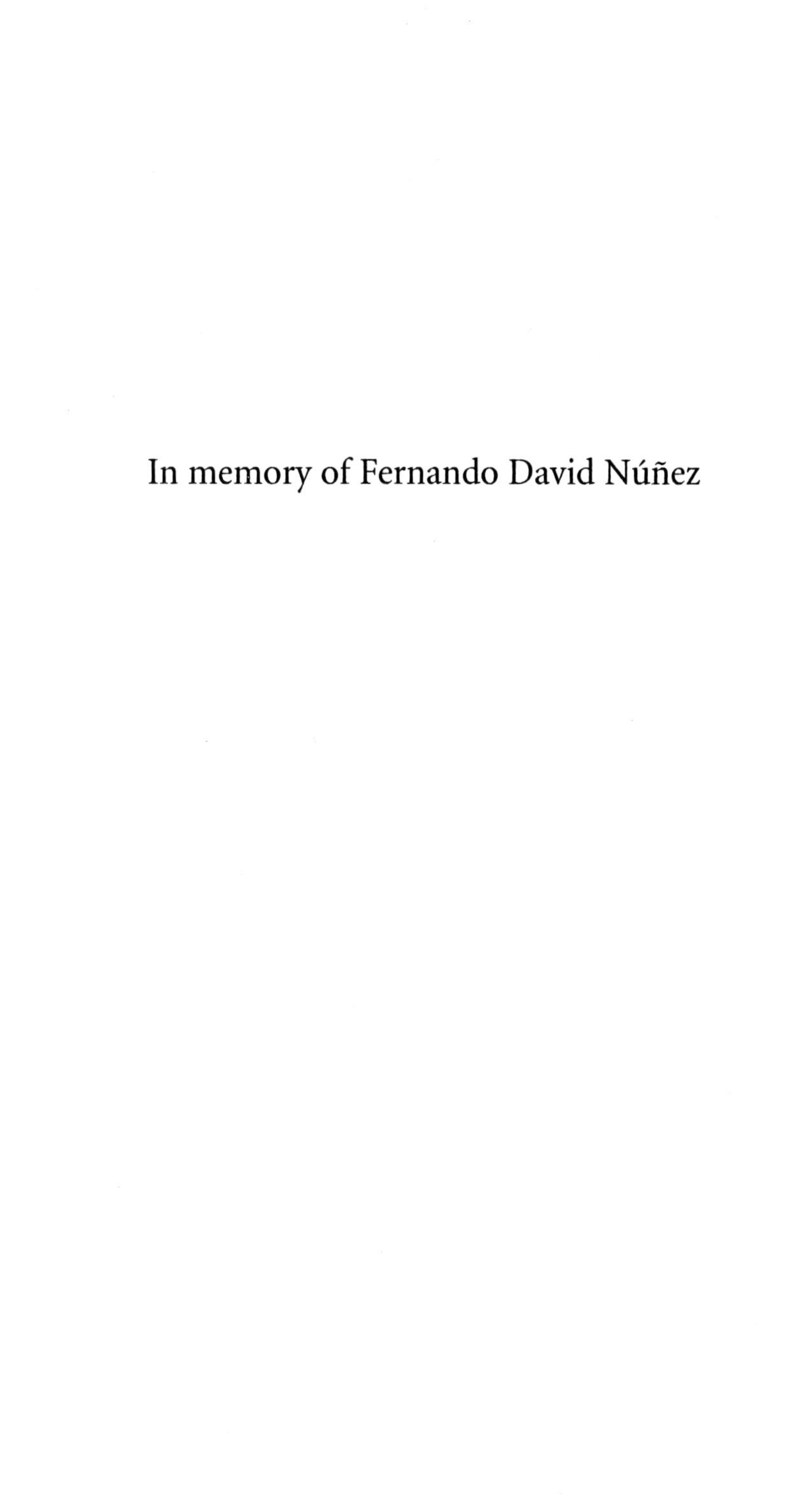

In memory of Fernando David Núñez

# ACKNOWLEDGMENTS

The authors would like to thank the following people for the information, advice, and help they so generously gave us.

Inspector Tony Camilleri, of the San Francisco Police Department's homicide detail, explained the basics of a homicide investigation to us and showed us a "typical" homicide inspector's office. (Note to readers: As Inspector Camilleri will no doubt be the first to notice, we've taken literary license with the information he gave us. This book is not a police procedural.)

Peter G. Neumann, Principal Scientist in the Computer Science Laboratory of SRI International and Moderator of the Internet Risks Forum, discussed hacking and computer security with us.

Bob Nahum, an avid surfer, provided insight on the sport and steered us to the best surfing sites in Santa Cruz.

Chuck Finney, Deputy District Attorney, San Mateo County, California, and host of the syndicated radio show "Your Legal Rights" on PBS station KALW 91.7 FM, advised on matters of criminal law and procedure.

Nina Davis, Elaine Migliore, Cheryl Schroder, and Hildreth Willson all read early drafts of the novel and provided valuable feedback.

Cherie Schaller, Kay Lowell, and Ann Inglis pitched in with practical favors, making it possible for CN to keep writing during a difficult stretch.

On a personal note, CN wishes to express her deep gratitude to the following individuals: Frank Hanley, Marilyn Irovando, Lori Johnson, Phil Moore, Asunta Pacheco-Kennedy, Stephanie So, Cathy Stone, James Stump, Adel Younoszai, and the caring members of the UCSF PICU staff.

Finally, the authors are forever indebted to their spouses, Georganne and Ray, for their unconditional love, support and patience.

This book is a work of fiction, and therefore names, characters, and incidents are products of the authors' imaginations. Any resemblance to actual persons, living or dead, or actual events, is entirely coincidental.

# Prologue

The man looked at what he'd just written and smiled. It was a brilliant piece of programming, and he knew it. Better than that, soon a lot of people would know it. With this last piece of code, he was through tweaking his software program. It was far enough along now to start showing to the money men. His first meeting with a venture capitalist was in two days, and he could hardly wait. He knew what a technological leap forward his program represented. He'd get the funding with no problem, and in less than a year, he'd be worth millions. Not bad for a twenty-three-year-old hacker.

He turned off the computers in his office, packed up his knapsack, and flipped off the lights. He was in such a good mood, he decided to skip the elevator and take the stairs instead. He jumped them three at a time, stopping to swing off the handrails wherever the stairway curved. The stairwell resounded with the rhythmic thumping of his heavy steps.

He burst out of the building into the balmy air. It was a short walk to where he'd parked his bike several hours earlier. There were a couple of streetlights out, so he had to fumble with his lock for a couple of minutes before he was able to undo it.

Finally, the lock clicked open, and he removed the chain that secured his bike to the stand.

The computer genius rode through the parking lot at a relaxed pace, entertaining himself with visions of his future. Once he had funding, and a name for his company, he'd tell his parents what he'd been working on these past couple of years. He'd considered talking to them about it earlier, but neither of them was very technical. They wouldn't have understood the significance of what he was doing. They couldn't fully understand it even now, but they would know what it meant to be president of your own company, and that was all that mattered.

The young man exited the parking lot and pedaled leisurely down the road. At this hour of the night, the street was empty, except for a green town car parked next to the curb. The hacker barely noticed it, and skirted around the long vehicle automatically, still daydreaming of the company he would build.

The future entrepreneur was so preoccupied with his thoughts, in fact, that he paid no attention to the car's engine starting up behind him. The driver of the car, on the other hand, was completely focused on the cyclist in front of him. He put the car in gear and approached the man on the bike, slowly closing the gap between them. A few moments passed as the driver waited to make sure the timing was right. Then suddenly he floored the accelerator as he swerved the car to the right, making sure to hit his victim with full force.

The hacker prodigy never saw it coming. He was dead before he hit the ground.

No one in the surrounding area saw the car. But a few other late-night programmers heard the noise. They peered out their windows, and spotted their colleague lying still on the ground, several feet away from his bicycle. The people who ran down the stairs arrived before those who took the elevators, but it didn't matter. Someone called the police.

A year passed, and the locals began to forget about the tragedy that had claimed one of their own. The posters around town announcing the $10,000 reward for information were tattered and mud-specked. And the police now had other priorities.

Another year passed. All the posters were gone now, and even the young man's parents, who had thought they would never survive the loss, were starting to recover. Life was hard for them—dull, gray, and full of aching memories—but one day they managed to notice that they were still alive. It was time to move on, to accept what the police had said long ago: only a lucky break would lead them to their son's killer.

# Chapter One

It'd better happen this week.

That's the first thought that pops into my head as I open my eyes. I've got half an hour until the alarm sounds, but I'm ready to hop out of bed and race to work.

I'm not usually this energetic on Mondays. Today is different, though, because sometime this week—if all goes well—I'll get to interview Arthur Hays, an industry legend, and more importantly, the CEO of a brand-new Internet company. Rumor has it that Hays plans to leverage his reputation as a technical genius to take his little startup public and cash in big. The company is so hot that the stock price is expected to quadruple on the first day, maybe even set a record. But despite the hype swirling around Hays Software, Hays himself has been so secretive about his company's one and only product that no one in the media has been able to write much about it. Until now.

The bed sheets start to move. I look over, and watch Michelle slowly join the waking world, admiring for the thousandth time the freckles on her cheeks, the red and gold of her hair, and the curves of her body under the blanket. Two minutes later I'm looking into the world's most perfect green eyes.

"Did the alarm ring?" she asks, moving closer. I put my arms around her. "Not yet, I just couldn't sleep," I say.

"That Hays thing, right?"

"Yeah, I've got a tentative appointment for this week. I'm hoping to firm it up today. If I can get this interview in on time, Mitch plans to make it the cover story for the September issue. And I want that cover."

"Another coup for Steven Cavanaugh," she says, kissing me. "Did I tell you that Arthur Hays was the featured speaker at our annual meeting last month?"

"Any juicy tidbits you'd like to share?" I ask in my most seductive voice, gently caressing her shoulders.

But Michelle knows this ploy too well.

"I don't know a whole lot. I don't even know how much we've invested in his company," she says sleepily. "Besides, you know I can't divulge any information about the firm's business."

"You can't blame a guy for trying."

I pull Michelle closer and start kissing her neck. I figure if we're not going to discuss Arthur Hays' latest venture, maybe we can do something else.

"Umm," she sighs. "I wish we had more time. But I've got to get going."

She sits up, runs her hands through her hair, and yawns.

"I've got to give a presentation at the partners' meeting this morning," she explains. "I want to get to the office early so I can check a couple of details. The man himself is going to be there, and I want everything to be·perfect."

"The man" is Marcus Turner, as in Grimshaw, Turner & Willson, Silicon Valley's most prestigious venture capital firm. His name may be second in the list of partners, but in recent years, Turner has become the firm's real power broker. His unfailing instincts in picking and promoting Internet companies have made Turner the most powerful venture capitalist in Silicon Valley, maybe even in the whole venture business, and certainly the man to impress if you want to get ahead at Grimshaw Turner.

Michelle swings her legs over the side of the bed and is about to get up when I put an arm around her waist and pull her back down. She laughs and pushes me away, but not very hard. I go back to kissing her neck, and then start working my way down.

Michelle closes her eyes and smiles dreamily.

"I really don't have time for this," she says in a voice that suggests otherwise.

I stop what I'm doing and sit up.

"I understand," I say with mock resignation. "And I certainly don't want to adversely affect your career."

I toss the covers off me, get up from the bed and start walking away. I've gone about three feet when I feel a pillow bounce off my backside.

"Hey," Michelle says. "Get back here."

I can't help grinning as I walk slowly back to the bed, where I lie down next to Michelle. I prop myself up on my elbow so I can look into her eyes.

"I thought you were too busy," I say to her.

Michelle doesn't say a word. She gives me a long, slow kiss, and pulls me on top of her.

I love Mondays.

*Digital Business* has its offices on the top floor of a refurbished warehouse, not far from San Francisco's Mission district. Visitors to the magazine often comment on the irony of housing a cutting edge, high tech publication in an historic landmark. But I think that's precisely why Mitch, our publisher, chose this place—he likes to be contrary.

I drive hurriedly through the area's ever-busy streets, trying to make up for my late start this morning. Soon I'm pulling into the parking lot *Digital Business* shares with the brewery next door. I rush into the building, only to find both elevators already engaged. Instead of waiting, I opt for the stairs, and arrive at the fourth floor at the same time as the slow-moving lifts.

I'm walking down the hallway to my office when I hear someone call my name. I turn around to see Matt Appleby, a fellow senior editor, approaching me.

"You dog, you," he says to me slyly. "How do you always manage to swing these deals? Tina just told me all about it."

"Told you about what?" I ask, puzzled.

"That you get to train that gorgeous new staff writer Mitch just hired," he replies.

"What are you talking about?"

"Her name is Angela Madrigal, and she'll be helping you with your articles," he says with just a touch of jealousy in his voice. "Don't tell me you didn't even ask for this. You mean they just gave it to you?"

"There has to be some mistake," I say, "Mitch knows I work alone."

"You might feel differently after you get a look at her."

"I don't care what she looks like," I say, starting to feel angry. "I don't work with other writers."

"I do," Matt says wistfully as I walk past him down the hallway.

I backtrack past the main lobby towards Mitch's office, ready to have it out with my boss. Mitch may be a great publisher—*Digital Business*is never out late, and we've turned a profit almost since the beginning—but he does have a weakness for pretty women. Normally, I couldn't care less, but it's not my job to babysit his latest conquest.

I blow through the double oak doors that lead to Mitch's corner office.

"Is he in this week?" I ask Charlene, Mitch's overworked secretary.

"You're in luck," she replies without even bothering to look up from her paperwork.

When I walk into Mitch's office, he has the phone receiver in his hand and is about to dial. He puts the receiver down as soon as he sees the look on my face.

"What's the matter?" he asks with a concerned voice.

"What's this about me tutoring your new hire?" I practically shout.

"Oh, is that all," he says, relaxing.

"Look, Mitch, I've got a lot on my plate these days. I don't have time to show this kid the ropes. Have Matt do it. Or Liz. They're both good writers."

"Yes they are," Mitch says agreeably. "But they're not you. And Angela specifically wanted to work with you. She's quite familiar with your writing, and happens to think that yours are the best-researched articles in the field."

I open my mouth to tell Mitch that flattery will get him nowhere, but he beats me to the punch.

"Besides," he continues, "How many times have I heard you complain that no one helped you out when you were first starting?

And how you plan to mentor young writers once you're established? Well, for your information, you are now an established journalist. Go mentor."

Mitch's biggest drawback, and virtue, is his excellent memory. I consider his comments for a moment.

"You're right. Maybe it is time for me to live up to my grandiose ideals and take on a protégé," I say. "But Matt says this new hire is supposed to help me with my articles. That's not mentoring; that's collaboration, and I don't do that."

A few years ago, I got beat to a great story because I said too much to the wrong person, the sister of a writer at a competing magazine. Since then, I've developed the habit of keeping information to myself. And I have no intention of changing now.

"You know, Steven, journalists thrive on contacts, including other writers," Mitch says. "It could conceivably be to your advantage to work with her."

"I don't think so."

"Fine, do things your way. In any case, I wasn't expecting you to actually collaborate with her. Officially, she reports to Tina, who'll be overseeing her assignments. But I do want Angela to spend about six months helping you out and learning more about the industries we cover."

"But now is not a good time…."

"Just think of her as a free research assistant," Mitch says, interrupting.

I pause a moment to mull it over.

"Alright," I finally say, graciously accepting defeat. "But you owe me one."

"Agreed," he replies, picking up the phone. Our conversation is over.

Leaving Mitch's office, I pass Charlene again. There's a barely disguised smirk on her face, like she knows I just lost my argument with Mitch.

When I get to my office, I call Tina, our managing editor, and tell her to send the new writer to see me today at four o'clock. There's no reason to delay the inevitable. It's also occurred to me that Mitch was right about one thing: I could use a research assistant. I have some assignments coming up that require reading through lots of boring white papers. A perfect job for a novice writer.

Angela Madrigal shows up promptly at four. My door is open, as usual, but she knocks on it anyway.

"Come in; have a seat," I say, gesturing to a chair.

"Thanks," she says in an open, friendly voice.

She slides into one of the chairs in front of my desk. I can see right away why Matt is so enthusiastic about her. She's very pretty, about twenty-five, with large brown eyes, long black hair, and full lips. But while I can understand Matt's interest in her, she doesn't strike me as Mitch's type. It takes me a moment to figure out why: she's not the least bit coquettish. She's dressed simply in a pair of slacks, and when she crosses her long legs, she does so casually and unselfconsciously. If she's aware of how attractive she is, she doesn't let it show.

"Tina tells me you did grad work at Columbia, then landed at *The Chronicle*," I begin.

"That's right."

"How did you get interested in journalism?"

"I was an English major at Santa Clara University, and I started writing for the campus paper in my junior year."

She slides a sheet of paper across my desk.

"Here's my résumé; it gives more detail."

I take the paper and scan it quickly. Tina has already told me most of what's listed here, but one item catches my eye.

"I see you played soccer in college. All-American." I look up from the paper, curious. "Were you in the Olympics?"

"I tried out for the team, but I got cut," she says simply. "How about you, play any sports while you were in college?"

"Football."

She nods, waiting for me to continue.

"I was the starting tight end for Cal in my junior and senior years," I add.

"Two years; that's impressive," she says. "I'm surprised you didn't go pro."

"I busted up my knee at the end of my last season," I explain.

"That's too bad," she says sincerely.

I shrug my shoulders.

"So, what attracted you to *Digital Business*?" I ask.

"I wanted to work for a publication that covers the technology business in-depth, especially the Internet revolution," she says, giving the answer I expected. She hesitates a moment before adding, "And, I really like your writing. Especially that piece you did on spinning IPO stock. How did you find out that Tom Whitcomb was illegally distributing those SaveNet shares?"

"I followed him all over Silicon Valley for a week. Once I saw who he was meeting with, I had a pretty good idea of what he was up to. Then it was just a matter of finding enough sources to verify my suspicions."

Angela leans forward slightly in her chair.

"In your article you made it sound like Tom Whitcomb was just being a typical investment banker," she says. "Is that true? Do all the bankers set aside stock to give to people they want to do business with?"

"Not all of them," I answer. "But you can see how tempting it is: Banker X wants to do business with Company Y. So he offers one of the board members of the company some free shares in a hot little startup his bank is taking public. It costs the bank nothing—remember, they control the stock distribution. Pretty soon, of course, those shares will be worth a lot. The board member can cash in big, and all he had to do was recommend that Company Y work with Banker X."

"You scratch my back, and I'll scratch yours," she says. "Everybody's happy, except the rest of us who have to pay for our stock."

"Exactly."

I catch myself smiling at her, and decide to change the subject.

"I've got a full day," I say, looking at my watch. "So let's get to work."

"Right. What would you like me to help you with?"

I pull open a desk drawer and take out three files.

"Start with these. I need you to read through them, and then write up a one page overview of each one for me."

Angela takes the files from me and thumbs through them.

"Oh, white papers," she says, deflated.

"They're research for some articles I've got coming up."

"Is this all you want me to work on?" she asks plaintively, indicating the folders.

It's a lot to do, actually, but I know what she means. Nothing in those files is particularly appealing. She seems so disappointed, I almost feel guilty for foisting all my grunt work on her. So I decide to let her in on a piece of real journalism.

"I could use your help developing some interview questions for the CEO of a little company called Hays Software," I tell her. "I have a tentative interview set up for this Wednesday."

"Hays Software," Angela muses. "As in Arthur Hays?"

"The same," I say, impressed that she could make the connection. "What do you know about him?"

"I know he's famous in technical circles," she replies. "And that he did some really innovative work at PCI Labs back East. But I'm not sure exactly what he did."

"He developed one of the first industry standards for networking," I explain to her. "It's outdated now, but at the time it was quite a breakthrough."

"And now he's come up with another breakthrough?"

"Apparently," I say. "I'll try to get the exact story from Hays when I talk to him. It won't be easy though. I'm told he's pretty secretive about his new product. Which is one more reason why it's so important to be prepared."

I grab a couple of thick folders from the corner of my desk and hand them to Angela.

"Here's some background information on Arthur Hays and his new company," I explain. "I'd like you to go over it today, and then help me finish up my questions tomorrow morning. Can you meet at ten?"

"Sure," she says sweetly as she adds the two folders to her pile of material. "And then when do we interview Arthur Hays?"

We? That's not what I had in mind. She's lucky I'm even letting her in on this project.

"I'll be going by myself," I tell her. "I'd like you to get more experience before you start joining me for interviews."

Angela's smile falters.

"But just how am I going to get interview experience if I don't go to any interviews?" she asks.

I have to admit, that's exactly what I would have said. Nevertheless, the Hays story is too important to use as a training exercise.

I'm about to explain to Angela exactly why she can't come along when my phone rings. I pick it up and am greeted by Michelle's voice.

"Hey, we're at the ballpark," she says. "Aren't you coming?"

"The playoff game," I say. "I can't believe I forgot."

My daughter Chloe's softball team, the Belmont Broncos, is facing the Portola Valley Panthers in what's sure to be a tough championship game.

"Don't worry about it," Michelle says to me. "You can miss a game if you have to. I'll tell Chloe you had to work late."

"No way," I reply. "That's the same damn excuse my dad always gave me. Tell her I'm on my way."

I hang up the phone and pick up my briefcase.

"I'll see you tomorrow," I say to Angela as I leave my office.

But my new protégé tags along beside me.

"I know you're in a hurry so I'll make this quick," she says, jogging slightly to keep up with me. "It just seems to me that if I'm going to stay up all night reading this stuff, and then help you come up with interview questions, I should be able to participate in the interview."

I look at her in frustration, but I don't have time to argue.

"Okay," I concede. "Go ahead and come with me, but I'll ask the questions. These CEOs have to be handled a certain way. And this is too big an interview for me to take any chances."

"Sounds good to me," she says as I step into the elevator.

The doors close and I start my descent, half-regretting what I just agreed to. I knew I shouldn't have let Mitch talk me into this mentoring job. My new research assistant is already more trouble than she's worth.

# Chapter Two

I get to work earlier than usual today so I can prepare for the Hays meeting, and spend the bulk of my morning carefully reviewing my notes on his company and its product. I've just finished drafting some preliminary interview questions when Mitch strolls into my office.

"How's it going?" he asks me. "How's Angela working out?"

"She's not," I reply.

"Well, I'm sure you'll get it to work," he says glibly. "Here, I want you to look at this."

"What is it?" I ask, taking a slick white folder from him.

"It's the press kit for an e-commerce startup in Marin. They're called Yogi.com," he informs me. "I was playing golf at the Olympic Club the other day and I met their CEO. Smart guy, says that Yogi will be the Amazon of the sporting goods market."

"And what do you think?" I ask him.

"I'm not sure, which is why I want your input," Mitch says, already on his way out. "If they're viable I'm thinking of running a corporate profile on them for the August issue. Look their stuff over and give me your take on it this morning."

I groan inwardly; it's dicey profiling young companies nowadays. I know that only a few startups will survive the Darwinian shakeout that inevitably happens in the wake of an industrial boom. The vast majority of these dotcoms will implode and go out of business. The odds are heavily stacked against an Internet company like Yogi.

I open up the press kit anyway and spend about half an hour skimming through the material. When I'm done I have to admit that the company does look pretty good, not necessarily the also-ran I expected. As much as I hate writing corporate profiles, this is probably a startup *Digital Business* should cover, even if it's just to illustrate what's happening in the electronic commerce market. I call Mitch and tell him I'll get started on the piece, then toss the press kit on top of my "To Do" pile and get back to the Hays information.

A few minutes later my phone rings.

"Steven, how are you?" Leticia Morgan asks me when I pick up. Leticia is the PR director at Hays Software, and my one and only contact there. Fortunately, she's also a good friend.

"Not bad. What's up?"

"I have good news and bad news," she answers. "Ask for the good news first."

"Okay," I say. "What's the good news?"

"I just discovered the greatest CD," she says excitedly. "It's by this woman named Emily Remler. She's an astounding guitarist."

I almost laugh. It's just like Leticia to consider music good news.

"So when do I get to hear it?" I ask.

"How about Friday?" she replies. "Are you free for lunch? It's been a while, you know."

I've known Leticia since high school. One day at the beginning of my junior year, we happened to sit next to each other in U.S. History class. Back in those days I was something of a class clown; it was the only way to stay awake in my more boring classes. Leticia found my jokes funny, so I immediately decided that she was both perceptive and intelligent. We soon discovered a common interest in jazz, and have been sharing our favorite artists with each other for nearly twenty years now.

"Friday lunch sounds good," I say, replying to her question. "How about Cafe Borrone at 12:30?"

"It's a date."

"Now tell me the bad news."

"We have to reschedule tomorrow's interview," she tells me. "Arthur has an emergency board meeting."

"Damn. What are my options?"

"I can get you in next Thursday. Or he could meet with you today, if you're up to it. His 11:00 appointment canceled."

I look at my watch. If we leave right away, Angela and I can just make it.

"We'll be there today," I answer.

"We? Who else is coming?"

"One of the new staff writers is working with me. I'm showing her the ropes here at the magazine."

"In other words, you have a free research assistant," Leticia says.

This time I laugh out loud. Leticia knows me too well.

"Not exactly," I say. "She's hardly a pushover. In fact, you'll probably like her. She's almost as stubborn as you are."

"Thanks a lot," Leticia replies. "Maybe I should give this exclusive to a more deserving journalist."

"Don't you dare," I say.

"It would serve you right," she answers teasingly. "But don't worry, a promise is a promise. Just be sure to be nice to us in your article."

"You know me, I'll be fair. But if you've got any skeletons, be sure to hide them before I get there."

"Very funny. We haven't been around long enough to have skeletons, so I guess we're safe," she says. "Oh, one more thing. When's this story coming out?"

"September."

"That should be okay."

"Okay for what?" I ask.

"Keep this to yourself: we're in our quiet period."

"So, the rumors are true."

Leticia has just told me that Hays Software is going public, most likely before the end of this month. The "quiet period" is an SEC regulation: privately-held companies are required by law to refrain from certain types of publicity for about three months before an IPO to about one month afterward. The law keeps startups from using the media to inflate their stock value.

"Yes, the rumors are true," Leticia confirms. "And I don't need to tell you that we don't want to be mentioned in *Digital Business* any time soon."

"Don't worry; I'll keep my mouth shut. See you in an hour."

I hang up the phone, grab my files and stuff them in my brief-case. I'm putting on my jacket when Angela arrives for our ten o'clock meeting. Right away I notice how different she looks today—she's wearing a business suit and sporting high-heeled shoes. She seems uncomfortable in the outfit, and is less than sure-footed in the pumps, but she looks good nonetheless.

"Change of plans," I say to her. "The Hays meeting has been moved up. We're leaving now."

Angela is clearly flustered by this.

"But I'm supposed to go with Tina to a trade show at 11:30," she tells me.

"I understand if you can't make the interview," I say as I pick up my briefcase and head for the door.

"But I want to," she says, a supplicating tone in her voice.

I turn to look at her.

"Tell you what. I'll call Tina from my car and explain," I say, surprised by my own response.

"Great idea," she says happily. "Thanks."

We walk out of the office together and I close the door behind us.

"At least I'm wearing a suit today," Angela says.

"That's all you need," I tell her. "Everything else you can wing."

"I need you to check something for me," I say to Angela. We're in my car, heading south on 280 to Santa Clara County, the heart of Silicon Valley. "I keep my tape recorder in the glove compartment. Could you make sure the batteries are still working?"

Angela takes out the recorder and tests it.

"They're dead," she informs me.

"I've got some spare batteries somewhere in my briefcase."

Angela reaches over to the back seat and hauls my briefcase into the passenger seat with her. She unzips the main compartment and starts digging around inside it.

"I have some questions about Hays Software," she says, still rummaging through my stuff.

"Ask them."

"Okay," she begins. "The way I understand it, Hays Software has found a way to use artificial intelligence to create the most powerful Internet search engine ever. They call their product Cheetah, supposedly because it's fast and precise."

"Right," I say. "According to them, Cheetah can search through all the information on the Internet and retrieve specific data—useful stuff like the best stock prices, restaurant reviews, whatever. You could use it to research just about anything."

"Sounds like a big deal," she says, pulling a couple of batteries from my briefcase.

"It is," I tell her. "If Cheetah really works, then it will be the universal standard for a new breed of intelligent search agents. All the big hitters—AOL, Yahoo, and AT&T—will want to incorporate it into their software. It'll revolutionize the Internet."

"Finally, the search engine that could," Angela says jokingly. Then she gives me a skeptical look. "But doesn't every technology company claim their product will change the world?"

"They do," I agree. "The trick is to weed through their rhetoric and look for actual facts."

"That's just it," Angela replies. "I read through the press materials twice last night, and there's no technical data. They don't even tell us what programming language Cheetah is written in, which makes me wonder if the product is even real. There are a lot of Internet companies that sound great, but don't actually make anything."

"I know," I reply. "They're called concept plays. And if it were anyone but Arthur Hays, I'd be ready to write him and his company off. But Hays is a solid researcher. I'm willing to bet his product is real; I just need to get enough technical details to prove that to my readers."

Angela tosses the tape recorder into my briefcase.

"I hope you're right about Cheetah," she says. "Every time I use the Net for research, I spend hours tracking down the right Web sites. I'd love to have something that does the work for me."

"You and a hundred million other people."

# Chapter Three

Hays Software is located in a nondescript technology park in Cupertino. There are about ten buildings in the complex, and they all look the same. I drive among the sand-colored structures until I see one with a Hays Software sign outside. It's a typical Silicon Valley office building—a bland, three-story structure with a small lawn and a bit of foliage. The one distinguishing characteristic is the row of large glass windows in front. They run together so closely they form a glass wall. I can see the whole lobby from the car.

Angela and I get out of the car and walk through the front doors, which are also made of glass. Inside, a receptionist is sitting behind a long, high mottled desk. She has on a black headset and is working the switchboard.

"Hays Software, where may I direct your call?" she says pushing the buttons. "That line is busy, would you like voicemail?"

We approach the desk, our shoes clicking lightly over the faux marble floor.

"We're from *Digital Business*, here to interview Mr. Hays," I say to the receptionist.

She glances at us, and looks more than a little harassed. Lights are flashing all over the switchboard.

"You'll have to sign in here," she says, pointing to a large binder. Angela picks up the attached pen and signs us both in while the receptionist reaches into her desk and hands me two official-looking stickers.

"Please fill out these name tags. I'll buzz Mr. Hays' assistant. She'll need to escort you back to the meeting area."

Angela looks at me, "Top security, huh?"

"Software companies are all like this. Their main capital is their ideas, so they're careful about who sees what. Last month when I was at Simplex, they even had someone tag along with me to the bathroom and wait for me to take a leak."

Angela laughs.

"That's hilarious. I guess only the paranoid survive."

"That's the theory," I say, handing her a name tag.

She peels off the backing and attaches the sticker to her suit jacket.

"I guess we might as well sit down," she says.

We make our way across the floor to a comfortable alcove next to the glass wall. For a startup, Hays Software has some pretty plush furnishings, at least in the lobby. The chairs Angela and I sit down on are overstuffed and expensive-looking. There's an oak coffee table in front of us, with various trade publications scattered across it. And under our feet is a richly detailed Persian rug. Hays is hardly roughing it in his new venture.

The door of the inner sanctum bursts open, and a long-legged young woman in a short skirt emerges.

"Steven? Angela?" she asks as she approaches.

"That's us," I say.

"I'm Savita, Mr. Hays' assistant. He's ready to see you now."

We follow Savita through a winding path that takes us past a number of office cubicles shoe-horned into a single large room.

Judging from the snippets of conversation I pick up as we walk by, it seems that most of the employees here are programmers. A lot of the desks are littered with Coke cans and jars of salsa, and I can smell microwave popcorn. Most of the cubicles also have toys in them—Nerf balls, mini-basketball hoops, battery-powered *Star Trek* phaser guns, and other distractions.

Most, though not all, of the programmers are men. But male or female, they share the same approach to work attire: comfort, not fashion, is what matters. A few of the programmers are dressed in such ragged outfits, in fact, that they look homeless. It's hard to believe that when Hays Software goes public, most of these nerds are going to be millionaires, at least on paper.

"Here we are," Savita says.

We've arrived at a spacious, well-appointed conference room. In the center is a long table made of heavy oak, just like the coffee table in the lobby. It's surrounded by a number of black leather swivel chairs. There's a large screen projection system at one end of the room, and a wet bar next to it.

I take a seat near the head of the table, next to where I presume Hays will sit. Angela seats herself on my right. Savita offers us something to drink. I ask for water; Angela declines. Savita goes over to the wet bar, puts ice in a glass, and removes a bottle of mineral water from a small refrigerator.

"Here you go," she says, handing me the drink. "I'm going to check on Mr. Hays and Ms. Morgan. I'm sure they're on their way."

Savita closes the double doors quietly behind her when she leaves.

Two minutes later the doors swing open abruptly. In walks Hays, with Leticia at his side.

"Steven, it's so good to see you. And you must be Angela," Leticia says, shaking hands. "This is Arthur Hays."

He shakes our hands firmly, gives us a perfunctory "Nice to meet you," and then sits down at the head of the table, just as I expected. Leticia sits on his left.

Leticia and Hays are a study in contrasts. He's of average height, balding and dumpy. His clothes are hardly distinguishing—gray pants and a blue business shirt, neither of which fit him particularly well. He must have weighed ten pounds less when he first bought them. Hays is wearing glasses and a faraway look on his face, like his mind is dealing with another matter entirely. Leticia, on the other hand, is completely in the present. She smiles warmly at Angela, and immediately makes her feel more at ease.

Leticia is dressed in her usual bright colors; a striking red business suit with lipstick to match. Her outfit is sharply tailored, and accented with a large multicolored scarf. She wears her hair short and natural, which makes her sculpted cheekbones and dewy black eyes stand out even more. Her face is further accented by an unusual-looking pair of 22 karat gold hoop earrings. Leticia has always had a flair for the exotic. People often ask her if she's from Nigeria or Kenya or some other foreign land, but in truth she was born and raised in East Palo Alto, just a few miles from where we are right now.

"Arthur is on a very tight schedule today, so let's get started," Leticia says, very business-like.

I start the interview by asking Hays about his career at PCI Labs, his overall take on the information technology industry, and how he recruited the talent for Hays Software. By the time we get to the heart of the interview, Arthur Hays has begun to warm up, and has lost that faraway look. He's obviously happy to be talking about his company.

"How was it you came up with the idea for Cheetah?" I ask him.

"It's something I thought about a good deal when I was at PCI. Then I took early retirement and joined the University of Texas at Austin, as a guest lecturer. That gave me more time to follow up on my ideas."

"How different is Cheetah from the other search engines already on the market?"

"It's a lot more than just a search engine." Hays spits out the last two words, as if the term "search engine" were an insult. "It incorporates elements of both fuzzy logic and artificial intelligence. That's why I call it an intelligent agent."

"But don't other companies make programs that incorporate some of the same features?"

"They claim to," Hays says, raising his voice slightly. "But frankly, compared to what we've done, they're just stumbling around in a dark cave. Consider this: if you go to a library and ask the librarian to help you research a subject, say, like the chicken pox vaccine, and she gives you 60,000 citations to sift through, that isn't very helpful, is it? But that's exactly what these other programs do. They're very crude products. Cheetah is far more precise, and that's one of the reasons why it's so revolutionary."

I like the way he refers to his competition as being stuck in the Stone Age. It will make a great pull-out quote for the article. Now let's see if I can get some real news.

"So how does the program work?" I ask him.

Hays shakes his head.

"I can't give you any specifics on the program itself—I don't want to tip off the competition. Suffice it to say that Cheetah works and that's what counts."

"But that's not good enough for my readers. They're pretty sophisticated about these things," I insist.

"Sorry, that's all I can tell you about it at this point; it's proprietary," Hays says emphatically. His eyes narrow and he gives me a sharp look.

"Perhaps we can move on to some other questions," Leticia suggests, smoothing things over. She warned me that Hays can be obstinate, and that he likes to play his cards close to his vest. She's obviously concerned that this is going to cause tension and spoil the interview.

"Of course," I say agreeably, already looking for another way to get the information I want. "Who are the investors in Hays Software?"

"Grimshaw Turner has been in on both rounds of financing."

"Anyone else?"

Hays nods.

"A couple of individuals, but they prefer to remain anonymous."

"Why's that?" I ask.

"You know how these angel investors are," he says. "They want the payoff from their investments, but not the publicity—like to keep a low profile."

Having come to another dead end, I decide to switch directions.

"So Cheetah is going to make the Internet finally pay off?"

"Absolutely!" Hays declares, slapping the desk for emphasis. "Up until now the Internet has been an extremely inefficient way to get information or conduct business. But with an intelligent agent like Cheetah, the Net will finally live up to its expectations as a forum for research, electronic commerce, and other transactions. The gold rush will be here at last."

Hays sounds like a commercial, but I can tell he really believes what he's saying. He's glowing as he describes his vision of the Internet.

If I were less experienced, I'd be thrilled with this interview. Hays has given me a dozen provocative sound bites that I can weave into an entertaining story. But despite my prodding, he's given me almost no substance. It's time to wind this up and rethink my strategy.

"So, what's it like running your own company? Do you find Silicon Valley congenial after working at PCI?"

It's a standard question. I try not to yawn as I ask it.

"Most of the time," he replies. "The hard part is dealing with all these damn government regulations."

"What exactly do you mean?"

"I think one of the biggest problems in business today is government interference," Hays says, leaning forward and putting his elbows on the table. "There's too much of it, and I think the free market has to be defended at all costs. Socialism doesn't work."

Oh no, not this. Not a lecture on his social philosophy. It happens sometimes when I interview CEOs; some of them just can't resist including their political opinions. I try to avoid these discussions, but it's too late now—Hays is just getting started.

"Just the other day, I got a letter from some committee or other on investment responsibility, already bugging me about whether or not I have a suitably diverse board of directors," Hays says, clearly annoyed. "I'll appoint whomever I want! I don't need someone who doesn't understand my business trying to tell me what to do."

Leticia rolls her eyes, and Angela fidgets in her chair. Hays doesn't notice.

"Do you believe some sense of responsibility to the community is part of good business?" I ask, trying to get the conversation back on track.

"Not really. It's irrelevant." Suddenly he asks me, "Have you read the works of Ayn Rand?"

What does that have to do with intelligent agents? Hays is on a soapbox, and he's decided to use it to push his brand of politics.

"I read a couple of her books in high school."

"She's completely right, especially about business," Hays asserts.

This last statement is too much for Angela.

"But isn't Rand's philosophy rather immature—the virtue of selfishness and all that?" she asks, politely but firmly. Angela seems to have forgotten that she's supposed to listen and learn here, not ask questions.

"Not at all, young lady," Hays replies, looking even more annoyed than before. "It's very realistic. Man's ego *is* the fountainhead of all human progress. And I'm convinced that if all the intelligent and talented people withdrew from civilized society, everything *would* grind to a halt."

Angela looks ready to respond. But I am not about to let this interview degenerate into a political debate, so I jump in before anyone else can say anything.

"Okay," I declare. "It seems we're out of time. This is a good start, but I know once I begin writing I'll have some more questions. I'd like to meet with you again in a week or so. When would be a good time?"

It takes Hays a moment to shift his gaze from Angela to me. He's clearly irritated by her remarks, but he's still friendly enough, at least to me.

"I'm awfully busy these days, as you can imagine," he says. "But I'll see what I can do."

He stands up. I rise as well, and we shake hands.

"Thanks again for your time, Arthur. I'll talk with Leticia about scheduling a followup."

"You do that."

Hays leaves the room without another word. Angela stirs in her seat, stacks her notes and gets ready to leave. Leticia heaves a deep sigh.

"Don't tell me, Steven. I know you didn't get what you came for," Leticia says, raising her hands in resignation.

"I'll be honest with you," I say to Leticia. "If you want any coverage in *Digital Business* then you have got to get me more to work with. I'm not going to do an article on Cheetah without any technical data. No one would believe it's a viable product, and I'd look like a gullible idiot."

"I know that," Leticia says, frustrated. She looks at me and asks, "Can I tell you guys something off the record?"

"Sure you can," I reply.

"Hiring a PR director was not Arthur's idea. He would prefer to work in privacy and then announce the product when it's completely finished, bug-free, and ready to ship. He had this idea of just dropping it on the public like a bomb, and having the PR campaign start *after* it was available."

"You mean he was planning to finish the product before selling stock in his company?" I say. "How old-fashioned."

Before Leticia can reply, Angela asks her, "If hiring you wasn't Hays' idea, then whose was it?"

"Marcus Turner's," she answers. "He feels it's time to hone the pitch for the big investors. You know, prep for the road show. So a couple of months ago he approached me about working here. It seemed interesting, and they offered me a lot of stock."

"I've heard of road shows, but I don't know what they're for," Angela says.

"They're a quiet way to build interest in a company right before its IPO," I explain.

"Executives in a startup hit the road with their investment bankers," Leticia adds. "Together they visit the institutional investors—the Fidelities and the Vanguards—and pitch the virtues of the startup to them."

"The big investors are the ones who make a killing in an IPO," I tell Angela. "Because they get in before anybody else. By the time the little guy manages to buy into an IPO, the stock price has already skyrocketed."

"But it's an IPO," Angela says. "An initial public offering. Doesn't an initial stock price apply to every investor?"

"You'd think," I reply. "But in reality, some IPO stock is more 'initial' than others."

I look over at Leticia.

"So Hays Software is one of Marcus Turner's projects," I say. "That explains the push to go public."

Leticia nods.

"He sits on our board," she tells me. "And he's decided it's time. I'm sure Arthur would rather wait, but there's no arguing with Marcus."

Leticia's revelations are not that unexpected. All venture capitalists play a guiding role in the companies they've invested in, but Marcus Turner is known to take his mentoring duties to an extreme. He has a reputation for getting company founders to do things his way—hire the staff he thinks best, issue stock when he wants, even sell the company when a good offer comes along. Predictably, Turner is also known for driving entrepreneurs up the wall. They put up with him only because he controls the purse strings.

"Something tells me that Hays isn't going out of his way to make your job easy," I say.

"You've got that right," Leticia says. "I knew from Marcus that Arthur was kind of eccentric, but I didn't count on him being paranoid. The man loves to talk about his product, his company, and himself. But I can't get him to approve a simple spec sheet."

"Which raises some obvious doubts," I tell her.

Leticia looks at me earnestly.

"Steven, Cheetah really works. We weren't exaggerating in our press materials."

If any other marketing exec said this to me, I would take it with a grain of salt. But I've known Leticia for years. She wouldn't lie to me.

"I know," I reply. "Because I know you. But I can't base an article on the promises of a PR director."

I shake my head, exasperated. Cheetah could be the story of the year, maybe the decade. Researchers in corporations and universities have been working on something like Cheetah for nearly thirty years. And Arthur Hays has finally figured it out. It's a great story, but I can't print it, all because I can't get my hands on some very basic product specifications.

"Unless you can find a way around your boss, I'm going to have to junk this story," I say to Leticia, more forcefully than I'd intended.

"I know, I know," she says, rubbing her forehead. "And I was hoping that once we were past the quiet period, I could kick off our media campaign with a cover story in *Digital Business*."

Leticia thinks for a moment, then comes to a decision.

"When would you need the information?" she asks me.

"By the end of this week. Mitch is expecting to see a first draft by next Friday."

"I'll get you what you need, as long as it's not truly proprietary. What exactly do you want to know?"

"Just the kind of stuff you'd find on a spec sheet," I tell her. "Like what language Cheetah is written in. I assume it will be compatible with Windows NT and UNIX. That kind of data."

"If I can get you that, will we get the September cover?"

"I can't guarantee it. That's Mitch's call. But I don't see why not."

"Okay, it's a deal."

"Great," I say, glad to have that problem solved. "Now when can I see the demo?"

"We don't have one ready for the press yet," Leticia tells me. "It'll be a couple of months."

"What?" I say. "I can't write about a product I haven't even seen, Leticia. Any chance of a sneak preview?"

"Maybe," she answers.

Leticia taps her pen against the table, considering her options.

"We do have a working version of Cheetah," she says at last, "But if anyone saw you guys looking at it, Arthur would have my head."

"So we're back to square one," I respond, disappointed.

"Not exactly," Leticia continues. "I think I know a discreet way for you to try it out."

She opens the clipboard she's been holding, pulls out a sheet of paper, and writes something down.

"I'm going to trust you with something very important," Leticia says, looking me straight in the eye. "I'm giving you access to a server running Cheetah, and I'm counting on you not to look at anything else but the product."

She folds the piece of paper and hands it to me.

"I've written down the phone number you'll need to dial up the server, and I've given you the passwords for both the server and the demo."

"Great, thanks," I say. "I really appreciate this."

"Just don't do anything that gets me into trouble," she replies in a serious voice.

"I promise I won't," I say, folding up the paper and putting it in my wallet. I pick up my briefcase and give my friend a smile. "Care to walk us out?"

We make our way back through the maze of cubicles towards the lobby. I can hear explosions and simulated gunfire coming from one of the cubes. Someone must be playing an action game over the Net.

We stop at the lobby to say our goodbyes. The two women shake hands, and I give Leticia a peck on the cheek.

"Don't forget lunch Friday," I remind her.

"I've got it on my calendar," she assures me.

Leticia turns quickly on her heel and walks back through the oak doors that separate the lobby from the rest of Hays Software.

"What was that kiss all about?" Angela asks me as soon as we step outside. "Is that how you get all your big interviews?"

"Hardly. Leticia and I have been friends for years."

"Oh," Angela says, comprehending. "For a moment there, I was wondering about your investigative methods."

"That reminds me," I say, giving Angela a stern look. "Never, ever, argue politics during an interview. Especially when it's *my* interview. Got that?"

"I've got it," she says grudgingly. "But you've got to admit—Arthur Hays might be brilliant, but he's kind of strange."

"That's your opinion. Most of Silicon Valley would disagree with you."

# CHAPTER FOUR

Breakfast meetings are my favorite, especially when they're close to home and I get to miss rush hour traffic. That's why I'm in such an upbeat mood as I negotiate the winding road to Buck's Restaurant.

I'm on my way to meet with Kevin Cheng of Redwood Capital, a top-tier venture capital firm. In keeping with my vow to be a good mentor, I've invited Angela along so that she can meet a real-life venture capitalist.

Today's meeting was Kevin's idea. Redwood Capital has put a big chunk of change into a communications company called Neptune Wireless, which plans to provide wireless access to the Internet, and Kevin wants to make sure the press knows all about them. That's why he wants me to meet Carl Jensen, Neptune's founder and current CEO. If what Jensen has to say is interesting enough, I'll do an article on his company.

I pull into the restaurant's parking lot and spot Kevin Cheng sitting in his BMW. The guy in the passenger seat next to him must be Carl Jensen. Both of them are talking into cellular phones—they look like they're having a walkie-talkie conversation with each other at close range.

They could be on the phone a while, so I'd better let them know I'm here. I approach the driver-side window and rap on it. Kevin starts and gives me a frightened look, like he's expecting to get mugged right here in the sedate town of Woodside. He takes a breath, nods, and points to the front door of Buck's to indicate that he'll join me inside when he's finished.

When I walk through the door I see Angela sitting alone in a booth. She's sipping coffee and going over some notes.

"Been here long?" I ask as I take a seat next to her.

"About half an hour. I wanted to get here early to review for the meeting. Where are they?"

"In Kevin's car, talking on their cell phones."

"Oh brother, boys and their toys. How long are they going to be?"

"Another couple of minutes at least. I banged on Kevin's window and gave him quite a scare. It was kind of funny."

"Speaking of funny, what is this place?" Angela asks, looking around.

I'm not surprised by Angela's reaction. Buck's is hardly a typical restaurant, and its faux western decor always confounds first-time visitors. The lamps hanging from the ceiling look like bronzed cowboy hats and cast a yellowish glow over the tables. In one corner, a countrified Mona Lisa, complete with Stetson and bandanna, grins at the diners. A couple of huge marlins and a miniature prop plane hang from the ceiling, and all around the main dining area is a series of cartoonish murals. For me, the kitsch decor is entertaining, and the best thing about Buck's.

Despite the restaurant's outlandish atmosphere, the menu is pretty simple and straightforward. Maybe that's why Buck's is so popular. Whatever the reason, it's frequented by some of the most powerful people in Silicon Valley, especially at breakfast time. Buck's is a place to see and be seen, a networker's heaven.

"Buck's is a funny place, but everybody comes here," I tell Angela.

Even as I say that, I notice the president of a Fortune 500 company sitting three tables away, digging into a stack of buttermilk pancakes. Across from him is an older man—probably the chairman of the board, or maybe a leading shareholder.

Just then three guys walk in the front entrance, decked out in the latest cycling outfits and holding aerodynamically perfect helmets. They look like they're training for the Tour de France, but I suspect they're just out for a short ride before going to the office. They head for a table on the other side of the restaurant, their shoes whooshing softly across the carpet as they walk.

"Hey, that woman over there looks familiar," Angela says.

I follow Angela's gaze across the room. Standing up from her seat, getting ready to leave, is one of the few women CEOs in Silicon Valley.

"That's Alice Barlow," I say. "She founded a graphic tools company that was recently acquired by a much bigger outfit. Now she's running another startup."

A waitress stops by the booth, leaves some menus and hurries off.

"So tell me about Kevin Cheng," Angela says, taking another sip of coffee.

"In VC circles, he's considered a rising star."

"By 'VC,' you mean venture capitalist?"

"Right."

Maybe I should start at the beginning.

"How much do you know about venture capital?" I ask Angela.

She pauses to think before answering.

"I know that venture capital firms give startup money to entrepreneurs in exchange for partial ownership of their companies."

"That's the basic arrangement."

"But what I can't understand," Angela continues, "is why a company founder would give up so much control in exchange for money. Why not just get a business loan from a bank?"

"Because most banks aren't willing to take on that kind of risk," I explain. "The majority of new high-tech companies never see any profit."

"So why does anyone invest in a startup?"

"Because when a company does succeed, the payoff can be huge."

"Hey, two men just walked in," Angela says suddenly. "Is that them?"

I glance at the entryway, and see that Kevin and Carl have finally emerged from the parking lot. Like Angela, Carl has apparently never been here before. He's staring at the huge jar of pickled lizards next to the cash register. They're fake, of course, but it takes a moment to realize it the first time you see them.

"Sorry about the delay, Steven," Kevin says as he nears the booth. He slides in right after Carl. "That was probably the most important call I'll get this week. The guy is going to be out of the country for the next couple of weeks and will be impossible to reach."

At thirty-five, Kevin is the youngest partner at Redwood Capital. He's had one enormous hit from a company that went public earlier this year, as well as a lot of smaller successes. But he knows he can't rest on his laurels, and is hoping that Neptune will be his biggest deal yet.

"This is Carl Jensen," Kevin says, motioning to his right. Carl is young too, about thirty, but unlike Kevin, he looks tired.

"Let me introduce you to Angela Madrigal," I say. "She just joined *Digital Business* and is going to be helping me out for the next few months."

"Nice to meet you both," Carl says, shaking our hands. He looks at Angela, "When did you join the magazine?"

"This is my first week. I used to work the technology beat at the *Chronicle*."

No doubt she said this to let Carl and Kevin know that while she may be new to venture capital, she does know something about the high-tech industry.

"That's interesting," Kevin says without paying attention.

Kevin doesn't like to spend time on chit-chat, and is already squirming in his seat, a bundle of nervous energy. Twitching and rocking as he speaks, he's a classic manic personality. Carl, on the other hand, simply looks exhausted. He's probably been up since 5 AM, and running around with Kevin certainly can't be restful.

The waitress walks up to our table.

"Hi, what can I get you folks this morning?"

"I'll have a bowl of oatmeal," Kevin says.

The rest of us scramble to open our menus and decide what to get. Carl orders up a breakfast just as Spartan as Kevin's—orange juice and an English muffin. I could never make it through the morning on that. I order a full breakfast: eggs, sausage, and home fries. Angela asks for the buckwheat pancakes.

"So tell me what Neptune is up to right now," I ask Carl as the waitress walks away with our order.

Carl starts to respond, but is interrupted by a loud beeping.

"Oops, there goes my pager!" Kevin says. He grabs the little device off his belt and reads what's on the screen. "I've got to check my e-mail; I'm expecting an important message. Do you mind?"

"No, go ahead," I say. "We'll talk with Carl."

Kevin plugs his laptop into his cell phone and immediately becomes absorbed. He taps his foot rapidly on the floor as he waits for his computer to connect to the network. The modem in his laptop chirps loudly and then makes a whining sound. No one in the restaurant even notices.

"So how close are you to releasing your new wireless device?" Angela asks Carl.

"Pretty close. We just finished our beta testing, and we're ready to ship the final version to some of our bigger customers. I have the specifications right here."

He hands her the spec sheet.

Kevin must still have an ear on the conversation; he pulls something from a file and slides it across the table.

"Here's the first draft of a press release announcing Neptune's new customers," he says, barely moving his eyes off his laptop's screen.

"Great," Angela says, picking it up.

"Are you going to be doing any more rounds of funding soon?" I ask Carl.

"Yes, Redwood will be putting in more money, and Excel Partners will also be investing in the second round. Some big corporate partners will be adding money, too. Here's a tentative list. We won't be formally announcing this for a few more weeks, so I'll have to ask you to keep this under your hat."

"No problem," I say, taking the list from him.

Carl fills us in on a few more details and gives us the names of some others at Neptune to interview about their product. Kevin is still busy with his e-mail. It looks like he's reading all of his messages, not just the supposedly crucial one. Angela seems surprised by his rude behavior, but I know to expect this whenever I meet with one of venture capital's hungry young stars. A shark has to feed constantly if it wants to keep swimming.

After another twenty minutes of conversation with Carl, the interview draws to a close.

Kevin finally logs off his computer.

"So, Steven, did you get the information you need?" he asks me as he puts his laptop back in its case.

"For now."

"Neptune is utterly unique, you know. We've got a big jump on the competition," Kevin says.

"It looks like it," I reply, humoring him.

If you go by what VCs and entrepreneurs claim for their products, everything they make is "utterly unique."

The waitress passes by and Kevin asks for the check. When it comes, he leaves it sitting on the table. I know I'm not supposed to pick it up, so he must be planning to leave it to Carl.

"I look forward to getting more information as it becomes available," I say, closing my notebook. "Keep me in the loop."

"Of course!" Kevin declares.

He gathers his things and prepares to depart. Carl looks more fatigued than ever.

As Kevin jumps out of the booth, Carl slides gingerly down the seat and rises slowly, check in hand. Kevin strides to the door; he already has his cell phone out, ready to make the next call. Carl moves towards the cash register and pulls out his wallet.

"Does Kevin ever quit?" Angela asks me. "He must not sleep."

"As a matter of fact, I've gotten e-mail from him that he sent at four in the morning. Rumor has it he never takes a vacation. His work is his vacation."

"What a nut," Angela says softly as she watches the two men depart. Then she looks back at me.

"So what do you think of Neptune?" she asks. "Aren't there a lot of other wireless companies out there, with competing standards?"

"That's right. It's a crowded field."

"If there are so many startups doing the same thing, how do they all find venture capital firms to back them?"

"VCs are funny," I tell her. "They've been called vultures, but a lot of times they act more like sheep, everybody doing the same thing. But Neptune might be a viable company; it looks okay so far."

I check my watch.

"It's getting late, we'd better get going."

Angela and I slide out of the booth, make our way past a painting of Roy Rogers, and exit through the front door.

"See you at the office," Angela says to me in the parking lot.

I get in my car, start the engine, and prepare to back out. When I look in the rearview mirror, I spy Angela getting into a bright red Mustang convertible. It's a classic, probably a '65 or a '66, and in mint condition. I have to wonder how someone just barely out of grad school can get her hands on a car like that.

The first thing I do when I get to the office is check my voicemail. I have about six messages, including one from a stockbroker I've never heard of, pitching some Internet stock fund he's put together. He leaves his number and asks me to call. I delete the message.

The rest of the messages are pretty routine, until I get to Leticia's voicemail.

"Steven," she says in a tired voice. "Listen, we need to talk. I . . . found something. I have it tucked away, but I'm not sure what to do with it, and I could use your advice. So call me when you get in tomorrow morning."

What could that mean? According to the voicemail system, she left me the message at about midnight last night, and marked it private.

I continue playing messages. The next one is also from Leticia, and according to the time stamp, she left it at 9:20 this morning. She sounds more energetic this time, more like her typical self.

"Hey buddy, where are you?" she asks. "Well, I woke up this morning and decided I should just hand everything over to you. You are the investigative journalist, after all. And you're going to love this story, believe me. So call me . . . but not at Hays Software—I resigned. And actually, I'm not sure when I'll be home either—I'm going over to my sister's today. So I guess I'll just try you again later. Talk to you soon."

This is exciting news. An exclusive interview is great, but inside dirt from a hot startup is better. And it must be something big for Leticia to quit such a good job so abruptly.

I immediately call Leticia at home, on the off chance she's still there. No answer, and even her machine doesn't pick up. Then I call home for my messages—nothing from Leticia. Damn, I wish I had her sister's number.

I'm about to replay her voicemail when Matt walks into my office and plops himself casually into a chair.

"How'd the interview with Kevin Cheng go this morning?" he asks me.

"Not bad. It looks like he's funded an interesting company for the wireless market."

"No kidding," Matt says without much enthusiasm.

I've known Matt long enough to realize that he wouldn't drop by just to talk shop.

"So what's on your mind," I say, trying to help him get to the point.

Matt hesitates, then blurts out: "I wanted to ask you about Angela."

He glances at the doorway, as if to make sure she's not headed this way.

"Go ahead."

"Does she have a boyfriend?" Matt asks, plowing forward. "I've asked her out to lunch a couple of times, and she seems to be giving me the brush-off."

"We've never talked about it."

"I was wondering if maybe she'd hooked up with Mitch," he says. "Do you think they're together?"

"I used to, but I don't anymore."

"Why not?"

"I don't think she's the type."

"I see."

He falls silent.

"Anything else?" I ask.

"Oh no. Do me a favor, okay? Let me know if you find out anything."

"She doesn't tell me about her personal life."

"Just thought I'd ask. Catch you later."

Matt gets up from the chair and leaves.

With my office once again free of distractions, I turn my thoughts back to Leticia's messages. I listen to them once more, but don't gain any new insights. Finally I decide it's useless to speculate. Besides, pretty soon I'll be able to talk with Leticia herself.

Except for lunch and a brief meeting, I spend the rest of the day at my desk, grabbing at the phone every time it rings. But Leticia doesn't call. Knowing her, she's at the beach, or maybe a cafe somewhere. I guess my story will have to wait one more day.

# CHAPTER FIVE

I race to the office this morning, hoping to hear from Leticia. There was nothing more from her when I checked my voicemail last night, so she's certain to call sometime soon. I feel excited and impatient, anticipating an even bigger story than the one I started with. I park myself at my desk, determined to stay there until she calls.

I try to review my notes from the Hays interview, but I keep reading the same sentence over and over—it's just too hard to concentrate when I'm expecting the phone to ring any minute.

"Am I interrupting anything?" says a voice from the hall.

I look up and see Angela standing in the doorway, holding a couple of coffee mugs. She walks in and takes a seat in one of my office chairs, without even waiting to hear my response.

"Come on in," I say facetiously. "I'm just going over my notes from Tuesday's meeting with Hays."

"Here, I brought you a mocha," she says, handing me a mug. "I've noticed that usually your first stop when you get here is the coffee maker. But this morning you breezed right past it."

I take a sip.

"Thanks."

"I also figured that if you were as busy as you look, then maybe you have other projects you'd like me to help you with."

I have to give Angela credit; she doesn't miss a trick. Given her drive, she'll probably have her own byline in less than a year.

"I might need more help from you in the near future, but I don't right now. In fact, it's not even work that got me in early today. I'm expecting an important phone call, and I want to be here when it comes."

"Oh really?" she says, raising her eyebrows as if to ask me what the call is about.

But I'm not talking.

"Really. So I'm planning to stay put for a little while."

Angela nods and takes another sip.

"So when are we going to look at the Hays demo?"

I flip open my calendar.

"Does 3:30 work for you?"

"Sure does. And then when do you think we can start writing up the interview?"

We? Where does she get these ideas? This is my project; she's just along for the ride.

"I'll probably start writing it Monday," I say pointedly. "I'm still waiting for that product information Leticia promised us."

"Oh, I see."

My message that this is my article, not *our* article, got through to her, and her disappointment is obvious.

"Mitch tells me you're a great editor. I want you to edit my first draft once I have it written," I say, trying to make her feel better.

She's about to respond when the phone rings. I stare at it for a couple of seconds. It's Leticia, I'm sure of it. And I don't want anybody overhearing this conversation.

"This is the call I've been waiting for. I'll see you at 3:30," I say to Angela, verbally pushing her out the door.

Angela is no dummy. While I'm sure she'd like to know who I'm so anxious to talk to, she knows better than to ask. She's out the door just as I pick up the phone receiver.

"This is Steven," I say quickly, expecting to hear Leticia's voice.

Instead, I'm greeted by a total stranger.

"Steven, this is Will Clayton at Stallion Securities. I left you a message the other day, but you must not have gotten it, or I'm sure I would have heard from you by now, because the Internet fund I represent is too good to be believed." He's using a real friendly tone of voice, as if we've been buddies since grade school.

This guy picked the wrong day to call. I'm not about to lose out on what could be the scoop of the decade so he can try to sell me overvalued stock.

"Don't ever call me again." I practically spit out the words, in a calm but angry voice. "If you do, I'll report you to the authorities." I doubt placing a sales call is a crime, but I like the sound of the threat.

Mr. William Clayton of Stallion Securities does his best to stutter out some sort of conciliatory reply, but I cut him off almost as soon as he begins.

"Goodbye," I say simply and hang up.

It was a completely unprofessional way to deal with him, I'll admit, but it was immensely satisfying.

By one o'clock I decide that I've spent enough time holed up in my office. Hunger has driven me to the common sense conclusion that even if I miss her call, Leticia will simply leave a message; hopefully, with a phone number this time. I head to the nearest deli for a quick lunch.

When I get back from the deli I notice that something is causing a stir in the office. Some of the staff have gathered at Craig's cubicle for what looks like an impromptu conference. Craig is a production supervisor, so having several people in his office at once is normal. What's unusual is their behavior. They're whispering to each other, and glancing across the hallway at the large glassed-in conference room.

Being just as curious as my fellow workers, I take a quick look into the conference room as I pass Craig's cubicle on the way to my office. I do a double take and almost stop in my tracks. When I get to my office, I sit down behind my desk and try to make sense of what I just saw.

One of the people in the conference room was Angela. I didn't see her whole face, but I recognized her profile. She was seated at the head of the long table, moving her hands lightly as she talked. She seemed to be explaining something. To her right, listening attentively, was an older, weathered man in a rumpled suit. His hair was liberally streaked with white—he must be about sixty. He looked at me briefly as I walked by, and then turned his attention back to Angela.

I caught a glimpse of one other person, a man leaning against the old-fashioned chalkboard Mitch likes to keep in the conference room. In contrast to his associate, this man was stylishly dressed. His suit was immaculately pressed, and looked expensive. His hair was slicked back, and he seemed much more polished than his companion.

"Maybe he's the one in charge," I think to myself. But in charge of what? They don't look like the type of people we usually get in here. They're wearing suits, so they're not technical gurus or reporters. And despite the younger guy's fashionable attire, they don't look like VCs or investment bankers either. I'm just curious enough to consider asking Craig what's going on. But I decide against it; Leticia could call at any minute. Besides, I'm sure Angela will tell me later.

I open a drawer, pull out a stack of reports on electronic commerce, and begin reading. I'm in the middle of a critique on Web advertising, when suddenly I get the feeling that someone is looking at me. I look up and see the well-dressed guy from the conference room standing at my office door.

"May I help you?" I ask.

"Yes. I'm Inspector Rick Morrison. Could you come with me," he states, rather than asks.

"What's this about?"

"Inspector Kamimoto will tell you all about it," he says, looking grave. I guess he's not the one in charge, after all.

"Well, okay."

I'm gripped by a sense of foreboding as we head to the conference room. When we arrive, the older man turns toward the door and watches me enter. Angela is just getting up from her seat. She's worn out and has a troubled look on her face. She moves past me as I enter the room and clutches my arm.

"You're not going to believe this," she says in an intense whisper.

I'm about to ask her what's going on when she's ushered out by Inspector Morrison.

"Steven Cavanaugh?" the older man says, standing and putting out his hand.

"That's me," I answer, shaking hands automatically.

"George Kamimoto. I'm an inspector with the San Francisco Police Department."

"Uh-huh," I say as I take the seat Angela just vacated.

Morrison has come back and resumed his position against the chalkboard.

"Time is critical, so let me be direct," Kamimoto says bluntly. "When was the last time you saw Leticia Morgan?"

"Why, what's happened?"

"Please just answer the question, Mr. Cavanaugh."

"I saw her Tuesday afternoon. I was interviewing her boss, Arthur Hays. She was there at the meeting."

"Where was the meeting?" Kamimoto asks.

"At Hays Software, in Cupertino."

"Have you seen her or talked to her since then?"

"No. Why?"

"What was her mood at the time?" Kamimoto continues.

"It was fine," I answer curtly, annoyed that he won't answer me.

Morrison clears his throat. I look at him, expecting a question, but he just stares at me.

"Does Ms. Morgan have problems getting along with anyone?" Kamimoto asks me. "Is she seeing anyone?"

"No."

My apprehension is growing stronger by the second.

"What's going on?" I say forcefully. "I demand to know before I answer any more questions."

George Kamimoto leans back in his chair and crosses his arms.

"Ms. Morgan is dead," he tells me.

It takes a few seconds for the news to sink in. It can't be possible. I stare at the conference table, completely unaware of my surroundings. I just saw her. She just left me a message yesterday!

"I've known her since high school," I say to no one in particular.

It takes me a couple of minutes to think of the obvious question.

"How? How did it happen?" I ask Kamimoto.

"Somebody killed her," he states simply.

I stare at him, stunned.

"It can't be," I protest weakly.

"That's why I was asking you if she was having difficulties with anyone," Kamimoto says, continuing in a businesslike fashion. "Are you sure she wasn't involved with someone?"

"No. She would tell me," I say, shaking my head. "We've been friends for years. I know all about her personal life." I can't bring myself to speak about Leticia in the past tense.

"How often did you see her?" he asks me.

"We have lunch once or twice a month."

Kamimoto makes a couple of notes on the small writing tablet in front of him. Morrison is watching me intently, like a scientist scrutinizing a lab specimen.

"Is that all?" Kamimoto asks.

"We see each other at birthday parties, that kind of thing."

"You never saw her any other time?"

"No, we were both too busy."

I'm getting tired of the inspector asking all the questions.

"When did it happen?" I ask him, taking the offensive.

"I'm not at liberty to provide details," Kamimoto says, and then moves on quickly. "Do you know why Ms. Morgan decided to skip work yesterday?"

I open my mouth to tell him about her last couple of messages, but then I stop. He's not telling me all he knows, so why should I tell him? I decide to sit on the information, at least for now. I need time to sort this all out.

"I wouldn't know," I answer.

Kamimoto writes this down.

"I just have a few more routine questions to ask, and then you can go," he says amiably.

"Fine," I reply, less amiably.

"What was your schedule yesterday?" he asks me.

"I had a breakfast meeting, and then I spent most of the day in my office writing."

"Did you have any other meetings during the day?"

"I met with Tina Davis—she's our managing editor—in her office at around 3:00, and then I stopped by Craig Nelson's desk on the way back to my office."

"Did you leave the building at all during the day?"

"I went out at lunch time."

"Anyone go with you?"

"No. I just went to the corner deli, ate a sandwich, and then came back to my office."

"To do more writing."

"That *is* what they pay me for," I reply, losing patience. What makes him think he can get away with asking me all these questions, and then not tell me anything about my friend's death?

"We're almost finished," Kamimoto says in a conciliatory tone.

I don't know if it's because he's picked up on my frustration, but Kamimoto changes his style of inquiry. He stops asking about yesterday, and his questions get more personal, even friendly: Where did I grow up? What do I do for fun? How long have I been married? and so on. I don't see what this has to do with a murder investigation, and before long I start getting angry again. Right about then Kamimoto terminates the interview.

"That's it for now, Mr. Cavanaugh," he announces. "You're not going anywhere soon, are you? I'd like for you to be available for any further questions I might have."

"I'll be around."

"Good," he says in a congenial voice. "Here's my card. Give me a call if you remember anything you think may be relevant."

I take his card and shove it in my pocket. I don't plan to use it.

I stand up abruptly, almost knocking over my chair. I don't like these people. I resent the fact that my friend is dead, and they won't give me any but the barest details.

I walk to the door and open it. But before I leave, I turn around and give the detectives one more piece of information.

"You've got chalk on your jacket," I say to Inspector Morrison. As the door closes behind me, I catch a glimpse of him furiously brushing himself off.

# Chapter Six

The minute I step out of the conference room, Craig and his gossip-hungry pals look my way, hoping I'll stop by and tell them what just happened. Craig is a decent guy, but there's no way I'm telling him about the interrogation I just got. I head straight to my office. Once I get there, I do something unusual for me—I close my door.

Almost immediately, there's a knock. Great, just when I want to be alone. No doubt it's some busybody wanting to know what happened.

"Can I come in?" says a voice from the other side.

It's Angela. The one person in the office I wouldn't mind talking to. At least she's in this with me, even if it wasn't her friend who got killed.

"Go ahead," I say. "Just close the door behind you."

Angela walks in and shuts the door.

"Everybody's been asking me what's going on," she says. "But I've told them we're not supposed to talk about it."

"Good idea."

Angela takes a seat in front of my desk, and leans forward, putting her elbows on the desktop.

"I'm really sorry," she tells me.

"Thanks. I am too."

Someone raps on the door. I ignore it. But I wonder how many more knocks on the office door I'm going to be ignoring today.

"Let's go to the Aztec Cafe," I say to Angela. "The one on Mission. I don't think we'll run into anyone we know there."

The walk to the cafe is a dreary one. Normally, I like the Mission district: its diversity, its energy, its gritty charm. But today it just seems menacing. The shoppers and cafe goers brush by me with complete indifference. And the homeless people seem aggressive today, even the regular smoking a cigarette atop "his" garbage can.

"Here we are," Angela says as the cafe comes into view.

"Let's see if we can find a place away from the crowd."

We choose a table next to the far wall, underneath a large painted mural of Aztec warriors drinking chocolate from golden goblets. The tabletop is littered with copies of *SF Weekly*, one of the local papers, and someone has left an empty cappuccino cup. Angela picks it up and moves it to the vacant table next to us, setting it on top of an abandoned copy of *La Prensa*

"I'll get us something to drink," she says.

Within minutes Angela is back, carrying a mug in each hand. She sets a steaming cup of coffee under my nose. It's not exactly what I had in mind, but it will do.

"You were in there with the police a lot longer than I was," she informs me as soon as she sits down.

"I was?"

"Yeah, I was only in there about ten minutes. You were there at least half an hour. I know because I kept waiting for you to come out."

"So what did they ask you?"

"Not much," she says. "Just about our interview with Hays. How well did I know Leticia; had I seen or heard from her since the meeting. What about you?"

"Kamimoto grilled me on my relationship with Leticia. I think he thinks we were having some kind of affair."

Angela leans back in her chair, a thoughtful expression on her face. Absentmindedly, she clicks her fingernails against her mug of hot chocolate.

"Really," is all she says.

"Leticia and I were not involved," I say emphatically, angry that I even have to explain myself.

"I know that," Angela says. "But I can bet what the police are thinking: if you two had been lovers, then it would give you a motive for killing her. You *are* a married man, and if Leticia threatened to talk...."

She lets her sentence trail off.

"Wonderful, this is all I need," I say. "On top of everything else, now I'm a suspect."

"Don't take it personally," Angela counters. "I'm sure you're not the only one with a possible motive. Whenever there's a murder, the police start by suspecting everybody."

She sips her drink, momentarily lost in thought.

"Even the family," she adds quietly.

"Still, I don't need this," I say, pushing away the coffee mug. "It's bad enough knowing someone stalked her and killed her."

"It may not have been premeditated," Angela points out. "It could have happened during a robbery attempt or something."

I shake my head.

"No, that's not it."

She looks at me questioningly, but says nothing. I hesitate for a moment, and then tell her about Leticia's messages. Angela is quick to comprehend the implications.

"That's too much of a coincidence. Leticia resigns, and then gets killed. It has to be connected," she says. "What did Kamimoto say when you told him?"

"I didn't."

"Why not?"

"I didn't like the fact that he wouldn't tell me anything about Leticia's death. So I figured, two can play that game."

I rub my temples and try to think.

"What I need," I tell Angela, "is more information. There's got to be a way to find out what happened."

Angela watches me in silence. I'm trying to come up with some sort of game plan, but I can't think of anyone I know who has experience tracking down murderers.

"I have an idea," she volunteers. "But . . . it's not entirely legal."

I look at her, surprised. For a moment, I consider telling her to forget it. But right now my options are pretty limited.

"Let's hear it," I say.

Angela leans closer and lowers her voice.

"I know a hacker who might be able to help us out. His name is Dan Guerra," she says, rolling the double R in a way I'll never master. "And he used to work for NetGuard Associates."

"The security firm?"

Angela nods.

I've heard of NetGuard. For a small fortune, their consultants will go into your company and show you all the ways your computer network is vulnerable to infiltration or attack. Then they recommend the best ways for you to safeguard your network from hackers.

"I see what you have in mind," I say. "You want him to break into the police department's computer system."

"Exactly. I was thinking he could check the SFPD's files. Maybe sniff out the details Kamimoto won't give."

I sit back in my chair.

"You're right," I tell her. "That's completely illegal." I think for a moment. "But highly effective. How good is this guy?"

"He's a geek hero," she says enthusiastically. "Been hacking since he was twelve years old and knows all the tricks. I'm sure he could do this."

"But will he want to?"

"Sure he will. When do you want to meet him?"

"The sooner the better," I reply.

"I'll try for tomorrow," Angela says. "Will that work for you?"

"I'll make it work. Here, let me give you my number. Call me when you've set it up."

I write my phone number and address on a napkin and hand it to Angela, who sticks it in her pocket. Then she picks up a discarded receipt from the floor, writes her address and number down on the back of it, and hands it to me. I put the slip of paper in my wallet.

Now that I've got a plan of action, I feel like I can face the rest of the day.

"Let's go," I say to Angela. "We can't spend all day hiding out here."

I walk Angela to the office and then head to my car. I'm not going back to work today.

I drive home on automatic pilot. My mind is filled with thoughts of Leticia. I remember our high school days, our friendship, her kindness and her stubbornness. I try to push the memories away, to stay focused, but I can't—I miss her too much.

I walk to the front door of my house, feeling numb and run down. I'm glad to have a couple of hours to myself; I need to be alone for a while. I think I'll get a beer from the fridge and sit in the back yard. Maybe then I'll be able to make some sense of this mess.

I open the door, and discover I'm not alone in the house. I can hear the sound of typing just a few feet away. I walk down the hall into the office, and find Michelle sitting at the desk, engrossed by something on the computer screen.

"Hi," I say softly.

Michelle spins around in her chair and gives me a startled look.

"Oh, thank God, it's just you," she says, relieved.

"It's good to see you too."

"You know what I mean. You scared me half to death. I wasn't expecting you home so early."

"I know," I say, walking closer. "What are you doing here?"

"Research," she says, turning back to her keyboard. "Jack wants a report on the technology buyout market. He thinks there's a lot of opportunity breaking lucrative divisions away from larger companies—the way Lucent was spun out of AT&T, remember? Anyway, Jack needs the report by next week, and it's just too hectic at work right now. I figured I'd get more done at home."

"I see," I reply, sitting down on a chair.

Michelle stops typing and looks at me, a concerned look growing in her eyes.

"So what's going on?" she asks.

"It's a long story."

Michelle gets up from her seat and walks over to me.

"What's wrong?"

I take her hand and hold it in mine.

"Leticia's dead," I say simply.

"What?!"

"It's true."

"Oh, my God. I'm so sorry," she says, putting her arms around me. "What happened?"

I tell her the whole ugly story, including the interview with the police, and everything I know regarding Leticia's death. Michelle is understanding and sympathetic, until I mention my plan to tap into the SFPD's computers.

"Are you crazy?" she says when I tell her. She pulls away and looks at me, uncomprehending. "You can't hack into a police computer; you'll be arrested for sure. What are you thinking?"

"I'm thinking I need to know what's going on," I say defensively, standing up and walking to the window.

"And then what will you do with the information, assuming you don't get caught?" she asks, following me. "Hunt down the killer yourself?"

I think back to my last conversation with Leticia. "Just don't do anything that gets me into trouble," I remember her saying. Somehow, I've let her down.

"Michelle," I say, turning around to face her. "I have to do this."

She gives me an angry look.

"I don't know why I even bother trying to talk to you," she exclaims. "No matter what I say, you're going to do what you want, just like you always do."

She walks back to the desk and sits down.

"Just don't expect me to visit you in jail," she says, staring at the computer screen.

This is not how I want to leave things. I walk over to Michelle and bend down so I can whisper in her ear.

"Will you at least write to me?" I ask facetiously.

Michelle shakes her head.

"Damn it," she says, turning around and giving me a tight hug.

# Chapter Seven

Angela called last night to say she'd talked with her hacker friend and arranged for us to meet with him this morning. She's picking me up at home and then we're going to his place in Santa Cruz. I'm glad Angela volunteered to drive. I don't feel up to it today, and the idea of kicking back and watching the scenery appeals to me.

At the moment I'm sitting in my back patio, sipping coffee, and watching a robin stalk worms while I wait for Angela to arrive. The bird hops along the dew-specked lawn and listens for movement under the sod, cocking her head to the side. All of a sudden she begins pecking away like a jackhammer. Soon she has a big fat earthworm clasped firmly in her beak. She flies off, no doubt to a secluded spot where she can devour her meal in private.

I hear the sliding glass door open behind me, and turn around to see Michelle leaning in the doorway, clasping a robe tightly around her.

"Aren't you cold out here?" she asks me.

"A bit," I answer truthfully. "Is Chloe still asleep?"

"Yeah, I just checked on her."

I hear the doorbell ring.

"I'll get it," Michelle says, retreating into the house.

I swallow the last of my coffee and go in a few moments later. I stop by the hall closet to retrieve a light jacket, and am slipping it on when Michelle walks up to me.

"You didn't tell me she was beautiful," she says, raising an eyebrow and looking at me archly.

"I hadn't noticed."

"Oh, you hadn't, huh?" Michelle says teasingly. She strokes my hair affectionately. "Hon, you are such a bad liar," she continues. "But I love you for trying."

Michelle puts her arm through mine and together we amble to the front hall. Angela is waiting in the entryway, the front door open behind her. She's thrown on a long-sleeved flannel shirt to protect her from the morning chill, but underneath it she's dressed for a day in hot weather: a tank top, sandals, and a pair of shorts that show off her tanned, shapely legs rather nicely.

"Hi Angela," I say, slightly awed by the sight of her.

"Hi," she says in a voice awfully chipper for 7:00 in the morning.

"You've met Michelle, right?" I ask.

"Yes, just now," she replies, and then facing my wife, she continues, "I've heard good things about you."

"Right," is all Michelle manages to say.

"I guess we'd better get going if we want to beat the traffic," I say, anxious to move out of the doorway.

I lean over to kiss Michelle goodbye. She pulls me close, wraps her arms around me, and gives me the kind of kiss we usually reserve for the bedroom. And they say men are territorial.

"Just don't tell me the car broke down," she whispers to me.

"Don't worry, I won't," I tell her, suppressing a grin. I don't think I've ever seen Michelle jealous before.

Angela has stepped back onto the porch and is studying the flower beds with great interest.

"Good luck," Michelle says to both of us.

"Thanks," Angela replies, looking embarrassed.

Angela and I walk to her car, which is gleaming in the daylight, the sun reflecting off its highly polished chrome accents. Angela certainly pampers this vehicle, I think to myself as I settle into the passenger seat.

It takes less then ten minutes to reach the freeway from my house, and soon we're on the open highway, with a couple of hours to kill before we reach Santa Cruz.

"How long have you known this hacker?" I ask her, trying to make conversation.

"Since I was a kid," she answers me. "He was my brother Rafa's best friend."

"Let me guess," I say. "They used to break into computer systems together."

Angela laughs heartily.

"Not at all," she says. "I don't think Rafa would have even made it through school if Dan hadn't helped him. They were an odd pair, those two, but somehow it worked. Dan helped Rafa with his homework, and Rafa kept the neighborhood kids from beating Dan up."

"They still keep in touch?" I ask.

Angela gives me an odd, anguished look, and then stares straight ahead at the road in front of her.

"My brother's dead," she says simply. "He was murdered when I was a teenager."

"Aw gee, I'm sorry," I say. "I didn't mean to pry."

"That's okay, it was a long time ago," she replies. "I can talk about it now. In fact, sometimes it helps to talk about it."

"What happened?" I ask gently.

"I'm not sure exactly how it happened," she begins tentatively. She pauses, reflecting on the past. "You know, when I was a kid, my brother Rafa was my hero. He looked out for me; he taught me things."

Angela glances at me.

"He's the one who showed me how to play soccer," she tells me. "And then when I got older, he made sure the neighborhood boys let me play in their games, even though they had a 'no girls' rule." Angela smiles to herself. "Nobody ever said no to Rafa. He was the biggest kid around, and very persuasive."

"He sounds like a nice guy," I comment, not sure what to say.

"He was," she agrees. "But I guess I didn't really know that much about him, especially once he was grown up." Angela sighs. "It turns out my hero wasn't exactly a model citizen. He was always 'between jobs,' and spent most of his time working on this baby," she says, patting the black dashboard of the Mustang. "I think he got by on charm and good looks. And that was his main problem—too much the ladies' man."

Angela pauses her narrative. I don't say anything, and the silence drags on for so long that I begin to think she's changed her mind about telling me her story. I occupy myself by gazing at the hills along the freeway.

"Ultimately, that's what killed him," she says finally, continuing as if she'd never stopped. "A few weeks before he died, he started seeing someone new. She never told him that she already had a boyfriend—a drug dealer."

"I can guess what happened," I say. "Did the police catch the dealer?"

Angela shakes her head.

"That's the most frustrating part," she says. "Everyone knew this dealer killed Rafa, but the only witness was the girlfriend, and she was too scared to talk."

Angela's expression belies a quiet, controlled rage.

"I swear," she says. "Those first couple of years after Rafa died, I could've killed the bastard who did it myself, if I'd known where to find him."

"I think I know what you mean."

# CHAPTER EIGHT

Dan lives in a white two-story wood frame house across the street from the beach. It's an older building and it could use a paint job, but it looks spacious. Dan rents the top floor from the house's owner, a retired widow who lives on the ground floor. Angela says that the owner likes Dan because he's polite and doesn't make much noise. Typical nerd, I think to myself.

Dan's apartment has its own entrance on the side of the house. We park the car and walk up the faded steps leading to his door. Angela knocks on the rickety screen door, but gets no answer. She opens the screen and knocks on the wood door behind it. Still no answer.

"Maybe he's asleep," I say to Angela.

"No, he's an early riser."

Angela knocks again. Behind me, I hear muted footsteps on the stairs. I turn around to see a man in his late twenties making his way up to us. He's wearing a wetsuit and carrying a surfboard. He's stripped the wetsuit down to his waist, so that the arms of the suit flap against his legs with each step he takes.

"We're looking for Dan," I say to the new arrival, who's still climbing the stairs.

Before he can answer, Angela steps forward and says, "Hi Dan. It's good to see you again."

"Same here," he responds, catching up with us on the landing. "It's been a while."

If this is Dan, then he's sure changed a lot since he was young. The man in front of me seems nothing like the geeky kid Angela described. He's short, which I somehow expected, but he's also muscular and fit, and his naturally brown skin has been made even darker by lots of time at the beach. He wears his wavy black hair in a Bohemian ponytail, and even the way he carries himself contradicts the mental image I'd already formed of him.

"You didn't tell me you were bringing someone," Dan says to Angela. He looks at me and says coolly, "You must be Jonathan."

"No, this is my friend Steven," Angela corrects him.

"I'm the one who needs your help," I add.

"Sure, I'd be glad to talk to you," he says, his voice friendlier now. "Let's get inside."

The little porch in front of Dan's apartment was not designed to comfortably hold three people and a surfboard. Angela and I have to move down a couple of steps just to give him enough room to unlock the door.

Once inside, Dan excuses himself and goes to a back room to take a shower and change. We're told to make ourselves at home.

At least the apartment looks like what I expected. To the left of the main hallway is a small living room. It has a fireplace, a big-screen TV, and a bookshelf in the corner. Across the hallway is the dining room, which has been completely taken over by computer equipment. There are at least three complete systems—a PC, a Macintosh, and a Sun workstation, all state-of-the-art. And in a corner, stacked up next to a surfboard, is a pile of miscellaneous equipment: a monitor, a couple of modems, and a few other peripherals. At least this guy's got the right set-up.

Angela and I decide to wait for him in the living room. I settle into a large, comfortable easy chair, and Angela takes a seat on the tired-looking sofa. Dan's living room is fairly neat and organized, but hardly a decorator's dream. The walls are bare except for a few posters. On the left wall, over the sofa, is a huge poster showing a dramatic photo of a surfer hanging motionless in the center of an enormous wave. The opposite wall sports a poster of Einstein playing a violin, along with another dramatic surfing photo. Over the fireplace is the only framed poster in the room; it's a colorful painting advertising a musical group called Mariachi Cobre, and it looks like it's been autographed by several of the band's members. A Dilbert calendar completes the room's decor.

A big old coffee table is sitting in the middle of the living room, just close enough to the sofa for someone to stretch out and put their legs on, which Angela does. I take a look at the reading material scattered on the table and decide that this guy is definitely not a typical programmer. In addition to the latest books on Linux, Java, and other programming languages, stacked on the coffee table are several issues of *Surfing Magazine*, as well as copies of *Gödel, Escher, Bach* and *A Brief History of Time*. I also spot a few issues of *2600: The Hacker Quarterly*.

"Dan isn't at all like I pictured him," I say to Angela as I thumb through a back copy of *Surfing*.

"What do you mean?"

"I don't know any other programmers who surf every morning before work."

"Oh that," she replies. "He picked it up when he came to Santa Cruz for college. I never thought of Dan as much of an athlete, but apparently he's become quite a surfer. Interesting, huh?"

"It's different," I agree, and go back to perusing Dan's magazines.

I've just picked up a copy of *2600* when Dan walks in fresh from the shower. He's wearing a pair of shorts, a faded T-shirt, and no shoes.

"Welcome to my place. Can I offer you guys something to drink?"

Both Angela and I decline, and Dan settles himself into a green bean bag chair behind the coffee table.

"So you're a computer consultant?" I ask him.

"Yeah. I like to call myself an international computer consultant. Sounds better. And I do travel sometimes—I've done jobs in Australia and Hawaii, wherever I can combine surfing and my work."

Dan leans back in the chair and stretches out.

"So what kind of problem do you guys need help with?" he asks, clearly expecting something run-of-the-mill.

"Where do we begin?" Angela says, looking at me for help.

"You can start with what happened yesterday."

"Right. Good idea."

Angela takes a deep breath and begins. Slowly and carefully, she explains to Dan the situation concerning Leticia and our recent visit from the San Francisco police. Dan is intrigued. As she talks, he shifts from his laid back position, and sits up as straight as one can in a bean bag chair. He doesn't even wait for her to finish before jumping in.

"I can appreciate the mess you're in," he says. "But I don't get it. What do you need a security expert for?"

"As I've explained," Angela answers, "The police refused to give us any details. And we need to know more." She falters, trying to decide how to phrase her request. "We need your help breaking into the SFPD database so we can look at the crime report."

"Whoa," says Dan. "That's not exactly legal."

"I know," Angela replies. She leans forward in her seat and looks at Dan beseechingly. "But I…we really need your help."

Dan doesn't reply right away. Instead he looks around the room, as if he's taking stock of his life. Suddenly it dawns on me just how much we're asking from this guy. Here he's worked his butt off to make it out of the barrio; he's finally set up his life the way he wants it, and Angela has just asked him to risk a few years in jail. What were we thinking? Any sane person would say no.

After a couple of minutes Dan settles his gaze on Angela. There's an obvious tenderness in his eyes when he looks at her, and something else that's less clear—longing. He's in love with her! And I bet he has been for a long time. I wonder if she knows.

"Sure," he says nonchalantly, "No problem."

"I knew we could count on you!" Angela says excitedly. She jumps up from the sofa and throws her arms around him exuberantly, nearly toppling him off the bean bag chair. Dan grins sheepishly under her embrace.

"When can you start?" she asks, finally unlocking her arms.

"Right now."

Dan and Angela head for the computer room. I follow behind, and overhear Angela thanking Dan once again.

"I'm glad to help you guys out," he replies, "But I've got to ask you: what does Jonathan think of you hanging out with Steven? Isn't he the jealous type?"

"Jonathan is never jealous," Angela says wistfully. "And it doesn't matter anyway. We haven't seen each other in a few months."

Dan's response is automatic and unfelt.

"I'm sorry to hear that."

Dan takes a seat at his desk and boots up the Sun workstation. I find a couple of folding chairs and Angela and I sit down to watch. Soon we see lines of code rolling across the monitor. Dan punches in a couple of symbols here, a line of code there, and the screen changes.

A few minutes go by in silence. Dan seems to have forgotten we're even here; he's completely absorbed by his work.

"We've hit a snag," he says at last. "I can't find any Internet links for the SFPD. Are you sure these guys are hooked up to the Net?"

"No, I'm not," I say.

"In fact, it would make sense if they weren't," Angela adds. "I'm sure they don't want to risk any computer breaches."

I should have thought of that. I guess I won't be breaking any laws today.

"Thanks for trying," I say to Dan.

"I'm not finished yet. There's still a couple of things I can try. Can someone get me a can of soda from the fridge?"

Angela volunteers and takes off down the hallway.

"And grab the bag of chips on the counter!" he yells out after her.

"How are you going to get into their system if they're not even hooked up to the Internet?" I ask.

"I'm counting on somebody there having a modem. Do you know the phone number for the SFPD?"

"I had a business card, but I threw it away."

"I've got the number," Angela says, entering the room with enough junk food for everyone. "Inspector Kamimoto gave me his card yesterday. I have it right here in my purse."

Angela puts down the food, gets her purse, and digs out the card.

"Here you go," she says, handing it to Dan.

"Great. This is all I need."

Angela resumes her seat and picks up a handful of chips. I feel like I'm back in college, pulling an all-nighter, except it's broad daylight.

"But what can you do with his phone number?" Angela asks him.

"It's called war dialing. It can take a while, but I know a couple of tricks to make it go faster."

"War dialing?" I ask. "What's that?"

It takes Dan a minute to realize I've asked him a question.

"I start with this number," he says finally, holding up Kamimoto's business card, "and then I check a couple hundred of the phone numbers closest to it. At least a few of those numbers will be for modems in the police department. Once I find the right one, we're in."

"I see."

He makes it sound simple.

We watch Dan execute a series of commands, and then sit back in his chair, relaxed.

"My little program is off and running," he says. "Now we just have to wait and see what it finds. I don't think it will take too long though."

Dan picks up a computer manual and starts thumbing through it, snacking as he reads. Occasionally, he looks up to check the progress of the program, and then dives back into his manual and junk food. Angela and I spend our time wandering around the room and looking at magazines.

After about half an hour, Dan's computer beeps. He puts down the manual and looks at the screen.

"This looks promising," he says to himself.

Dan starts typing in commands.

"I'm at a C prompt," he tells us. "Security is not strong on this box. This shouldn't take long."

Dan works determinedly for a few more minutes.

"We're in," he says at last. "I've gained control of the server for the public affairs office, and it seems to be part of a larger internal network."

"Congratulations," Angela says, patting him on the back.

He smiles up at her, then opens another bag of chips and continues working in silence. A short while later, he comes up for air.

"I've accessed the server for the homicide group," he announces triumphantly.

"Perfect," I say.

"I'm sure I can locate the police report," he tells us. "It looks like they organize them by chronology, type of crime, victim . . . how do you want me to search for this case?"

"Victim," Angela and I say together.

"Okay. What's the victim's name again?"

"Leticia Morgan," I reply, feeling a fresh pang of grief as I spell the name for him.

We fall silent again. For the next few minutes there's no sound in the room but the click-clack of the keyboard.

"Sorry," he says finally, "It doesn't look like they have a report for her in their database."

"They probably haven't added her file yet," I say.

Dan turns to me.

"Would you like me to check their e-mail?"

"You can do that?"

"Oh yeah, electronic mail is far less private than most people realize. Kind of like corresponding on postcards," Dan says matter-of-factly.

He turns back to his computer.

"If I can break into the mail management system, I shouldn't have much trouble locating this guy's e-mail," Dan says. "If he's like most people, he lets his mail sit on the server, where it's easy for hackers like me to get at."

Dan bangs away at his computer keyboard while Angela and I dip into a box of Ding-Dongs sitting on top of the printer. I can see why hacking lends itself to junk food consumption. When you're this busy, there's no time to eat much else.

"I think I've found what we're looking for," Dan says after a short while.

"What have you got?" I ask.

"It looks like two or three online discussions mentioning Leticia's name. Not too extensive, but it's better than nothing."

"Can we print them out?" Angela asks.

"Sure."

The printer starts cranking out copies of the e-mail. I pull out each page as it's printed and look it over. Leticia's name is sprinkled throughout the e-mails. There are also a lot of references to simply "the victim."

Once the printing is finished I gather up the papers and take them with me to the living room. Dan and Angela linger in his office. I know they must be nearly as curious as I am, and I'm grateful to them for letting me read this first by myself.

I lay the papers on the coffee table and arrange them chronologically. The first piece of mail I look at is a discussion between

Inspector Kamimoto and Lieutenant O'Hanna, who I guess must be Kamimoto's boss. Their conversation lays out the crime and the SFPD's investigation. It's hard for me to piece things together exactly, because it's a conversation between two people who already know what they're talking about. But there are enough references for me to get the basic facts.

It turns out Leticia was killed in her sister's house. The place was ransacked and some jewelry was stolen. Luckily, no one else was hurt—Leticia's sister and her family were out of the house at the time.

I stop reading and let my mind wander, remembering. I've met Leticia's sister, Mona. I even went to her house once. It's in the Marina district; one of those charming Victorians everyone associates with San Francisco. It's hard to picture it as a murder scene.

I shake the image from my mind and pick up the next sheet of paper.

It seems that at first, Lieutenant O'Hanna figured that Leticia's killing was a simple case of robbery gone wrong. But Kamimoto wasn't convinced, and upon further investigation, he found evidence that the murder was the work of a professional. Certain details about the "method of entry" and the relative lack of mess made it clear that the killer was well-practiced.

I reread that particular discussion. Leticia was killed by a professional. What the hell is going on?

I quickly read through the rest of the papers, hungry for more information. There are two other e-mail exchanges involving Leticia. One is an irrelevant discussion of some police protocol. But in the other one, Kamimoto is telling O'Hanna who he plans to interview as part of the investigation. I notice my name is near the top of the list.

I look over the papers again, but I don't learn anything new. Finally, I gather them up and walk back over to Dan's office.

"Well?" asks Angela. "Did you find out anything?"

I nod.

"Here, see for yourself."

I hand her the documents. Angela takes the papers and walks back into the living room. She settles into the easy chair and starts reading. Dan follows her out of the office and sits on one of the chair's arms. He leans in close to Angela so he can read over her shoulder.

I've stretched out on the living room sofa and am staring at the ceiling. There's a spider web in the corner nearest the fireplace. I watch it closely, wondering idly if its creator is still around someplace.

"Leticia was killed by a hit man," Angela says after she's finished reading.

"Apparently," I answer. "Which means that now I'm looking for two people—the killer, and his employer."

No one else says anything. Angela gathers the papers and lays them neatly on the coffee table.

"I think we should be going," she says at last. She gives Dan a goodbye hug and squeezes his hand affectionately. "Thanks for all your help. We couldn't have done it without you."

"Anytime," he says, not letting go of her hand. "Let me know if you need anything else."

"Sure will."

"I'm just sorry we couldn't find out more," he continues.

"You found out plenty," I interject from my perch on the sofa.

I swing my legs off the couch and stand up.

"I really appreciate all you've done for me today," I tell him.

I shake Dan's hand vigorously as I thank him. In truth, though, I'm not sure how grateful I really feel. I have the strange sensation of having crossed a line, as if this new information just pushed me past the point of no return.

Angela and I don't speak much the first half of the drive home. I stare out the window, trying to figure out my next steps.

"Do me a favor," I say to Angela after awhile. "If Michelle asks you what we found out today, just tell her the police don't have Leticia's case file in their database."

"You want me to lie to her?" she asks me.

"Just don't tell her everything we found out," I reply. "There's no need to burden her with the gory details."

"I see."

Angela gives me an appraising look.

"Tell me," she says. "Are you trying to protect Michelle, or keep her from interfering with your investigation?"

"Probably a little of both," I answer truthfully. "Just do me the favor, okay?"

"Of course."

Angela negotiates a sharp turn on the mountain freeway and goes back to driving one-handed.

"I just can't figure out who did it, although it must be someone connected to Hays Software," she says. "Why else would Leticia resign from her job?"

"That's the most likely scenario," I agree. "She found out something about Hays Software, and someone had her killed for it." I look over at Angela. "Somehow, we need to find out more about what's going on at that little startup."

"Maybe you can do some digging at the party tomorrow night," she replies. "I'm sure Arthur Hays will be there."

"What party?"

"You know, Jason Grimshaw's birthday party," Angela says, looking at me like I just asked her when Christmas is. "The social event of the season. I tried to finagle an invitation, but Mitch said senior staff only. You must be going."

With everything that's happened this past week, I completely forgot about the party. Jason Grimshaw, the founder and most senior partner of Grimshaw, Turner & Willson, is turning seventy this week, and to celebrate he's invited three hundred of his closest friends and business contacts—as well as lots of press and the entire staff of Grimshaw Turner—to a grand party at his golf club.

"Jason Grimshaw's birthday bash. I'd forgotten about it," I tell Angela. "You're right, Michelle and I are going. Maybe I'll be able to ask Hays a few questions."

"Just don't be too obvious. I don't trust him."

"Me neither," I say. "Don't worry, I'll be discreet. Sorry you won't be there."

"Me too," Angela replies with a sigh. "But I couldn't convince Mitch that it would be an advantage to *Digital Business* to have me there. I'm just a junior staff writer."

"You know," I say without thinking, "when I first met you, and Mitch made me take you on as my apprentice, I thought maybe you two were involved."

Angela's face is the picture of incredulity.

"In other words, you thought I slept my way into a job," she says with disgust. "What ever gave you that idea?"

"Hey, look at it from my perspective," I say, starting to feel defensive. "All of a sudden Mitch shows up with this new writer, who happens to be an attractive young woman, and he's giving her a special assignment. It just looked suspicious, that's all."

"What a sexist thing to say. It never occurred to you that I might be a talented writer, and *that's* why I was getting extra consideration?"

Actually, knowing Mitch the way I do, that would never have been the first thing I thought of.

"What a primitive remark," Angela mutters to herself.

"What was that?" I ask her sternly. "Listen, if you've got something to say, say it out loud."

"Fine," she replies. "I said it was a primitive remark."

I'm in no mood for this.

"You know, I don't need your feminist crap," I tell her.

"Crap, is it? I don't believe this. I get the world's best hacker to snoop for you, drive all the way to Santa Cruz, spend hours staring at a computer screen, and this is the thanks I get? What was I thinking helping you out?"

"What *were* you thinking?" I reply hotly. "If I'm such a damn Neanderthal, then why are you helping me?"

Angela looks at me; her expression has changed from one of indignation to bewilderment.

"I don't know," she says quietly. "I've never stopped to think about it."

We both fall silent. I go back to watching the scenery, impatient for this ride to be over. Finally, Angela starts talking. Her voice is calm now, her previous anger apparently forgotten.

"You know, when Rafa was killed, I tried desperately to get somebody to *do* something. The police didn't think they had enough evidence, so they gave up. The girlfriend was too terrified to do the right thing. Dan was off backpacking through Europe, and even my parents . . . I think they figured they'd already lost one kid, they didn't want to risk any more. They kept telling me to 'get on with my life, for Rafa's sake.'" She grips the steering wheel tightly as she tells me this. "I was sixteen years old, and had no idea how to even find my brother's killer. So eventually, I just gave up."

Angela looks at me earnestly before turning her attention back to the road.

"I guess the point is," she continues, "that I know what it takes for you to do what you're doing for Leticia. And knowing that, I can't *not* help you."

I stare at Angela, studying her face intently. Somehow, it's like I'm seeing her for the first time.

"Thanks," I say softly.

Angela simply nods her head.

"Besides," she says, adopting a lighter tone. "I don't really think you're a Neanderthal."

"That's good to know," I reply, just as lightheartedly.

"Yep, I'd say you're at least Cro-Magnon."

Angela's remark catches me off-guard, and I jerk my head to look at her, just in time to see a mischievous grin spread across her face.

"Okay, this is war," I announce with mock ire. I pick a paper cup off the floor and toss it at her. It lands on her forearm and bounces off harmlessly.

"No fair!" she protests laughingly. "I'm driving, I can't defend myself."

"You should have thought of that before."

"Alright, alright. Truce."

By this time we're both laughing, and I realize that it's the first time I've done so since Leticia died. It feels good.

# Chapter Nine

Angela was right about Jason Grimshaw's birthday party—it is the social event of the year. Michelle is acutely aware of this and is taking even longer than usual to get ready. She's pretty excited about the prospect of schmoozing with the who's who of Silicon Valley. She's even heard rumors that some VC hot shots from the East Coast are flying in just to attend this party (and swing a deal or two on the side, no doubt).

"Are you about ready honey?" I ask her.

"Yes, almost," Michelle replies, digging around in a drawer for a pair of pantyhose.

I have it easy. I simply put on the same tux I always wear to these formal gatherings. It takes me less than ten minutes to get dressed, except for tying the bow tie, which is always a headache. I've tried twice already, and I can't get it to look right.

"I'm really looking forward to this party," Michelle says from her corner of the room.

I stop fiddling with the stubborn bow tie and look over to where Michelle is standing. She looks ravishing. Her jade silk dress cascades from her shoulders down to her toes, accentuating every curve along the way. I don't know if it's the dress, or

Michelle's heightened mood, but her green eyes are more brilliant and catlike than I've ever seen them.

"Wow," I say. "You look great."

"So do you."

Michelle walks over to me, takes hold of the tie, and fashions it into a perfect bow.

"Thanks," I say, kissing her.

"Anytime."

We head downstairs to the family room, where we say goodbye to Chloe and the babysitter before heading to the garage.

"Tonight promises to be very interesting," Michelle says with a roguish look.

"What do you mean?"

"Jason and Marcus in the same room," she explains. "The grand old master and the upstart pretender, vying for the same audience."

"But it's Jason Grimshaw's party," I point out.

"That won't stop the ever ambitious Marcus Turner," she says, getting into the car. "Just you watch."

I close her door, walk to the other side of the car, and take my place in the driver's seat.

"I didn't realize there was such dissension in the ranks of Grimshaw, Turner & Willson," I say blithely.

"Not dissension," Michelle corrects me. "Full-blown jealousy. Marcus has been a little too successful lately, at least as far as Jason is concerned. I'm sure one of the reasons the old tiger decided to turn his birthday into such a media event is so that he can recapture some of the limelight."

"So what exactly can we expect from Mr. Grimshaw this evening?"

"I can't predict. But whatever happens, it should be fun."

Michelle is grinning from ear to ear in anticipation. It's great to see her this happy. Her job means a lot to her; it was a big deal getting hired right out of business school, and Michelle has worked hard to prove to her bosses that they made the right decision. After all that work, a party like this is like icing on the cake. She'll be shaking hands and networking the minute we walk through the door.

My goals are entirely different. What I want are some answers.

We arrive at Grimshaw's club and hand our keys to a valet before moving with a surge of the Silicon Valley elite toward the main building. At the door, we present our engraved invitations to the white-gloved attendant and are granted passage inside. While Michelle checks her wrap, I stand idly with my hands in my pockets and examine our surroundings. Even from outside the main hall, I can already spot several prominent venture capitalists and entrepreneurs.

"Ready?" Michelle says to me, putting her arm through mine.

"Absolutely."

I guide her to the grand entrance, where we make our way down a short flight of stairs and into the main ballroom. The room is cavernous, with several large windows that stretch halfway to the cathedral ceiling. Two enormous doors along the back wall are open, revealing a large patio, and further away, an immaculately groomed golf course. There must be two dozen crystal chandeliers hanging above us, all of them so brightly polished that they twinkle with the slightest breeze. Every wall is lined with a series of buffet tables, each one loaded with food and drink.

"Would you care for champagne, Ma'am?"

I turn around to see a waiter dressed in black trousers and a white waistcoat offering Michelle a glass of champagne from a silver tray. She takes a glass and the waiter then proffers the tray to me. I pick up a drink and the waiter moves on.

"Who do you want to talk with first?" I ask Michelle.

"I'm not sure. Let's just start circulating and see who we run into."

Gazing about the crowd, which looks like it's already around three hundred people, I spot several more familiar faces, most of them well-known in Silicon Valley. If I wanted to, I could probably meet more rich and famous people here tonight than I do in a typical year working at *Digital Business*

"There's Bob Spenlow from Carmel Capital," Michelle says. "Let's go say hello to him. I want to see if he's really as hard-nosed as everyone says he is."

Spenlow is widely known as the curmudgeon of west coast venture capitalists, and is famous for cutting people off by simply stating to them that he does "not suffer fools gladly." More than one hopeful entrepreneur has been denied funding from Spenlow with precisely those words.

Spenlow is standing alone near a buffet table, wearing a gray suit that matches his gray hair. He's helping himself to some of the hors d'oeuvres on the table, all the while surveying the party with a dour expression on his face. No doubt he'd prefer to be at his office right now, looking over another business plan, but it would be truly gauche not to show up for Grimshaw's birthday celebration.

Just as Michelle and I are approaching, Spenlow bites into a cracker piled high with what looks like some sort of Cajun crab dip, so now he'll have to greet us with a mouth full of food. It turns out to be even more awkward than I anticipated. Before we can say hello, Spenlow starts to cough.

Michelle and I stand off to the side, politely waiting for Spenlow to clear his throat. But instead the coughing becomes more pronounced. Then Spenlow starts gagging and turning red. He bends over; tears are running down his cheeks and snot is coming out his nose. Should we call a waiter? Dial 911? I haven't updated my CPR certification since Chloe was born, but I think I remember what to do.

Right as I'm about to put my CPR training into practice, Spenlow looks up at us and manages to gulp down some air.

"Spice," he gasps. "It's the spice."

Somebody should have told him that Grimshaw likes exceedingly spicy food. Michelle warned me that there are always a couple of "killer" dishes at his parties, and unfortunately, you never know which ones they are until some hardy—or naive—soul discovers them by accident.

Spenlow downs some water and wipes a napkin across his face. I guess he won't be dropping dead at our feet after all. No doubt Jason Grimshaw would be pleased to know that. I'm sure that after all the trouble he's gone to with this party, he'd hate to see his thunder stolen by a dead man.

Since Spenlow is showing signs of recovery, we decide to move on and let him recover without an audience.

"Excuse us," I say as I walk away with Michelle.

"That was embarrassing," she says to me.

"I guess even the elite can succumb to a strong enough pepper. Remember, avoid the crab dip."

"You'd better believe I will."

As we move across the room, Michelle spots one of her colleagues from Grimshaw Turner.

"I should go say hello," she tells me.

"Go ahead. I'll keep making the rounds."

I watch Michelle glide off into a group of well-dressed partygoers, then turn my attention to the crowd around me, planning to begin my search for Arthur Hays. Instead, I'm greeted by Franklin Albright, a rising young executive at Van Ness Securities, one of the better known investment banks in San Francisco. At 29, Albright is already a managing director at the bank, which is why Mitch likes to call him "the Wonder Kid of investment banking."

"Steven Cavanaugh," Albright says, extending his hand to me. "It's good to see you. I'm so looking forward to lunch on Friday. I can't tell you how flattered I am that my favorite business publication wants to interview me."

"Mitch is convinced that you're destined to become CEO of Van Ness," I state simply. "And we like to interview all the up-and-comers."

"Really?" Albright responds. "I must say, I feel humbled to be included in such a group."

I doubt it, I think to myself. Albright is known for a lot of things, and humility is not one of them.

"How are you enjoying the party?" I ask him.

Despite Albright's impressive credentials and successful career, I'm surprised to see him here. He's an important executive, of course, but most VCs think of the service people—

accountants, lawyers, and investment bankers—as just a bunch of leeches living off other peoples' ideas and industry, and only grudgingly tolerate them as a necessary evil. Then I remember that Albright is the son of John Albright, a former executive at some of the biggest companies in Silicon Valley. The senior Albright accrued a lot of stock options during his career, retired rich, and has become a new player in venture capital. No doubt it was John Albright who was invited to the party, and the son, well aware of the networking opportunities, decided to tag along.

"I hear that everybody who's anybody is here tonight," Albright says, taking a sip of his drink and looking around the room. "But I haven't run into anyone I don't already know yet, have you?"

"I think I saw Jenny Noto just a couple of minutes ago," I say, throwing out a lure that I'm sure will get Albright to move on.

Jenny is the president and founder of Mambo Software, a red-hot Internet startup. Every investment bank in the nation would love to underwrite their IPO.

"She's here? I haven't seen her," Albright says with studied nonchalance.

"I'm sure I saw her somewhere over in that direction," I say, gesturing toward a table laden with a variety of silver and crystal punch bowls.

"Oh good, I was on my way to freshen my drink. Maybe I'll run into her," he says.

He shakes my hand politely and then moves smoothly into the crowd, strolling in an unhurried yet determined fashion towards Jenny.

Now that I'm free of Albright, I take a moment to look around the grand hall. Despite the dense crowd, it doesn't take me long to catch sight of Arthur Hays. Standing conspicuously between two buffet tables, and holding forth to a small but growing group of people, Hays looks as happy as a lark. I decide to keep an eye on him and wait for an opportunity to talk with him when he's alone.

Not far from Hays and his admirers, a much larger group of people has gathered around Marcus Turner, laughing at his bon mots and occasionally even clapping. I see right away that Michelle was correct. Ever polished and sophisticated, Turner is once again stealing the spotlight from Grimshaw.

I catch a glimpse of green out of the corner of my eye and turn to see Michelle approaching me, a radiant smile on her face.

"I'm having a great time," she tells me.

"I'm glad. But I haven't seen the birthday boy yet, have you?"

"No, he's nowhere to be found. And it's his own party."

Just then a wave of laughter and smattered cheering ripples from the other side of the room and moves in our direction. It's soon apparent what's causing the commotion. The crowd parts slowly and Jason Grimshaw moves toward the center of the room . . . on a horse!

Grimshaw is dressed up in a royal medieval costume—two sizes too big for his diminutive frame—complete with an ornately jeweled crown. He looks like a frumpy King Arthur. The horse he's atop is huge and well-muscled, like one of those beasts you expect to see hauling a beer wagon. Grimshaw has to duck his head to keep it from hitting the chandeliers hanging from the ceiling.

I immediately wonder what they're going to do if this Trojan-sized horse dumps one on the floor, but I see a couple of janitors hovering behind the animal with pooper scoopers and plastic trash bags. The head waiter circles back and forth nervously behind them. Grimshaw swings his right leg over the saddle and alights on the floor. An assistant moves in quickly and takes hold of the horse's bridle to lead it away, but Grimshaw raises his right hand to indicate that he should stop. Grimshaw obviously wants to savor the moment and is in no rush to remove his best prop. The assistant furrows his brow, but says nothing.

"Ladies and gentlemen, loyal subjects," Grimshaw intones as he surveys the room. "I welcome you to my kingdom."

Grimshaw lifts a glass of champagne off the tray of a passing waiter and downs it with one swig. He smiles broadly at his audience, pauses dramatically, then waves his hand to signal his aide to take the horse away. The assistant leads the great animal out the back door, with the janitors following closely behind. The head waiter looks relieved.

I turn to Michelle to share a cynical observation, but she's already engaged in animated conversation with the woman next to her. They're whispering, so I can't make out what they're saying, but judging by the look on Michelle's face, it must be pretty funny.

Grimshaw pontificates to his captive audience for a few more minutes, all the while downing one glass of champagne after another. He looks irritated if there isn't a waiter at his elbow to provide a fresh glass whenever he wants one.

"Quite a spectacle, isn't it?" someone says to me.

I look over and am pleased to see Ambrose Hunter, a member of Silicon Valley's Old Guard—the generation of venture investors that funded the microchip and the personal computer. Ambrose is one of the few people I've interviewed whom I truly admire.

"It certainly is," I agree.

A waiter passes by and offers us champagne.

"Thank you," Ambrose says as he picks up a glass.

Ambrose is white-haired and courtly. He's about seventy, and is well-respected in the industry. I've always enjoyed his stories about venture capital in the 1960s, when he used to lunch with other VC pioneers at Sam's Grill in San Francisco. The VCs would routinely interview an entrepreneur during lunch, then end the meal by asking the entrepreneur to step outside while they passed the hat around to see how much money they could come up with.

Although today Ambrose could boast as much success as Jason Grimshaw—he started scoring big with early investments in Apple Computer and Intel—he's much less flamboyant. In fact, he prefers a low profile. "As long as the deal flow for our venture partnership is good," he once told me, "then we really don't need the extra publicity."

We stand there for a moment watching Grimshaw perform.

"So what do you think of all this?" I ask Ambrose.

He looks more amused than appalled.

"I've known Jason for years," he says. "I think I'd be disappointed if he didn't act like himself."

Just then a waiter approaches with a slip of paper on a small silver tray.

"Mr. Hunter, you have a message."

Ambrose picks up the note and reads it.

"I must be going," he says to me. "Business calls."

"The last time we talked you said you were retiring," I remind him.

"I was, but you know how it is."

He disappears into the crowd, off to make another few million dollars for his firm.

Meanwhile, back at center stage, Grimshaw has been speaking and drinking for over half an hour, and the effects of so much champagne are starting to show. His speech is slurring and he's becoming incoherent. He rambles on irrationally, throwing out random thoughts about his pet peeves—government regulation, taxes, investment bankers, and anyone that gets in the way of his prosperity. He's particularly incensed about some state proposition that will be on this fall's ballot.

"And what I am saying," Grimshaw spouts to his audience, "is that if Proposition 225 passes, Silicon Valley will be doomed. Those rascally lawyers will drain the lifeblood out of all our companies with their frivolous lawsuits!"

Grimshaw pauses after this momentous declaration, and Marcus Turner seizes the opportunity to step forward and join his partner. No doubt he's trying to keep Grimshaw from making a complete idiot of himself, not because he cares about Grimshaw's reputation, but because he doesn't want the firm to look ridiculous.

Lean and distinguished in a double-breasted Italian tuxedo, the composed Turner is a stark contrast to the rumpled Grimshaw in his baggy costume and ill-fitting crown. Grimshaw gives Turner a startled look as Turner raises his glass and addresses the gathering.

"Thank you, Jason, for your usual pearls of wisdom," Turner says with absolutely no trace of sarcasm in his voice. "Silicon Valley would not be what it is without you."

Turner beams at the crowd.

"I would like to propose a toast. To Jason Grimshaw on his seventieth birthday—our true king!"

"Hear, hear," say many in the room.

Grimshaw gives a drunken smile and looks around the room, obviously pleased.

What follows is a series of toasts and tributes, poems and roasting from various Grimshaw Turner partners. They're joined by some of Grimshaw's peers, although I notice that Bob Spenlow doesn't give a speech. As a junior member in the firm, Michelle is not called on to say anything. If all goes well, however, Michelle will be giving a toast at Marcus Turner's seventieth birthday party twenty years from now.

After about forty minutes, Marcus Turner returns to his post as self-appointed master of ceremonies. He brings the toasts to an end graciously, and then makes a final announcement.

"We have one last surprise for Jason tonight," he tells the assembled guests.

Grimshaw looks around the room like a kid on Christmas morning who can't wait to get the last, big present that's been saved for the end. From the direction of the kitchen comes the sound of a woman's voice singing—

*Don't let it be forgot,*
*that once there was a spot;*
*for one brief shining moment*
*that was known as Camelot.*

Grimshaw's head jerks in the direction of the singing and he blushes with pleasure. As the crowd parts, a young woman dressed up as Guenevere and showing some serious cleavage walks toward Grimshaw while she continues to sing. She moves forward and joins hands with Grimshaw; together they sing the conclusion of Camelot once again. Grimshaw's voice is surprisingly good.

Grimshaw's main philanthropic activity is sitting on the board of San Francisco's premier theater company; Guenevere is obviously its main representative tonight. I figure Grimshaw must have raided its closet to get his King Arthur costume. Where the horse came from, God only knows.

After a second round of "Camelot," Guenevere leads Grimshaw away, allowing him to exit almost as dramatically as he entered. With the main attraction gone, the crowd begins to break up into small groups, and a few of the guests head for the exit.

Michelle takes off for the ladies' lounge, leaving me free to search for Hays. I scan the room and spot him standing at a buffet table, spreading pâté on a cracker. For the moment, he's alone.

I walk over to him and extend my hand.

"So Arthur, how are you?"

Hays glances at my hand and makes no effort to shake it. He acts as if he doesn't recognize me.

"Remember me, Steven Cavanaugh of *Digital Business*?"

"Oh, right, right."

Hays gives me a half-hearted handshake. He seems far more interested in his paté than my company.

"Are you enjoying the party?" I ask, trying to break the ice.

"Pretty entertaining. Jason Grimshaw is always full of surprises."

It's getting late and I'm concerned Hays is going to get away, so I decide to skip the niceties and get to the point.

"Isn't that terrible about Leticia Morgan?" I say abruptly.

Hays looks surprised. Now I have his attention.

"What do you mean?" he asks.

"I'm talking about how she was killed."

"How do you know about that?"

"I was interviewed by the SFPD as part of their investigation," I reply.

"Oh, I see," Hays says, picking up another cracker. He continues talking while he loads the cracker with pâté. "Leticia meant a lot to Hays Software. She was a hard worker and a great person. I sure hope the police figure out what happened."

Hays stuffs the cracker into his mouth, downing it in two bites.

"Did anything unusual happen that day?" I ask him.

"What do you mean by 'unusual'?"

As I'm about to answer, Marcus Turner joins us.

"Steven," he says, patting me on the back. "I must congratulate you on your team winning the tournament. To be honest, I was surprised. I didn't think your team was that strong."

"The tournament?" I ask. I haven't played on a weekend league in a couple of years, so I'm not sure what Turner is talking about.

"The championship game between the Panthers and the Broncos," Turner clarifies. "I was at that game. My daughter Chelsea plays for the Panthers. I saw you and Michelle there, so I assume your daughter—Chloe, is it?—plays for the Broncos."

"Right," I say. "She just started with the team this year, but she really likes it. In fact, just this morning she was bemoaning the fact that the season's over."

"I didn't know you guys knew each other," Hays chimes in, his mouth full of beluga caviar.

Turner notices a couple of stray fish eggs on Hays' chin, and gives him a slightly disgusted look before responding.

"Steven is married to Michelle Trudeau. I don't know if you've met her. She's one of our associates."

"So your wife works at Grimshaw Turner," Hays says, his mouth still full of food. "That must make your job pretty easy."

I've heard this accusation plenty of times before, and I give my standard response.

"Michelle and I have a strict agreement about not sharing confidential information."

"Of course you do," Hays replies, clearly skeptical.

"We have complete confidence in Michelle's discretion," Turner says affably.

Thank you, Mr. Turner, I think to myself. I'd like to say something rude to Hays, but I need information from him, so it's probably not a good idea to tick him off. I opt instead to change the subject, and bring the conversation back around to Leticia.

"I was just talking with Arthur here about the tragic loss of Leticia Morgan," I say to Turner.

"Yes, I was shocked," Turner says, shaking his head sadly. "I personally recruited her for Hays Software."

"So she told me."

"I have no idea how we're going to replace her, at least any time soon," he continues. "She was among the best in her field—one of the few PR people I knew who actually understood the product she was pitching. She had a very strong background in programming."

"I know," I say. "Her bachelor's degree was in computer science."

"Steven wanted to know if Leticia was acting funny before she died," Hays interjects, directing his comment at Turner.

"Funny?"

"I guess it's just the reporter in me," I say, making light of my question. "I was just wondering, did she do anything odd, like get mad at anyone or quit her job, that kind of stuff."

"Not that I know of," Turner offers. "But you would know better, Arthur. Had she been acting differently lately?"

"No, not at all. Everything seemed perfectly normal."

That's the answer I expected, but I decide to press the issue anyway.

"So she wasn't thinking of leaving Hays Software to try her hand at something else?" I ask them both.

"Of course not," Hays answers. "She took her job very seriously. And we were going to give her a nice little chunk of stock. I can't believe she'd move on until the company had gone public."

I watch Hays down another hors d'oeuvre. He's lying, and I wish I knew why.

"What makes you think Leticia wanted to resign?" Turner asks me.

"Nothing specific," I lie. "A few times at lunch she mentioned that it would be kind of fun to run her own PR agency. And I got the feeling that lately she'd been leaning more and more in that direction."

"I had no idea," he replies. "How well did you know Leticia?"

"We went to high school together. We were pretty good friends."

"Then I am truly sorry for your loss," Turner says, realizing for the first time that this is more than just a story for me.

"So, I guess all this will delay publishing the interview," Hays says abruptly.

Turner gives Hays an astonished look. Apparently he finds his behavior as bizarre and callous as I do.

But Hays is oblivious to his patron's displeasure. He goes on to pitch the virtues of Hays Software, without giving any technical details, of course. Turner listens briefly, then checks his watch and decides it's time to go. As he's leaving, he makes a point of once again offering me his condolences.

After a couple of more sound bites about how his product will revolutionize the Internet, Hays bids me goodbye as well.

By now the party crowd has dwindled to about half its original size. Jason Grimshaw is nowhere to be seen. He's probably gone, no doubt safely nestled in Guenevere's bosom. I spy Michelle across the room, talking with someone I don't recognize. I decide to join her anyway, and spend the next few minutes pretending to listen while Michelle and a colleague discuss internal rates of return, management fees, and other esoterica of venture capital deal structure.

When midnight strikes, hundreds of gold balloons rain down from the ceiling, signaling the end of the fête. But this last spectacle only serves to further excite the hard-core revelers, who have been drinking champagne and liquor for over four hours now. They immediately start playing with the balloons, bouncing them off each other's heads and kicking them around the room.

A would-be soccer player bumps into Michelle and steadies himself by holding on to her, a little longer than necessary. I grab him by the collar and give him a shove back over to his pals.

"Let's go," I say to Michelle.

She gives me her hand and I guide her through a gauntlet of popping balloons and giggling guests to the nearest exit.

# Chapter Ten

The sun is shining through the skylight at full force this morning, bathing me in luxurious warmth as I lie propped up on a couple of pillows. I'm lounging in my favorite sweats, sipping coffee and reading the newspaper—doing my best to get my mind off the hunt for Leticia's killer, if only for a while.

Michelle is next to me on the bed, lying on her stomach and industriously working a crossword puzzle. Downstairs, Chloe is munching on toast and peanut butter and indulging in a favorite pastime: watching cartoons. Ah, the bliss of a lazy Sunday morning.

Our bliss is broken by an unwelcome sound.

"Was that the doorbell?" I ask.

"I didn't hear anything," Michelle replies without looking up from her crossword.

I go back to reading, but before I've finished the next paragraph, Chloe bursts in.

"Mom, Dad, there's someone at the door!" she exclaims.

I slide out from under the blanket of newspaper sections covering me and put on a T-shirt before heading downstairs with Chloe. As we approach the front door, we hear someone rapping on it insistently. I look through the peephole. It's Inspector Kamimoto!

I open the door.

"Mr. Cavanaugh, sorry to bother you on a weekend, but I'd like to ask you a couple of more questions," he says. "Mind if I come in? It will only take a few minutes."

"Why not," I say, feeling annoyed.

I let him into the house and then turn to Chloe.

"I need to talk in private with Mr. Kamimoto," I tell her. "Why don't you go keep your mother company for a while."

"But Rugrats is still on."

"Ask Mom if you can watch it on our TV."

Chloe trudges up the stairs, none too happy about being evicted from her favorite spot.

I usher Kamimoto into the living room, then take a seat opposite his. "Okay, Inspector, what can I do for you?" I ask him.

"I'll get right to the point," he says. "We checked with the phone company, and we know that Leticia Morgan called your office twice the day she was killed."

"That's right."

"Why didn't you tell me this when I interviewed you?"

"You didn't ask."

"Watch your step, Mr. Cavanaugh," Kamimoto says, losing his cordial demeanor for once. "I can always charge you with concealing evidence."

I shrug my shoulders.

"What did Ms. Morgan say to you?" Kamimoto asks.

"I wasn't there when she called. I never talked to her."

"So she must have left messages. What did she say?"

"That's private," I answer, crossing my arms.

The inspector gives me a stern look.

"Mr. Cavanaugh," he says. "You seem to have forgotten that we're on the same side."

"If that's the case, then how come you don't tell me what *you* know?"

Kamimoto considers this for a moment.

"Fair enough," he says. "You cooperate fully with me, and I'll tell you what I know in return. Is that clear?"

I don't like his military manner, but I want the truth about Leticia.

"You first."

For a moment, Kamimoto looks like he's going to object, but then he changes his mind. He takes out a notepad from his breast pocket, and flips it open.

"Ms. Morgan left her apartment sometime after 9:25 am Thursday," he says reading from his notes. "She went to her sister . . ." Kamimoto flips through his notepad, looking for a name.

"Mona," I say.

"Right. She went to her sister Mona Fairchild's place. No one was there when she arrived, but Ms. Morgan had her own key, so getting in wasn't a problem. When Ms. Fairchild got home at six that night, she found her sister dead. It had all the signs of being a professional hit."

Kamimoto relays the information like it was a recipe for biscuits. It's hard for me to be as detached about it, but I try.

"How did her killer know where to find her?" I ask.

"Ah, now that's interesting," he says, looking up from his notepad. "Mona Fairchild told us that she called her sister's apartment around 10:00 that morning. She got the answering machine, and left a message telling Ms. Morgan to go on over to the house whenever she wanted. When we went to examine the apartment, we found that somebody had beaten us to it. The whole place was torn apart, and the tape was missing from her machine."

I jump at this news. Leticia's apartment was ransacked. She was tracked to her sister's house. But how did the hit man know where Mona's house was? That information could be in her personnel file at work, I realize suddenly. I think back to my conversation with Arthur Hays last night and wonder.

"Whoever searched Ms. Morgan's apartment was very thorough," Kamimoto continues. "They even took the trouble to move the refrigerator."

The inspector is studying my face.

"Any idea what they were looking for?" he asks me.

"No. I haven't a clue."

Kamimoto sighs disappointedly.

"That's everything we know," he tells me. "Now it's your turn. What was in those messages?"

"Here," I say, "you can listen for yourself."

I go pick up the phone and bring it back to the sofa. I tap into my voicemail at *Digital Business*and let Kamimoto listen to Leticia's messages. He asks to hear them a couple of more times and takes notes. Then he finishes and hangs up the phone.

"No one at Hays Software said anything to me about Ms. Morgan resigning," he says, looking over his notes.

"Yeah, I know. I saw her old boss at a party last night and he denied it."

"So you've decided to do some detective work yourself, huh?" Kamimoto says, giving me a patronizing look.

"I have a right to ask questions," I reply.

"It is curious," he says thoughtfully, returning to the subject at hand. "It certainly doesn't jive with the voicemail you just played for me. But there could be nothing to it."

He puts his notepad back in his pocket.

"I'd like to go to your office tomorrow and make a copy of those messages."

"Be my guest."

"I'll be there at ten," he replies.

We stand up and walk towards the front door.

"Thanks for filling me in on Leticia," I say.

"I didn't exactly have a choice," he answers bluntly.

"Neither did I," I respond just as tersely.

Kamimoto looks at me, then cracks a smile.

"True enough," he concedes.

We walk a few more feet, and Kamimoto continues.

"Look, don't think I don't appreciate your help. I do," he says. "But now I need for you to stop asking people questions on your own. My partner and I are quite capable of interviewing witnesses. From now on, I want you to come directly to me with any new information."

"Understood," I say, even though I have no intention of stopping my inquiries.

I watch Kamimoto walk to his car and drive away. Then I go to the kitchen and pour myself a cup of coffee. I take it to the back yard and sit down under the Chinese elm. There I run through what little I know about Leticia's murder: it was done by a professional; it happened the day after she resigned from Hays Software; apparently, her assassin was looking for something.

I wonder if Arthur Hays would know how to hire a professional killer?

# Chapter Eleven

I'm late getting to the office today, but I don't care. I pull into the parking lot of our building, and manage to avoid hitting a homeless man who's searching the outdoor ashtrays for cigarette butts. Working in the city, I'm often treated to this kind of encounter. Not long ago near this same parking lot, I was nearly knocked down by a bike courier in hot pursuit of the man who had stolen his bicycle. The courier was a good sprinter, but after a couple of blocks, it was obvious that the thief was going to get away.

When I walk into the lobby of *Digital Business* I'm greeted by yet another new receptionist. It seems we can't hold on to one for more than six months.

"Hello," I say to her. "I'm Steven Cavanaugh, one of the editors."

"It's so nice to meet you," she says in what sounds like a well-practiced bedroom voice. "I'm Catherine."

Not surprisingly, Catherine looks as if she just walked in off the beaches of southern California. She's got long blond hair, a perfect tan, and a figure that could land her a role on *Baywatch*. One thing I'll say for Mitch, he's consistent.

"Welcome to *Digital Business*," I say to her. "Is the mail in yet?"

"Just arrived," she answers sweetly.

I stop by the mail room to gather my correspondence before continuing down the hall to my office.

As I approach my office door, I spy Matt out of the corner of my eye heading in my direction. He walks in to the room just as I'm settling into my chair.

"Hey," he says, sitting himself down in a chair opposite mine. "How was your weekend?"

"Fine," I say as I open a drawer to retrieve my letter opener. "How was yours?"

"I had a great weekend," Matt says enthusiastically. "Really, really great. Fantastic, in fact."

I can tell I'm supposed to ask him what made it so wonderful.

"What did you do?"

Matt hesitates.

"Maybe I shouldn't talk about this. There's another person involved."

Normally I wouldn't mind finding out who Matt bedded this weekend, but right now I've got too much going on to spend my morning gossiping.

"That's okay," I reply. "I understand."

"Well," Matt says quickly, "I guess I can trust you to be discreet. And it does involve someone you know."

I stop opening mail and look at him. Matt is beaming.

"This weekend," he begins, stammering slightly, "Angela and I . . . we . . . you know."

I'm not sure I want to know this, but I can't help asking.

"You what? Are you saying you slept with her?"

"And how!" Matt replies, clearly proud of himself.

"Angela Madrigal?" I ask, just to make certain. I can't believe Angela would sleep with Matt, of all people.

"Of course, Angela Madrigal, your little helper," he answers. "Why do you seem so surprised?"

Because I thought Angela had better taste, I think to myself.

"You told me she kept turning you down whenever you asked her out," I say to him. "I guess I figured you weren't her type."

"That's what I thought. But now I can see she was just playing hard to get. When we met at that party this weekend, she was all over me."

I don't know what to make of this. I don't usually think twice about Matt's abundant extracurricular activities. But Angela? It doesn't seem like her.

"Congratulations," I say, ready to end the conversation. I pick up another letter and open it.

"Thanks man."

Matt stands up. I guess now that he's through bragging to me, he's ready to move on to his next buddy's office. But before he goes, he puts his hands on the back of the chair he was just sitting on, and leans forward.

"It's funny, but I feel like I should thank you," he says. "I mean, Angela came here because she wanted to work with you, and now I've got her."

I look up from my mail at Matt's smug face, and for some reason, I feel like punching him.

"I guess so," I say curtly.

"You know," he continues, "maybe I'll take her to Vegas this weekend. There's this hotel there that you just wouldn't believe. . . ."

"I bet," I say, cutting him off. I've heard about the hotel before; many, many times before.

"Well, I've got to get going."

But before Matt has gone two steps, Angela comes barreling into my office. She stops dead in her tracks as soon as she sees Matt.

"Oh, I'm sorry," she says to me. "I didn't realize you were busy. I'll come back later."

"No, that's alright," Matt says. "Steven was just giving me some help with a piece I'm doing on encryption technology. We just finished up."

He walks over to her.

"How about lunch today?" he asks her. "There's a new place over on 16th I think you'll like."

Angela looks at him. Her mouth is open, but there are no words coming out. She has a blank expression on her face. I have the distinct impression that she does not want to have lunch with Matt.

"Well," Angela says.

But nothing follows. It's silent again.

"It's just that . . ." Angela tries again. But she stops before she finishes her sentence.

I can't take this anymore. I decide to speak up and rescue Angela from this awkward encounter.

"Angela and I are already booked for lunch today," I lie. "We have to go over my initial draft of the Hays interview."

"That's too bad. Maybe next time," Matt says to Angela, resting his hand momentarily on her waist.

As he walks away, I see Angela flinch. She quickly closes the door behind him, and leans against it.

"Oh God," she whines. "What have I done?"

I'm not sure what to say. None of this is my business.

"Bad weekend?" I ask.

"Awful."

She walks over to the chair Matt just vacated and sits down.

"You're not going to believe what I did this weekend."

I raise my eyebrows questioningly, but don't say anything.

"I slept with Matt," she laments, "Can you believe it?"

"If you say so."

"You're probably shocked. I know I am."

I consider lying for a moment, but decide that in this case, honesty is probably the best policy.

"Actually, Matt just told me."

"He told you?" Angela looks desperate. "Do you think he'll tell anyone else?"

"To be honest, I think he'll tell everyone else."

"Great, this is just what I need," she says. "When I made my escape yesterday morning, I asked him to please be discreet. I should have known better."

"Matt's concept of discretion is to not describe your anatomy."

It's a harsh thing to say, but it might help prepare her for the coming office gossip.

Angela sinks dejectedly into the chair.

"I knew better than to expect anything else," she says simply, burying her face in her hands.

"Then why did you do it?" I blurt out.

She lifts her head and looks at me.

"Revenge."

"What do you mean?"

Angela takes a deep breath and begins her story.

"Saturday night I went to this huge party that my friend Andrea throws every year," she tells me. "I knew Jonathan—my old boyfriend—would probably be there, and I was sure I could handle seeing him again. Unfortunately, I didn't count on him showing up with a new girlfriend."

"That bothered you?"

"It must have, because when Matt happened to show up, I started hanging all over him, just to get back at Jonathan."

"Did it work?" I ask.

"Who knows? But even if it did, it wasn't worth it."

Angela shakes her head woefully.

"Somehow, things got out of hand. The next thing I know, I'm waking up in Matt's apartment with a splitting headache. I must have had too much to drink," she confesses.

"We all make mistakes." I know it's trite, but I'm not sure what you're supposed to say in these circumstances.

Angela rubs her forehead ruefully.

"I bet you've never done anything that stupid," she says.

I think back to my reckless days in college, before I met Michelle.

"Not recently," is all I can say.

"I was hoping I would get to work and he'd just pretend it never happened," Angela continues, lost in her woes. "But now he wants to see me again. What am I supposed to do?"

I don't understand what Angela is so worried about.

"Just because you slept with him once doesn't mean you have to do it again," I remind her. "Tell him you're not interested."

"Yes, of course." She smiles at me. "Thanks for listening."

"You're welcome."

Angela starts to get up, ready to leave, then suddenly she sits back down in the chair.

"I forgot to ask you about Jason Grimshaw's party," she says excitedly. "How did it go? Did you get a chance to talk with Arthur Hays?"

I tell Angela all about my conversation with Hays, including his assertion that Leticia never resigned.

"I guess it's possible she never got a chance to officially hand in her resignation," Angela says.

"Oh, yes she did," I say. "Here, listen to this."

I pick up the phone, tap into voicemail, and queue up Leticia's messages. Angela takes the receiver from me and listens intently.

"You're right," she says when she's finished. She replaces the receiver and continues, "Hays is definitely covering up something. I bet he hired the hit man."

"Yeah, probably," I agree. "I'm just not sure how to prove it."

Angela looks pensive.

"Hey, what about your wife?" she asks suddenly. "She works at Grimshaw Turner, right? And they're a big investor in Hays Software. Maybe she can do a little investigating."

"Nothing doing," I say. "Even if she wanted to help us, Michelle doesn't have access to the information. Hays Software is one of Marcus Turner's pet projects, and he handles those on his own."

"So much for that idea," Angela replies, disappointed.

"It just means we have to figure out something else."

"Any ideas?" she asks.

I think for a moment. I have the vague sensation that I've forgotten something crucial, but hard as I try, I can't recall what it is.

"Not yet," I say slowly. "But I'll think of something."

"Let me know," she says, standing up.

She takes a couple of steps towards the door, but then stops and turns around.

"Thanks for helping me out earlier," she says to me. "You know, with Matt."

"No problem."

A few minutes later there's a knock on my door. It's probably Craig being nosy, or Matt come to brag again.

"Come in," I say, resigned.

The door opens and Angela enters.

"Guess who I bumped into?" she says, stepping aside.

In walks Kamimoto and Morrison, with a middle-aged woman in tow. I wonder why Catherine didn't buzz me to let me know they were coming.

My phone rings and I pick it up.

"Yes?"

"It's Catherine," she says in a breathy voice. "A Mr. Komodo from the police department is on his way back to see you. He said it was urgent, but he didn't say why. Said you were expecting him."

"Thanks."

I hang up and turn to Kamimoto and his colleagues.

"This is Masha Kolmeyer," Kamimoto says, introducing the woman. "She's a private investigator I work with from time to time. She'll record the voicemail messages you played for me yesterday."

I guess even the police department outsources these days.

Kolmeyer puts down the large briefcase she's carrying and shakes hands with me. She has a firm grip and a friendly face, and reminds me of my third-grade teacher.

"Here's the phone," I say, gesturing to it. "Go right ahead."

She walks to the telephone on my desk and inspects it. Almost all the phones at *Digital Business*are the inexpensive, standard business issue, the ones that look like rotary phones with push buttons. Mine is no exception.

"So how does this work? Is it complicated?" Angela asks the detective as she watches her pick up the receiver and use a small instrument to pop off the plastic shell.

"Not at all," Kolmeyer informs us. "I simply insert the bug into the phone and record the voicemail directly."

Kolmeyer gets back to work, and Angela hangs over her, watching everything she does. She seems to find the whole procedure fascinating. I look away from the phone and turn my attention to the police inspectors.

"Any new developments in the case?" I ask them.

Morrison shakes his head.

"Nothing," Kamimoto tells me. He's about to say something else when he's interrupted by Kolmeyer.

"George!" she says. She points to the opened handset. I think I can discern a small black object about the size of a pea stuck inside the phone's receiver, but I'm not sure. Kamimoto motions to Kolmeyer to put the phone back together, then signals for all of us to follow him out of my office.

We file out silently. Kamimoto closes the door, and leads us down the hall away from my office.

"This is interesting," he says.

"What's interesting?" I ask.

"Someone has bugged your phone."

I figured as much already, but hearing Kamimoto say it makes the truth hit home.

"Why don't you search the office for more bugs," Kamimoto says to Kolmeyer.

The private investigator nods and walks away to start the search. There's a bounce in her step; she seems happier than when she first walked in here. The routine task she came here to perform has suddenly gotten more challenging.

"Have you talked with any one on the phone about the murder?" Kamimoto asks me. "About any of the things I told you Sunday?"

"No, but I did replay Leticia's messages for Angela just this morning. And she listened to them on my phone."

Kamimoto and Morrison exchange glances.

"Well then," Kamimoto says. "I'd say whoever killed Leticia knows she was trying to reach you before she died. And for all they know, she might have talked with you before they got to her."

I get a funny feeling in the pit of my stomach.

"Is there any way to track down who planted the bug?" I ask him.

"Not unless the guy left a calling card."

Kamimoto scans the sea of cubicles next to us, then glances down the hall towards the lobby.

"One thing's for sure," he tells us. "This place is an easy target for surveillance. You guys have zero security. No ID badges, no electronic locks. Whoever did this could have just waltzed in and done it in broad daylight."

"I could question the employees," Morrison says to his partner. "Someone might have seen something."

"Waste of time," Kamimoto replies. "I'm sure whoever did it had no trouble getting in and out without being noticed. We're better off helping Masha. Let's go see how she's coming along."

The two men walk away without another word. Angela and I are left standing in the hallway, with nothing to do but wait.

But patience is not one of my strong points. After a couple of minutes spent restlessly pacing the hallway, I take off after the inspectors.

"Hey, wait a minute," Angela says, catching up with me. "I don't think we're supposed to go in there."

"I don't care," I reply without slowing down. "It's my office."

We reach the office and I open the door abruptly. The first thing I see is Morrison on his hands and knees, examining the lower shelf of a metal bookcase. He looks up from his task and immediately gestures for me to leave.

"I want to help," I announce from the threshold.

Kamimoto pops his head up from underneath my desk and furrows his brow, annoyed.

"This work requires special training . . ." he begins.

"Well, not everything," I hear Kolmeyer say from behind the door.

Angela and I step inside and I close the door behind us. Kolmeyer is standing in front of my pine bookshelf.

"Help me move this, will you?" she says to me with a motherly smile.

I pick up one end of the bookshelf and move it away from the wall. Kolmeyer walks around it and crouches down. I look over the bookshelf and see her examining a couple of electronic devices taped to its back. Each of these contraptions is small and boxy, with a black wire connecting it to a nearby wall socket.

"Pretty much what I expected," she murmurs.

The rest of the group have joined me at the bookshelf.

"What did you find?" Kamimoto asks Kolmeyer as he bends down for a closer look.

"The whole setup," she answers. "It's all right here."

"So what are those?" I ask, pointing to the gadgets.

"Those," says Kolmeyer, "are a receiver and a transmitter. They've been hardwired into this electrical outlet behind your bookcase. They're used to pick up the transmissions from the phone bug and send them to a remote listening post."

"And where's that located?" I ask her.

"My guess is that it's in one of the warehouses in this neighborhood. But I'm afraid it's impossible to trace the outgoing transmission to its final destination."

"There's probably a voice-activated tape system at the listening post that records everything from the phone bug," Morrison muses.

"No doubt," Kamimoto agrees, scrutinizing the equipment. "Hold on here. Masha, what's that on the receiver?"

Kamimoto is pointing to a pair of blue and green wires coming off the larger of the two devices.

"That's the other bug," she tells him. "Or rather, where it would have been. Look."

Kolmeyer's delicate hands carefully trace the wires to their destination.

"See this?" she says. "Someone started to wire some kind of wall bug into the receiver, and then gave up. I'm not surprised, really. This whole setup is pretty sloppy, the work of some amateur."

"They must have had problems getting it to work," Kamimoto says, "or maybe they felt they were going to be discovered, so they cleared out before they got caught."

Kamimoto stands up.

"In any case," he says to me. "It looks like your office is clean."

"That's good to know," I say.

I walk to my desk and sit down on the corner, gazing contemplatively at the telephone.

"So now what happens?" I ask Kamimoto. "What do I do about my phone?"

"I don't want to remove the bug," he says. "I think it's better not to let them know that you've discovered it. You'll just have to be careful about the calls you make. Keep it strictly business."

"I can do that," I say.

"And just in case," he continues. "Watch it on your cell phone, too. Those calls are a breeze to listen in on." He looks at Morrison. "Let's get this office back in order."

Morrison pushes the bookcase back against the wall while Kolmeyer gathers her tools and puts them back in her briefcase.

"George," she says, picking up the case, "Do you need me to check his house?"

"That would be wise. What do you think, Mr. Cavanaugh? Masha could go over there right now if you want."

"No, not today. My wife is working at home this afternoon, and I don't want to worry her about this. How about tomorrow morning?"

"What time?" Kolmeyer asks me.

"Nine o'clock."

"Works for me. I'll bring my staff."

"Masha will let me know if she finds anything," Kamimoto tells me. "In the meantime, I want you to contact me right away if you get any new information."

"I will."

Morrison and Kolmeyer leave my office without another word. Kamimoto follows them to the door, but stops at the threshold.

"And remember what I said about playing detective," he warns me. He gives me a long, searching look, as if he knows I might be up to something. Then he turns and walks away.

# Chapter Twelve

As soon as Kamimoto and his colleagues have left my office, Angela closes the door behind them. Then she walks to my desk and sinks into a chair.

"I can't believe someone was able to just walk right in and plant a bug in your phone," she says. "You'd think someone would have noticed a complete stranger walking around."

"Hey, we've been hiring so many new people lately, I don't recognize half of them myself. As long as the person walked in acting like they belonged here, I'm sure they would have no problem. And you know I don't keep my office locked."

"I suggest you start locking it."

"I intend to. Although I don't know what good it will do me now."

"Who do you think placed the bug?" Angela asks.

"I'm not sure. I'm suspicious about the way Hays was acting at Grimshaw's party, but I can't picture him . . ."

I stop in mid-sentence. Suddenly, I remember what it was that was so important.

"Damn! We are so stupid," I say, reaching behind my computer and turning it on.

Angela gives me a "speak for yourself" look and asks, "What do you mean?"

"Here we've been going nuts trying to find out more about Hays Software, and we've had access to their internal network all along."

"What do you mean?" Angela asks, confused. "How?"

"Remember the Hays interview?"

"That's right," she says, comprehending. "Leticia gave you those passwords."

Angela moves her chair over to my side of the desk and leans in close so she can read the computer screen. I pull out my wallet and remove the paper with the phone number and the passwords Leticia gave me.

In less than three minutes I've connected to the computer network at Hays Software.

"Okay, so far so good," I say. "Now, what I want first is information about Arthur Hays. I wonder which of these servers he uses."

There are about a dozen servers that make up the Hays Software network, each one named after a Greek god. I click on the icon for a server called Zeus, figuring that's probably Hays' domain. Right away I get a prompt for a password.

I try entering the passwords Leticia gave me. No luck. Then I take my best guess and type in "HaysSW," but as soon as I hit the enter key the screen goes blank.

"What happened?" Angela asks.

"We lost the connection," I explain. "It must be part of their security protocol: each server has its own password. You get three shots at it, and then you're tossed off the network."

"I don't believe this," Angela says. "I've never heard of a startup with this kind of internal security."

"Even Dan couldn't get through this," I say, dialing into the network again. "It looks like we're limited to what we can find on the marketing server."

As soon as I've reconnected to the network I go straight to the marketing department's server, looking for something, anything, that might be helpful. I stop when I notice a file called "Cheetah demo."

"Of course," I say, opening the file. "This is it."

"The product demo?" Angela asks. "What good is a canned presentation going to do us?"

"It's more than a demo," I answer. "Leticia called it a 'working version' of the product, which means we've got our hands on the greatest research tool ever invented." I look over at her. "Let's see what we can dig up on Mr. Hays."

I initiate the program and am immediately asked for a password.

"Not again," Angela moans.

"No problem," I answer. "Leticia gave me this one."

I type in the password—011MPUS—and am greeted by a box marked "Search Criteria." I type in "Arthur Hays" and click on the "Search" box.

The logo for the Cheetah program is, of course, a Cheetah, stylistically rendered in bright yellow. The Cheetah logo begins to run, indicating that the search is launched.

We watch the screen anxiously. The search takes quite a while, and as soon as the list of articles appears on the screen, I can see why. There are over five hundred articles included.

"So much for Cheetah's laserlike precision," I say sarcastically.

"Here's the problem." Angela taps the screen. "Some of these citations go back thirty years. Try narrowing the search."

I use the program's sort function to limit the selections to the past five years.

"That did it," I say when the new list appears. "It's down to thirty-two articles. That's manageable."

Angela and I spend the next half hour skimming through the articles. Most of them are from trade publications, and are heavy on product and industry information—not very helpful. But one article from the *Wall Street Journal* stands out.

"Check this out," I say, scrolling through the article. "It looks like Hays was involved in some kind of lawsuit."

It seems that when Hays was still at PCI, he developed an enhanced version of an existing networking technology. PCI filed for patent protection, and drew up plans to market the device. Soon after, however, a PCI competitor called Newport Systems started selling a similar product. PCI sued, claiming patent infringement. As the developer of PCI's product, Hays was directly involved with the suit.

"No wonder Hays is so paranoid," Angela says. "He's had his ideas stolen before."

"It looks like it," I agree.

"I wonder what the jury decided," she muses.

"Let's see if we can find out."

We discover our answer in a *Wall Street Journal* news brief, dated six months after the original article.

"Looks like it never got to a jury," I say. "They settled out of court."

"Newport Systems probably backed down," Angela says. She leans forward and rests her elbows on my desk. "I guess that's it then."

"As far as Cheetah is concerned." I exit the demo and return to the server window. "I want to look at the rest of these files."

I browse through the server's directory until I come across a file folder labeled "Hot Partners." I open it and discover a number of preliminary press releases. Apparently, Hays Software has already signed partnership agreements with some of the biggest players in the online world, including Microsoft, Yahoo!, America Online, and IBM.

"It looks like Hays has deals with all the major Internet companies," Angela says, reading over my shoulder.

"I haven't heard anything about this before," I say. "I'm sure nobody else in the press knows."

"Look at the dates on these press releases, the end of next month. We're not supposed to know about these agreements yet."

"No we're not," I say. "Let's see if there's anything else here we're not supposed to know."

Angela and I spend another hour reviewing the rest of the files on the marketing server, but don't turn up anything else unusual.

"That's everything," I say finally.

The early afternoon sun is shining brightly through the window. Angela is reclining in her chair, her arms stretched over her head, and her feet resting on an open desk drawer.

"I'm not sure we've learned very much," she says, bringing her feet down to the ground with a heavy thud.

"We've learned enough," I say, determined not to let two hours worth of work go to waste. "The news about the partnerships is pretty hot, so naturally, I need to call Hays to get his comments on the matter."

"You're going to call Arthur Hays?" she asks, unbelieving.

"Sure am. And in the process of asking him about these deals, I plan to slip in a question or two about Leticia."

"But, you can't just say, 'Congratulations on your strategic alliances. Did you by chance hire someone to snuff out my friend?'"

"I don't know what I'm going to say," I tell her honestly. "I'll just start by asking about the partnerships and see where things go from there."

"I don't think it's such a good idea," Angela says.

"I can't sit here and do nothing," I insist. "It's time to ask some direct questions."

I flip through my Rolodex, locate the phone number, and am about to pick up my phone when I remember the bug.

"Let's go down the hall to make this call," I say.

We manage to make it to the conference room without anyone asking us about this morning's events. I lock the door and dial the number.

As the phone is ringing, I think for a moment of Inspector Kamimoto. He most certainly would not approve of what I'm about to do.

"Arthur Hays' office," the assistant says.

"Yes, is he in? This is Steven Cavanaugh from *Digital Business*."

"May I tell him what this is about?"

"Yes. I'd like to ask him about the new partnerships he has lined up, especially the one with Microsoft."

"One moment, please."

I put my hand over the mouthpiece and say to Angela, "That should get his attention."

I hear a click on the line as the call is transferred.

"This is Arthur Hays."

"Yes, Arthur, Steven Cavanaugh here."

"Right, how can I help you?" he says brusquely.

"I wanted to ask you about your deals with Microsoft, IBM, and the others."

"So my secretary told me. Just how the hell did you find out about those?" he bellows.

"Leticia told me about them," I say, introducing the real reason for my call.

"No she didn't. She couldn't have. She's dead, remember?"

"She told me the day we went out to interview you," I insist.

"And you waited until now to ask me about them? I don't think so."

I consider telling him about the server connection, but decide that would just cause more trouble. Hays jumps back in.

"All those agreements are tentative. They have not been formally announced," he growls. "Now, are you going to tell me your source?"

"I already have."

"I don't have time for this. I have work to do."

Hays slams down the receiver.

"That didn't go the way I'd hoped," I say, hanging up the phone.

"So I gathered," Angela says. I can read the expression on her face: I told you so. "It seems to me that all you've done is infuriate a man we suspect of murder," she adds.

"Hey, it had to be tried," I shoot back. "Nothing ventured, nothing gained. Besides, we're no worse off. So Hays won't talk to me now; it's not like he was talking to me before."

"I suppose that's true," Angela concedes.

Nevertheless, I realize she might have a point. But it's too late to worry about that now.

"Oh no," Angela says suddenly. She's staring at the clock on the wall as she jumps up from her seat. "I have a meeting with Tina in two minutes. She wants an update on my projects."

Angela dashes to the door.

"Don't say anything about Hays," I bark out to her as she exits.

I hear a muffled "Don't worry" as the door closes behind her.

I walk slowly back to my office, thinking. I know I should try to get some work done, but I can't seem to let go of this investigation, not even for a minute. So when I get back to my desk, the first thing I do is run the Cheetah program again. This time I take my time, carefully reading everything it turns up: the lawsuit, the settlement, Hays' retirement from the Business Solutions Group.

I pause to think about that last event. Somebody else I've heard of recently just retired from the same group. I can't remember his name, but I do remember how I heard of him. He was mentioned in the press kit Mitch handed off to me last week. The guy I'm thinking of just joined Yogi.com.

I rummage through my In Box until I find the Yogi press kit. I open the file and dump its contents on my desk, searching through them hurriedly. After ten minutes of speed reading I find what I'm looking for: Hank Pilsbury, the new chief technical officer for Yogi, used to work in the same PCI division as Hays. They must have worked together. Suddenly, the article on Yogi has become my top priority.

I dig through the papers on my desk and manage to find the phone number for Pilsbury's direct line. I pick up the phone and dial the number, hoping I might get lucky and catch him in his office.

I get his voicemail. I expected this, but I'm disappointed nonetheless. I leave a message, telling him about the company profile I'm writing and asking if it might be possible to interview him soon. E-commerce startups like Yogi depend on publicity even more than their storefront counterparts, so I'm betting I'll hear from Hank Pilsbury this afternoon.

I hang up the receiver and stare at the company literature and research reports spread out across my desk. I suppose if I'm going to interview Pilsbury about his company, then I should probably find out something about it. I pick up a document and start reading.

After a half hour spent skimming various reports and press releases, I'm starting to get a feel for the company. It's pretty simple really—Yogi hopes to become the Amazon.com of sporting goods, kind of a Sportmart on the Internet. Yogi is faced with all the usual Internet challenges of quickly establishing its brand in the mind of the buying public, while at the same time trying to keep Amazon and the other e-commerce behemoths from eating its lunch—not an enviable task. I stop to jot down a few of the facts I've learned, and then resume my research. But before I've finished the next press release, the phone rings. I pick it up immediately.

"Steven Cavanaugh," I say hopefully.

"Yes, Steven. This is Hank Pilsbury, returning your call."

"Thanks for getting back to me so quickly."

"I wouldn't want to keep a member of the press waiting," he says in a friendly voice.

"Thank you," I reply. "Listen, I'm on a pretty tight deadline. Is there any chance that we could meet soon? I'm free this afternoon."

"You certainly don't believe in wasting time," Pilsbury says with a chuckle. "Let me check my calendar."

I hear the sound of pages flipping, and then Pilsbury comes back on.

"We're in luck," he says. "All I've got is a staff meeting, and that's easy to move. When exactly did you want to meet?"

"It's about 3:20," I say, looking at my watch and calculating the distance to Marin County. "If I leave right away I could be there in about an hour, maybe less."

"See you then."

I slam down the receiver, and start stuffing background material and the few notes I've managed to take into my briefcase. I'm about ready to go when Tina walks into my office.

"Do you have a few minutes?" she asks.

"Not really," I say impatiently. "I'm on my way to an interview."

"Then I'll make this quick," she says, standing in the doorway and crossing her arms. "This afternoon I had a rather strange meeting with Angela. She was quite vague about the work she's doing for you. Other than talking about white papers, she didn't have much to say."

"Really?"

"Steven, Mitch asked you to keep her involved in your projects for a reason," Tina says, a scolding tone creeping into her voice. "Our turnover in the entry-level positions is way too high. That's why we teamed Angela up with you. We need you to help us make her job interesting."

"I'm doing my best," I say, anxious to move on. "I've even got her helping me with the Hays interview."

"Which brings me to the main reason for my visit," Tina says, taking a step closer. "How's that story coming?"

"Fine," I answer. "It's just a little more complicated than I'd originally anticipated."

"Yes I know," she says, giving me a concerned look. "I've heard about the police visits, and about what happened to Leticia Morgan. I'm sorry. I know you two were close friends."

"You do? Did Angela tell you that?"

"No," she replies. "I met Leticia Morgan last year at the Black Women in Technology Conference. We got to talking, and when I told her I worked at *Digital Business*, she asked me if I knew her good friend Steven."

"I see."

"Look Steven, if this story is too personal, then maybe you should hand it off to someone else."

I shake my head. Until this moment, I didn't realize just how much I've been using the Hays piece as a cover for my investigation. As long as I'm on the story, I can ask anyone anything about Hays. That's not a tool I'm ready to give up.

"Things were kind of . . . hectic, at first," I reply. "But they're back on track now."

"Are they?" Tina asks skeptically. "Frankly, it doesn't seem like you've written anything in over a week."

I smile nonchalantly.

"Don't worry," I say reassuringly. "I'm still writing. In fact, I plan to finish the first draft of the Yogi profile today. How about if I drop a copy off to you tonight?"

"That'd be great," she says, visibly relieved. "Just leave it on my desk."

"Will do." I look at my watch. "I've got to run."

"Oh sure," she says amiably. "Don't let me keep you."

# Chapter Thirteen

I'm so preoccupied with my upcoming meeting that I don't even notice the drive through the city—I'm halfway across the Golden Gate Bridge before I realize where I am. I look around at the scenery and try to snap out of my daze. As usual, the bridge is full of walkers and joggers. Beyond them, looming large in the background, I see Alcatraz and Angel Island. The wide blue expanse of the Bay is dotted with sailboats; I watch a couple of white specks disappear over the horizon.

Soon afterwards I'm in San Rafael, roaming the third floor of a large office building in search of Yogi.com. I wander through hallway after hallway of identical office suites, until finally I find the right door. I open it, and step into a huge room, sparsely furnished—a typical bootstrapped startup. There's a small receptionist desk right in front of me, but its occupant is missing. The rest of the room is made up of several cubicles, loosely grouped together. Each cube contains at least two computers, and a number of peripherals. The people hard at work on the computers are all wearing jeans or shorts—obviously programmers.

The room must not have been designed to handle this much computer equipment. I see outlets strained with octopus-like power cord adapters and extenders. A couple of the more inventive programmers have even run power cords up to the fluorescent ceiling lights.

I walk over to the nearest occupied cubicle.

"I'm looking for Hank Pilsbury," I say to a twenty-something man with dreadlocks.

He looks at me, but doesn't say anything. After a delayed reaction, he stands up, and adjusts his pants, which then immediately slide back down to his hips.

"Uh, he's around here somewhere," he says, walking out of his cubicle.

I follow the programmer across the room to the other side. There, against the wall, is a row of four, small glassed-in offices. These must be the executive "suites."

"That's him," the young man says, tapping on the window of one of the offices.

Hank Pilsbury looks up from his plain metal desk and smiles welcomingly. The programmer nods in response and then saunters back to his cubicle.

I open the door to the office and walk in.

"Steven Cavanaugh," the gray-haired executive says in a friendly voice. "Good to meet you."

Hank Pilsbury is clearly from the technical side of the business. Although he's wearing a suit and tie, he looks out of place in the outfit, as if he'd rather not have to bother. He's tossed the jacket onto a chair, and has his tie loosened and his sleeves rolled up.

We shake hands cordially, then I settle into a thinly-padded Army surplus chair. We exchange pleasantries while I pull out a notepad and set up the miniature tape recorder. Once that's done, I start the meeting by asking about Yogi's play in the electronic commerce market. Pilsbury is happy to show me Yogi's Web site on his office PC. He has me sample the site's selection of sporting goods and demonstrates how smoothly Yogi can fulfill product orders. He also brags about the company's customer service operation, and hints at upcoming endorsements by some big-name professional athletes.

Pilsbury also informs me that Yogi expects to go public sometime in the next six to eight months. The company plans to build up a financial war chest from the sale of its stock, and use the funds to establish their brand, capture market share, and stave off the competition. Yogi is especially hoping to cut into the customer base of brick-and-mortar operations like Big 5 and Sportmart.

After about an hour, I draw the interview to a close. I can't think of a graceful way to broach the subject of Arthur Hays, so I just ask him point blank.

"Yes, Arthur Hays," Pilsbury says, pronouncing the name slowly. "I haven't seen him in a long time. How's he doing?"

I shrug my shoulders.

"He's working on making his startup the next Microsoft."

"Aren't we all."

"I could use some background information on him," I say. "And I know you both used to work at PCI."

"That we did," Pilsbury replies. He puts his hands together in a kind of bridge and his brow furrows. I can see he's rewinding his memory back to a different era.

"Is this off the record?" he asks me.

"It is now," I say, turning off the tape recorder.

"What would you like to know?"

"For starters, did you work directly with him at PCI?"

"I did," he replies. "We were in the same division, although he worked on networking solutions, and I ran the applications group."

"What was he like to work with?"

"A real pain in the ass. Not a team player at all. And he'd stab you in the back if he thought it was to his advantage."

"Somebody must have liked him," I say. "He managed to stay at PCI for nearly thirty years."

Pilsbury shakes his head.

"Nobody liked him," he tells me. "But as long as he was making money for the company, the powers that be were willing to put up with him. As soon as he started costing them money, however, they cut him loose."

"What happened?" I ask.

"Let's just say that Hays got the company into a little legal trouble."

"The lawsuit against Newport Systems," I say.

Pilsbury looks at me, impressed.

"I see you've done your homework. Yes, that's exactly what I mean. That suit cost PCI a few million to settle."

"PCI paid?" I ask. "But I thought Newport Systems was at fault."

"So did Arthur Hays. When Newport came out with a competing product right after we'd announced ours, Hays assumed that somehow they'd managed to steal his idea. He accused just about everyone on his staff of being an industrial spy. Then he went to the legal department and managed to get them to file suit. They shouldn't have done it, but Hays is an industry legend, right? It never occurred to our lawyers that he was just nuts."

"So Newport Systems didn't steal his work?"

"Not at all," Pilsbury says. "Once the legal staff started doing their research, it became clear that it was a case of simultaneous development. Which wasn't really surprising—the device was a logical extension of an old product. The problem was that Arthur Hays was so arrogant it never occurred to him that someone else could come up with the same idea."

Pilsbury takes a sip from the glass of water on his desk.

"Anyway, after that Hays was pretty much ruined at PCI," he continues. "So when the company's stock dipped, the CEO used the opportunity to clean house and get rid of the guy. And there you have it."

Pilsbury looks at his watch. I'm sure we've met longer than he planned. It's time to go.

"Okay, Hank," I say. "Thanks for meeting with me on such short notice."

"No problem. Glad to do it."

We shake hands and I leave his office. I walk slowly past the cubicles and towards the exit, watching my step to avoid tripping on the snaked cords and surge protectors that criss-cross the floor.

The drive back to *Digital Business*gives me time to think about what I've just learned: Arthur Hays is an office backstabber, and egotistical as hell. But is he ruthless enough to kill?

By the time I return to my office it's after six, and I still have to write 1500 words about Yogi. It's going to be a long night. I call Michelle to let her know I'll be home late.

Two hours later, I'm halfway through a first pass on the article. It's amazing how fast you can write when you don't really care what you're doing. I'd planned to keep pushing until I finished the piece, but I've been getting hungrier and hungrier as the evening wears on, and it's reached a point where I can't ignore it. I consider running over to the all-night deli, but then I remember that a few days ago I left a bag lunch in the company fridge. If I'm lucky, it's still there, and still edible.

The walk to the kitchen is eerily silent. Everyone is gone but me. Someone even turned off some of the lights when they left, no doubt thinking they were the last to leave. I walk into the kitchen and switch on the light. It flutters to life as I make my way to the refrigerator.

I don't think anyone has cleaned out the fridge in at least five years, so it takes some digging to find the week-old lunch. Finally, I locate it under a box of half-eaten pizza. I open it up and examine the contents. The banana is long gone, but the salami seems okay, and the chips can last forever. I dump the banana in a garbage can and head back to my office to have "dinner" while I write.

By midnight I've managed to pound out a rough draft. It's not the best writing I've ever done, but it's serviceable. I walk to the printer to get the hard copy, then drop it off on Tina's desk before heading out. I'm tired, and the salami sandwich didn't entirely agree with me, but at least I got the article done.

The elevator glides quietly to the lobby floor. I walk leisurely through the empty lobby and into the cool night air. I can't wait to get home, take a hot shower and fall into bed.

The large parking lot next to our building is nearly empty at this hour of the night. My footsteps ring loudly in the open space, reverberating off the surrounding buildings. Other than that, it's completely silent.

I squint my eyes and in the distance I can barely make out the silhouette of my car, parked next to the high chain link fence that surrounds the lot. I'd forgotten just how dark this place can get. The street lights in this part of town are few and far between.

I continue in the direction of my car, pulling out my car keys as I walk. My feet crunch on some broken glass, and the brittle scraping sound fills the parking lot.

When I get to within fifty feet of my car, the doors to a black sedan swing open and three men get out. I must have stumbled into the middle of a drug deal. This has happened to me before here, so I don't think much of it, at first.

Without slowing my pace, I glance over at the three men. All of them are dressed in dark clothing. Two of them look like tough guys from a fifties movie. They're tall and wiry, and are wearing blue jeans, boots, and black leather jackets. The third guy is short and stocky, and wearing a long coat.

They're looking in my direction. I turn my eyes away from them and try to mind my own business.

Thirty seconds later I hear their footsteps coming towards me. I wonder if I should sprint for my car. If I unlock the car without disabling the alarm, the blaring might scare these guys off. Or maybe running would just make things worse.

I start to walk faster. The footsteps get louder, and now I can see the trio out of the corner of my eye. These guys aren't here for a drug deal; they're after me.

I'm only ten feet from my car now. I'm about to make a dash for it when suddenly the two tall guys come out of nowhere. They plant themselves a few feet in front of me, blocking my way to the car.

We glare at each other in the darkness. I can barely make out their faces, but they look like they're in their twenties. One has closely-cropped hair and the other looks as if he's shaved his head bald.

"Steven Cavanaugh?" someone says from behind me. The voice is low and gravelly.

"What's that to you?"

I try to get around the two goons, but they move to intercept me. The short guy comes around from behind and looks me over. He gives me a tight thin-lipped smile, and his small eyes seem to disappear into his face.

"We have a message for you, Cavanaugh," he says to me.

"And what's that?"

"Just this!"

The bald guy swings at me with a huge, hammy fist. But I manage to block his punch, and land one of my own, right on his jaw. He staggers back, but before I can land another blow, somebody chop-blocks me at the knees. I fall hard on to the asphalt, dazed. I roll over to my side and regain my senses just in time to see the blur of the short guy's black-booted foot swinging towards me. He nails me in the stomach. I start to gasp and cough.

All of them are standing over me now. I brace myself for the next blow, but it doesn't come.

"Our message is simple Cavanaugh—back off!" the short guy says to me.

"Who sends the message?" I manage to ask, wheezing.

"That doesn't matter," he replies in a grating voice. "Just give up your snooping. Got that?"

"But . . ."

One of them kicks me in the stomach again.

I feel nauseous and dizzy, and almost vomit.

"Just shut up," the short one says. "And do what we say."

There's a long pause.

"Alright, that's enough for now," the trio's leader finally says.

The men stomp away noisily. I raise my head long enough to see them get back into the black car. It looks like a BMW, but I can't make out the license plate number. The headlights come on and blind me with their glare. Then the driver revs the engine and starts driving right at me, tires squealing. At the last second he swerves and leans on the horn. It leaves a deafening ring in my ears.

I roll over and cough. After a minute or so, the ringing in my ears fades and I'm aware of the spooky silence all around me. I've got to get out of here. I stand up slowly, fighting hard to keep my balance. My head is spinning. As I walk toward my car, I stumble and fall on to the chain-link fence. I hold on to it for dear life.

I feel nauseous. Suddenly my salami sandwich comes up with a great rush and I vomit all over the fence. I wipe my mouth with my sleeve, take a deep breath, and begin walking to my car once again.

I open the car door and collapse on to the driver's seat with a groan. I rest a few seconds, then take a deep breath and try to regain my senses. After some measured breathing, I can finally focus well enough to drive home.

I pull out of the parking lot and on to the main street near our building. Then I make my way quickly through the gloomy streets of the neighborhood to the freeway.

The miles pass by as if in a dream, and soon I'm at my exit in Belmont. All is quiet as I pull into the driveway of my house. I walk in and stop at the downstairs bathroom to examine myself for signs of damage. My reflection in the mirror looks tired and pale, and there's vomit on my sleeve, but nothing worse than that. I lift my shirt and look at my stomach. Amazingly, there's no sign of serious injury, only a couple of red marks.

I snap off the bathroom light and then trudge up the stairs, into our bedroom. Michelle is asleep. As I enter the room, she rolls over in bed, but doesn't open her eyes.

"Steven?" she says sleepily.

"It's me; I'm home," I say in as normal a voice as I can manage.

"How did it go?" she asks, yawning.

"I got the first draft done."

"Great," she says and rolls over again.

I peel off my clothes and gingerly slip into bed, trying not to disturb Michelle any further. I rub my hand across my stomach one last time. I hope there won't be any obvious bruises by morning time.

The day's events blur together as I drift into a fitful sleep.

# Chapter Fourteen

When I wake up this morning I feel groggy, like I had too much to drink last night. I roll over to stretch my back, and realize I'm all alone in the bed. Looking at the clock, I see it's an hour and a half later than I usually get up. No wonder Michelle is gone. I have a vague recollection of her trying to wake me earlier, but I mumbled something about being exhausted and needing to sleep, and she gave up. The house is quiet, so I assume that Michelle has left to take Chloe to school and then head to work.

I sit up in bed, and immediately wince from the pain. I lie back down and stretch out slowly in an effort to assess last night's damage. I'm sore as hell, but I'll live.

I sit up again, slower this time, and try to collect my thoughts. I replay last night's events in my head, straining to remember everything that was said. It must have been Hays, attempting to scare me off. But it won't work. All it's done is make me more determined.

I look over at the clock again. Masha Kolmeyer will be here in less than twenty minutes. I'd better get moving.

I shower and dress quickly, then go down to the kitchen for some coffee. I take a mug from the cabinet, and go to fill it up. Next to the coffee machine, I find a plate with a bagel, some cheese, and a banana. There's also a note from my wife: "Steve, I'm sure you're planning to skip breakfast. At least take this with you. Love, Michelle." I take a bite of the bagel and then carry the plate of food to the dining room.

But before I can even sit down, the doorbell rings. I leave the food on the table and go to the front door.

"Good morning," Masha says to me when I open the door. She's got two young people with her, a man and a woman; they must be her staff. They're both dressed in blue jeans and T-shirts, and don't look much like surveillance experts, but like their boss, they're each carrying a large black briefcase.

I show them into the living room.

"This is Tasha, and this is Rudy," Masha says, indicating her companions. "They'll be helping me today."

"Nice to meet you," I say, shaking their hands.

I'm struck by how much the assistants look like their employer. They all have the same curly hair and brown eyes. They must be related.

My suspicions are confirmed almost immediately.

"Hey Mom, how about if I start in this room," the young man says as he puts his briefcase on the sofa and opens it up.

"Go ahead," Masha replies.

Then she looks at the young woman who I bet is her daughter.

"Tasha, why don't you take the kitchen. I'll do the bedrooms."

Tasha nods and walks down the hall.

"This shouldn't take long," Masha says over her shoulder as she ascends the staircase. "In the meantime, just go about your usual routine. It won't affect what we're doing."

"Can I help?" I respond, anxious to do something.

Masha turns around, an indulgent look on her kind face.

"We'll let you know," she says.

I can take a hint. I walk back to the dining room to eat breakfast.

It's kind of hard to stick to a normal routine when your house is being taken apart one small piece at a time, but I do my best. I sit at the table, eating my bagel and reading the paper, while all around me furniture and picture frames are removed, examined, and replaced, and everything electrical is checked with a fine tooth comb.

True to her word, Masha does call on me a few times to help move furniture, but for the most part, all I can do is sit and wonder what the detectives will find.

Finally, Masha comes into the dining room to tell me they've finished.

"The house looks clean," she informs me, sitting down in a chair next to me. "We checked the obvious places, and the not-so-obvious ones, and didn't find a thing."

"That's great," I say, relieved. It's nice to know that Arthur Hays hasn't been eavesdropping on my bedtime conversations.

"It is good news. I guess whoever bugged your office isn't too interested in your house."

"We do have an alarm system. Maybe that's what kept him away."

"Yeah, I took a look at it," she tells me. "It wouldn't keep a professional out, but like I said yesterday, I think this guy is an amateur. Maybe it scared him off."

Just then I hear a low buzzing. Masha takes a pager from her belt and checks the message.

"Do you have any questions?" she asks me as she's putting the pager back.

"Not that you can answer."

Masha smiles and pats my hand. Then she stands up and pushes her chair back under the table.

"I'll call George right away and give him my report." She pulls a business card from her pants pocket and offers it to me. "Give me a call if there's anything else I can do for you."

I take the card from her and look at it.

"Nothing personal," I say to her, "but I hope I never need the services of Kolmeyer & Associates again."

"A lot of my clients say that," she states simply.

I walk Masha to the front door. Her kids are already waiting for her in the hallway. I thank all of them for their work and show them out.

After they're gone, I walk around my house. It's a relief to know it's bug-free. For the moment, at least, my home is safe.

Despite my busy morning, I manage to get to work before noon. I nod hello to Catherine when I reach the lobby, and stride quickly towards my office.

"Oh, Steven," she calls after me.

"Yes?"

Catherine smiles coyly and lowers her eyes.

"I forgot to put this message in your box yesterday," she tells me in a school-girl voice. "It's from a man named Patrick Nagel. He dropped by yesterday afternoon while you were out. He wants you to call him as soon as you get a chance."

I walk to the receptionist desk and take a pink message slip from Catherine. The message shows my visitor's name and number, but nothing else.

"Did this guy say what he wanted?" I ask Catherine. "I've never heard of him."

"He didn't say."

"Did he at least say who he works for?"

"No, he just said he wanted me to deliver the message to you personally," she answers brightly. She thinks for a minute. "He used to work at Hays Software, but he didn't tell me where he works now, so I didn't put it down," she adds, explaining her logic to me.

I leave the lobby without another word and head to the conference room to give Patrick Nagel a call. The door is open, and two people from the graphics department are sitting at one end of the conference table, eating pizza and going over what looks like next month's cover design. They look up and give me a questioning look when I walk in and pick up the phone. Neither of them says anything, however.

I dial the number and wait, half expecting a message machine. But after two rings, someone answers.

"Patrick Nagel?" I ask.

"Yes, yes," he says, sounding almost out of breath.

"This is Steven Cavanaugh from *Digital Business*."

"Oh, very good, right, right," he replies nervously.

"You dropped by yesterday?"

"Yes, it's somewhat urgent."

"How so?"

"I heard through the grapevine that you're working on some kind of story about Arthur Hays," he says. "I used to be the chief programmer at Hays Software, and I have some information that I think you'll find useful. That is, if you're interested in the full story."

"Of course I am. And I want to hear what you have to say, but I can't get into it on the phone right now."

I glance at the graphic designers at the other end of the table. They're downing one slice of pizza after another, and seem completely unaware of me. But I don't want to take any chances.

"Could we meet somewhere?" I ask.

"Sure," he says. "I'm in Berkeley. I could drive over to the city and meet you someplace there . . ."

"Sounds good."

"Except that my car's in the shop," Nagel adds sheepishly.

"Why don't I come your way, then," I say. "Where do you want to meet?"

"How about Cafe Anastasia? It's on Telegraph Avenue, just south of the Cal campus."

"Okay, I'm taking off now. See you there."

I hang up the phone and pull my briefcase off the conference table. I consider dropping by Angela's cubicle to invite her along, but then I remember that Tina has her covering a trade show at Moscone Center this morning. So I go straight to my car instead, and head east across town to the Bay Bridge.

It doesn't take long to reach Berkeley. I drive slowly down Telegraph Avenue until I spot Cafe Anastasia, then I turn on to the nearest side street and park.

I hop out of my car, jaywalk across the street, and make my way past a homeless man and a couple of guys passing out handbills. I enter the cafe and look around. At a small round table to my left, I spot a red-headed guy with an earring. He's holding a newspaper in one hand, and there's a latté and some kind of croissant sandwich in front of him. But he's neither reading nor eating. Instead, he's tapping the table nervously with his index finger, and looking out the cafe window. Something tells me that's Patrick Nagel.

I approach his table.

"Patrick?"

He starts, and looks at me inquisitively.

"I'm Steven Cavanaugh," I say, extending my hand.

He stands up, and his chair screeches on the wood floor as it slides back from him. He's about 6'3" and husky, wearing faded black jeans and an untucked flannel shirt. We shake hands. In spite of his size, he has a soft handshake. I look straight at him, but he only glances at me sporadically. We stand there awkwardly for a moment.

"May I join you?" I ask, breaking the silence.

"Ah, yes, of course."

Patrick points to another chair, then sits down in his and drags it back up to the table. He starts folding up his newspaper to make room for me.

I sit down and notice he's been reading the classified ads.

"Looking for a job?"

"Yeah."

"It shouldn't be hard for you to find one. You were the chief programmer at Hays Software; that will get you into just about any Internet company."

"Search engines are what I know best, but I'm having to look for jobs in other areas," he replies.

"Why is that?"

"I signed this agreement when I joined Hays Software," he explains, bobbing his head up and down nervously. "It prohibits me from going to work for any competitor for three years after leaving Hays."

I've heard of these Machiavellian employment clauses. They're impossible to enforce in California, but Hays probably counts on most of his employees being too naive to know that.

"Those agreements are illegal in this state," I tell him. "You might want to consult a lawyer."

"I never thought of that," Patrick says, looking relieved. "That's great to know, because money's starting to get tight." Patrick sips his latté. "Not that I haven't tried," he continues, apparently concerned lest I should think him a bum. "I've been doing a little day-trading, hoping that would help, but I can't ever seem to get in on those hot offerings I keep hearing about. And then last month a friend of mine lost $5000 in a phony IPO. He thought he was getting in on this great offering—the next Microsoft—but it turns out the company didn't even exist. Some scam artist had just set up a fake Web site to sell shares."

Patrick is on a roll. I hear all about his friend's stock losses before he lets up long enough for me to get a word in.

"Day trading certainly has its risks . . ." I begin, planning to segue to a new topic.

"I don't like it; too much like gambling," Patrick interrupts. "Besides, I miss programming. That's why I want a real job."

"Speaking of jobs," I say quickly, "when did you leave Hays Software?"

Patrick pauses a moment, as if his brain were switching gears.

"I quit about two months ago," he tells me, "but I still keep in touch with my friends there. That's how I heard about your article on Arthur Hays. I just thought you should know the truth about the man. He's no hero."

"What makes you say that?"

"Uh, maybe I should just give you a quick summary of my experience working for him," he says. "It might explain why I had to leave."

"Go ahead."

"When I first came to Hays Software, I saw it as this incredible opportunity," he begins. "I'd spent a lot of time researching artificial intelligence in graduate school, and then after finishing my degree I joined a company specializing in expert systems and I knew a lot about . . ."

I let Patrick ramble on for another minute or so before pushing him back on track.

"You were telling me about when you went to work for Hays Software," I say, interrupting him.

"Uh, yeah. Well anyway, it looked like Hays Software was going to finally come up with an intelligent agent that works. I had visions of glory, you know, heading up the team that makes this great thing a reality."

"You mean Cheetah?"

"Yeah, Cheetah."

"I tested it and it really does work," I say.

"Oh it does. That wasn't the problem."

"So what was?"

"Arthur Hays."

Patrick's head stops bobbing and he actually makes eye contact with me.

"Something weird is going on," he tells me.

"Like what?"

"I'm not sure. But this is what happened with Cheetah. When we started, we were given a huge corpus of beautifully written code to build on. Most of the main software engine was already in place. It was our job to plug it into the existing Internet technology and make it run."

"And where did the software engine come from?"

"Hays developed it on his own time while he was at PCI, and then put the finishing touches on it when he was at the University of Texas," Patrick says.

"I see, go on."

"As much as I hate the man, I have to admit, Hays is a great programmer. Which is why I could never figure out why he didn't want to talk about his work."

"What do you mean?"

"Hackers are just like everyone else," he tells me. "We like to talk shop, brag about what we've done, you know. But Hays never joined these conversations."

Patrick looks right at me.

"One time I was admiring this really sweet piece of code, and when I asked him how he managed to figure it out, he told me to get back to work. Can you imagine?"

Yes, I can. I already know that Hays is temperamental.

"What else happened?" I ask.

"Hays just kept getting more and more out of control. He was yelling at programmers and secretaries and everyone else for no reason. Then there was the time he started throwing things at me. What a psycho."

Patrick rolls his eyes in disgust.

"What brought that on?" I ask him.

"We'd been working seven-day weeks for about three months, and I knew we needed to hire more people," Patrick explains. "I thought it would be good to add a senior programmer to the team. Everyone else but me was right out of college. They were mostly Stanford grads, so they were pretty good, but they were still kind of green."

He takes another drink of his coffee.

"When I was a grad student at the University of Illinois, I used to tap into an online discussion group where researchers talked about what they were working on," Patrick continues. "I remembered talking with this guy who was doing some pretty impressive stuff with search algorithms, so I thought that if I could track him down, I might offer him a job."

"So what happened?"

"When I mentioned to Hays what I was planning to do, he blew his stack! He turned beet red and screamed at me. He said we had enough resources and didn't need anyone else's help and to get back to work. He got so mad, he actually threw his coffee mug at me. I had to duck or it would've hit me."

Patrick hunches forward and lowers his voice.

"I'm telling you man, there's something about Cheetah that Hays doesn't want anyone to know, not even the programmers."

I study Patrick's face. He's completely sincere. This is it, I think, whatever it is Hays is keeping so secret, Leticia managed to figure it out.

"So you quit because of this?" I ask.

"Officially I quit," he says, leaning back in his chair. "But in reality Hays got rid of me."

"How's that?"

"When I joined his company, he promised me certain stock options. But about a week after his big blowup, I got this letter from Hays Software outlining my stock plan. It wasn't even a tenth of what Hays had promised me. So I had no choice but to leave. I mean, who works for straight salary in this industry? I was counting on that stock."

I feel sorry for Patrick, but I don't have time to commiserate with him.

"So, anything more about Hays?" I ask.

"No, not really, only that I think he's up to something funny, and I thought you should hear my story before writing your article."

"I appreciate the information."

I stand up and extend my hand. Patrick gets awkwardly to his feet to shake hands. He's smiling now.

"Thanks so much for meeting with me," he says. "My brother's sister-in-law is a lawyer. Maybe he can call her about the employment contract Hays made me sign."

"Good luck."

I head for the door and am soon walking through a swarm of pedestrians and street vendors. As I glance back through the cafe window, I see Patrick swig the last of his latté and get ready to leave. He has a call to make. And I have more searching to do. At least now I can narrow the focus of my investigation. The answer lies with Cheetah itself.

# Chapter Fifteen

On the way back to the office I stop for fast food. I eat my meal on the road, which hardly makes for a great dining experience, but I'm too busy for anything else today. By the time I pull in front of the *Digital Business* offices, I'm downing the last of my soft drink.

I'm through the lobby and halfway to my office when I remember that I haven't picked up today's mail, so I loop back down the hallway to the mail room. As expected, there's a small mound of correspondence waiting for me in my mailbox. I gather it up without examining it, and then start sorting through the packages on a nearby table to see if there are any for me.

At first, it looks like the usual stuff—sample products, free magazines, and press releases that were too fat to fit into a regular business envelope. There's also a puffy brown envelope with a handwritten address. The handwriting catches my eye—it's from Leticia!

I let the mail I'm holding fall to the floor, and grab the small package. My heart is racing as I rip it open. In my haste I almost tear the thick envelope in half, and a small piece of paper flutters out. I pick it up and look at it. It's a receipt from the Greyhound bus station in San Jose, listing a locker number and an access code, and it's got last Thursday's date on it. I'm not sure what to make of it, but I already know I'll be making a trip to the bus station soon, just to check it out. I look inside the package and find a short note. It looks hastily written, but I can still make it out:

> Dear Steven,
> I'm thinking of taking my nieces to San Diego, so it could be a while before I see you. Since I know how you hate to wait, here's the key to my little discovery. The documents I found are pretty hot, so I put the copies I made in the safest place I could find that late at night—the bus station. I know you'll have a ton of questions, and I promise to call you when I get back from our trip. By the way, this is the best story I've ever given anyone. Have fun.
>
> Love, Leticia

My mind is racing by the time I finish the note. I knew Leticia had found something at Hays Software, but I never thought I'd see it. A week ago, those papers would have been nothing to me but source information for a great story. But now . . . now they might tell me why Leticia was killed, maybe even help me prove who did it.

I put the receipt in my wallet for safekeeping. Then I grab the envelope and exit the mail room, anxious to share my good news. I just hope Angela isn't still stuck at the trade show.

I hurry to Angela's office. Unfortunately, as I'm getting closer I hear Matt's voice coming from her cubicle.

"They have the best sushi in the city," I hear him say.

"I'm sure it's a great restaurant, but I really don't have the time," Angela replies tersely.

"That's right, she doesn't," I say, interrupting their conversation.

Angela looks delighted to see me. Matt, however, is far from glad. He sounded like he was trying to get her to go to dinner with him, no doubt so he could repeat last weekend's scenario. I guess Angela hasn't told him yet that she's not interested.

"Sorry Matt, but Angela and I are trying to finish up the Hays article," I continue. "I really need to talk with her."

Matt hesitates.

"Alone," I add.

He glares at me and walks off.

Angela breathes a sigh of relief, turns toward me, and scans my face.

"What's up?" she asks. "You look like something's happened."

"Something has. Take a look at this."

I hand her Leticia's note. Angela takes it and studies it for a moment.

"When did you get this?" she asks me.

"Just now. I found the note inside this package, along with an access code for a locker at the Greyhound bus station."

"You just got this today?" Angela asks, surprised.

"Yeah, but it's postmarked last Thursday. So either the Pony Express took a while to get it here, or I just didn't notice it in the mail room before."

"This is a real break," Angela says, reading the note again. She looks up at me. "So when are we going to the bus station?"

I smile. This time I don't mind her inviting herself along.

"Right now," I reply. I look at my watch. "I need to pick up Chloe on the way and get her home first. But I'm sure I can get my neighbor to watch her, so after that we can go straight to San Jose."

"I'm ready," Angela says, standing up and reaching for her purse. "Let's do it."

Twenty minutes later I'm cruising south on 280, on my way to Chloe's school. Angela is right behind me in her red Mustang. She must have her radio on. Whenever I glance in my rearview mirror, I see her bopping her head back and forth rhythmically, and singing out loud.

We continue on for a couple of miles. The next time I look in my rearview mirror I notice that a dark blue BMW sedan has moved in between Angela's car and mine. It reminds me of last night's episode in the parking lot. Automatically, I move over one more lane and pick up speed.

I check the mirror to make sure Angela has followed me. She's there, still singing along with the radio. But looking further back, I see that the blue sedan has now pulled in behind her. I tell myself that it's probably not the same car I saw the other night.

We go a few more miles. The BMW keeps a safe but constant distance from Angela. I see my exit coming up, and wait until the last second to move over and exit the freeway. I hear the squeal of tires behind me. Looking in my rearview mirror, I see Angela giving me a puzzled look and throwing up her hands. The BMW has taken the same exit and is still behind Angela's car.

It's a frequently used exit, I remind myself.

I go about a quarter mile and turn off on Ralston Avenue. Angela's Mustang follows close behind, and so does the sedan. It's getting hard to believe this is just a coincidence.

I glance back at Angela, trying to see if she's noticed the car behind her, but she's gone back to singing along with the radio.

I signal the next turn, slow down, and go right. Angela follows behind. The sedan keeps driving straight, and I breathe a sigh of relief.

When I drive up in front of the school, I see Chloe running around the playground with some of her friends. I get out of my car just as Angela is pulling in behind me.

"I didn't know you were such a reckless driver," she says to me. "What was that turn off the freeway? You almost lost me there."

"Sorry. I thought that maybe we were being followed."

Angela laughs.

"Now you're getting paranoid."

"Getting beat up will do that to you," I say with a shrug.

She gives me a serious look.

"What do you mean by that?"

I give Angela the five-minute version of last night's events. She listens intently, her eyes growing wide.

"This is getting serious," she says. "What do you plan to do?"

"I plan to keep investigating. I'm not going to let a bunch of thugs scare me off when I'm this close to nailing Hays."

"What does Michelle think about all this?" Angela asks.

"She doesn't know, and you're not going to tell her."

"Fine," she says. "It's your business."

"Dad, Dad," comes a voice from behind me.

I turn around and see Chloe running up to me with a friend in tow.

"Can Kelly come to our house for dinner?" she asks.

"Not tonight. We'll do it some other time."

Chloe looks disappointed, but fortunately doesn't make a big deal of it. Without another word to Angela, I go help my daughter get in the car.

# CHAPTER SIXTEEN

When I turn on to my street, I see Michelle's car parked in front of the house. I wonder what she's doing home so early; she was planning to work late tonight.

I park in the driveway and walk rapidly towards the house. Chloe jogs along beside me. The drapes are closed, and there don't seem to be any lights on in the house. I open the front door and step into the hallway. The house is eerily dark and silent. There's no indication that Michelle is even here.

Angela joins us in the hallway, bumping into Chloe in the darkness.

"Ouch!" Chloe squeals.

"I'm sorry," Angela replies. "I can't see in here."

I flip on the hallway light.

"Hello?" I call out as I walk farther into the house.

Angela is right behind me. Chloe darts ahead.

"Wait a minute," I yell out.

"In here Dad," I hear Chloe say.

I move toward her voice, down the hallway and into the den. I find her standing next to her mother, who's seated in her favorite spot, a big leather Winston chair. Chloe is leaning against her, and has put her small arms comfortingly around her neck.

Michelle is looking at Chloe and trying to smile. The lights are off and the shades have been drawn shut; nevertheless the afternoon sun manages to poke through in long glimmers, softly illuminating Michelle's face. She looks like she's been crying.

"What's wrong?" I ask.

Michelle look up at me, and says in a tremulous voice, "I got fired today."

I'm stunned.

"How? Why?"

Michelle tries to answer, but starts to cry before she can get any words out. I sit down on the arm of the chair and gently kiss her. The tears flow even harder.

After a few minutes, Michelle stops crying and asks for a tissue. Chloe dashes out of the room and is back in no time with a box of Kleenex.

"This afternoon, Jack called me into his office," Michelle tells us, wiping her eyes. "He said that they had overhired, and had too many people on the partner track." Her voice breaks as she speaks. "And I had to be one of the ones to go."

"Jack Jackson fired you?" I ask.

"Yep, he sure did," Michelle says in a low, angry voice. "Although according to Helen Farrell, he and Marcus Turner had a long meeting this morning. My guess is that Marcus is the one who really decided who to let go. But I don't know why they'd choose to get rid of me. I thought I was doing so well."

So did I.

"I'm amazed," I say. "I just don't understand."

"Me neither," Michelle says between sniffles. "They've given me six months' salary as compensation, which I'll get as soon as

I sign their termination agreement. They'll also give me a letter of recommendation."

"Who else got let go?"

"I don't know. Neither did Helen, but she said she'd call and let me know as soon as she did."

Good ol' Helen. She's been with the firm for years, most recently as Turner's assistant. She's always treated Michelle like a daughter.

I get up and switch on the overhead light. Looking at Michelle I can see the color returning to her cheeks. The initial shock seems to be wearing off.

"You could sue for wrongful termination," I tell her.

She smiles ruefully at my suggestion.

"Not if I want to work for another venture capital firm."

"I know. I'm so sorry."

"I'm not," she says defiantly.

"You're not?"

"No, not anymore," she replies. "Now I'm mad as hell."

She slams her hand down hard on the arm of the chair.

"I just want to hit someone, you know what I mean?"

I nod in complete understanding.

"I've worked my butt off, made Grimshaw Turner a lot of money, and now this," she says. "It's not fair!"

She springs to her feet, newly energized. I stand there, not sure what to expect.

"Chloe, could you go to your room and play?" she asks. "I'll call you when dinner is ready."

"Oh Mom, do I have to?"

"Yes, your Dad and I need to talk privately."

Chloe trudges off to her room obligingly, but none too happily.

Michelle faces me, "Do you still want information about that startup?"

"Sure."

"Good. I don't know anything about it, but I'm willing to go back to the office tonight and dig around."

"How will you get in?" Angela asks, coming forward for the first time. "Didn't they take away your keys when they let you go?"

Michelle stares at Angela, thrown off by her presence.

"I don't mean to be rude," she says. "But why are you here?"

Angela looks embarrassed.

"Steven and I were planning to go to San Jose this evening," she explains. "He got a package from Leticia today."

Michelle looks at me.

"From Leticia? What was it?"

"There was a letter in it, and an access code to a locker at the bus station," I tell her.

"What's in the locker?" she asks.

"Papers—that's all I know. But they must be important, which is why I think I should stick with my original plan. We can go to your office tomorrow night."

Michelle shakes her head.

"That won't work," she says. "I'm pretty certain that HR hasn't had a chance to tell security that I no longer work there. But we have to act now. They won't let me in again after tonight."

I'm suddenly struck by the full implication of what Michelle is proposing.

"Honey," I say to her, "I don't want you doing this. We could get caught."

Michelle looks at me and smiles happily for the first time since I got home.

"This from the man who eavesdropped on the SFPD?" she says lightly. "I can't believe you're worried."

"It's too risky," I say in a serious voice.

"Oh, I get it," Michelle responds, walking over to me. "It's alright for *you* to run all over the place and risk getting thrown in jail, but I'm supposed to stay home where I'm safe and sound."

Something like that, I think to myself.

"Look Michelle . . ." I start.

"No, you look, Steven," she says, putting her hands on her hips. "I want to do this. I couldn't help you before because I was bound by a promise I made to my bosses. The way I see it, now that they've broken their faith with me, there's no reason for me to remain loyal to them. I'm free to help you out now, and I intend to do it."

"But what happens if your former employers find out about your late-night visit," I ask. "Then what?"

Michelle gestures nonchalantly.

"Easy," she says. "I'll just tell them I went back to retrieve some personal items."

"That does sound plausible," Angela chimes in.

"I can do this," Michelle insists, looking at me earnestly. "I know I can."

I return her gaze, considering. Then I lean over and give Michelle a kiss on the forehead.

"What exactly did you have in mind?" I ask, resigned.

Michelle answers me excitedly, "I figured that since Hays Software is one of Marcus' pet projects, the best strategy is to focus our search on his office. He should have several files on the company."

"Great idea," I say, "but how exactly are we going to get into his office?"

"With this," Michelle says, pulling a key out of her pocket and holding it up for us to see. "Angela was right. They did take my keys when they let me go. But what they didn't know is that Helen gave me a key to her office last year so that I could munch on her homemade cookies whenever I worked late."

"Who's Helen?" Angela asks.

"Turner's assistant," I reply. "She works in his outer office."

"And I know I have a spare key to my office around the house somewhere," Michelle adds. "Just in case we actually need to get in there."

"I guess we're set then," Angela says cheerfully. She's stretches her back out, like she's getting ready for a jog. "We're going to break into an office. This is even more fun than reading police memos."

We spend the next three hours preparing for tonight's sleuthing: working out contingency plans in case we get questioned, getting someone to watch Chloe, and tracking down the elusive spare key to Michelle's office, which somehow found its way into my toolbox in the garage.

By nine o'clock, I'm more than ready to go. Chloe is asleep in her room, and the three of us are waiting impatiently for the babysitter to show up.

The doorbell rings and we all jump up at the same time to answer it. Michelle gets there first, and opens the door. Our neighbor Lois steps into the hallway, wearing an expression of deep concern.

"Oh, Michelle," she says, hugging my wife. "I'm so sorry to hear about your job."

"Thanks," Michelle replies. This must be difficult for her. Michelle doesn't like to talk about her setbacks with any but her closest friends, but she had to find a way to explain our late-night outing. So when she called Lois, she told her she'd been fired and was going back after hours to clean out her office. Lois was quick to say yes to babysitting, mostly because she's a friendly person and a good neighbor, but also because she likes gossip.

Lois steps back from Michelle. She's shaking her head back and forth, which sends her short straight hair flying in all directions, like a dog after its bath. Finally, she stops moving her head and notices Angela.

"I don't believe we've met," Lois says to her.

"I'm Angela. Nice to meet you."

Lois is about to ask a question, but Michelle preempts her.

"Angela is Steven's cousin. She stopped by for dinner, and offered to help us out tonight."

"Oh," Lois says to Angela as she looks her up and down. "Isn't that nice of you."

"We'd better get going," I say to Lois. "We don't want to keep you up too late tonight."

"Oh, it's no problem," she replies. "The kids are all in bed, and Frank is just watching the news. I'll be fine. You all take as long as you need."

"Thanks a lot, Lois," Michelle says, picking up her sweater and her briefcase. "We really appreciate this."

We file out the front door, and walk quickly to Michelle's car. She's practically gunning the engine as I get in next to her. Angela takes a seat in the back. As soon as the last door closes, Michelle pulls sharply away from the curb. In just a few minutes we're on the freeway, heading south to the prestigious offices of Grimshaw, Turner & Willson.

# Chapter Seventeen

Like many of the elite venture capital firms, Grimshaw Turner's offices are located on Sand Hill Road in Menlo Park. We make our way down the street and turn into a parking lot. The lot is nearly empty, but there are still a couple of cars parked in front of the building.

"Not everyone is gone yet," Angela says. "How are we going to get into Turner's office without bumping into somebody?"

"Don't worry," Michelle replies. "None of these cars belong to partners. I can bluff my way past anyone else."

Michelle parks the car under a tree. We get out and walk towards the front entrance. The Grimshaw Turner building has a high-pitched roof and a huge glass window above the front door. All it needs is a cross laid over the window and it could pass for a church.

Michelle approaches the main door and taps gently on the glass facade just to its right. She's trying to get the attention of the security guards without setting off the alarm, which is highly sensitive. At most VC firms, the alarm would be all we'd have to worry about. But Grimshaw Turner is protective to the point of paranoia, and has therefore taken the added precaution of hiring a security service.

After a minute or two, one of the guards hears the tapping and comes to the door. He cups his hand to peer through the darkened glass. There's a threatening look on his face as he looks us over, but then he recognizes Michelle, smiles, and signals her to wait. He punches a code into a pad on the wall, shutting off the alarm so he can open the door.

"Forget something, Ms. Trudeau?" he says to her pleasantly once the door is open.

"I sure did. We were out at dinner when I realized that I'd left some files in the office. I'm just glad I remembered before I got home."

"I understand. Come right in," he says.

We file past the security guard and he locks the door behind us. When he turns around again to face us I notice for the first time what a big guy he is. He must be at least 6'6," and looks ponderous in his navy blue blazer. I glance at his name tag. His name is Grant.

"There's some stuff on my computer I might need as well," Michelle says to Grant. "So it may take a while."

"No problem," he replies. "Just be sure you leave through the front lobby so one of us can let you out. All of the doors are alarmed."

"Will do," Michelle replies as we walk to the steps leading to the offices.

We get to the top of the stairs and continue walking down the expansive main hallway until we're out of sight of the lobby. Then, instead of turning right onto the narrow corridor that houses the associates' offices, we hurry forward a few more feet and make an abrupt left onto "Partners' Row."

"Here's Marcus' office," Michelle says, stopping in front of a glassed-in room about halfway down the hall.

The venetian blinds covering the windows on either side of the door are lowered but not closed, so we're able to get a pretty good look at the darkened outer office before we even go in. It's small, with a plain desk to the right, along with some file cabinets. On the other side of the room are more file cabinets, a printer, and a copy machine. I also see two chairs against the back wall, situated next to a door that undoubtedly leads to Turner's inner sanctum.

Michelle takes out a key and slides it easily into the outer door. There's a slight click, and the door opens. We file into the office quickly and I lock the door behind us. Then I close the venetian blinds, which leaves just enough light seeping through from the hallway for us to find our way to the other door.

Michelle gets to Turner's door first, and is about to open it when I put my hand out to stop her.

"Look," I whisper, indicating a subdued light coming from the bottom of the door.

But before Michelle can even reply, the door handle turns. We all freeze, and I hear a quick intake of breath from Angela. Michelle is completely silent, and standing as still as a statue. I don't know what to do: run or think up some excuse for being here.

The door starts to open. Michelle, Angela and I are still immobilized. We stand there like the Three Stooges, as the person from inside looks up to face us.

What a relief, it's the janitor. This is not a good development, but at least we're not face to face with Marcus Turner.

"Hi," Michelle says. "How are you tonight?"

"Hello," he says.

"Is this Marcus Turner's office?" Michelle asks innocently.

The janitor nods but doesn't answer the question. I'm not sure he speaks English. He's looking at us like he's not quite sure what to make of us, but clearly he knows we're up to something.

Michelle looks like she's about to say something else when Angela jumps in.

"Buenas noches, señor," she says to him.

"Buenas," he replies, still eyeing us suspiciously, but starting to warm up.

"Dejé algo muy importante en la oficina y lo necesito," Angela says.

"Bueno," he replies, amiably. "Pero por favor, no me la dejen tirada. Ya la limpié."

"Claro que no, señor."

I took Spanish in college, but they're speaking too fast for me to follow. I can only make out a few words like "important" and "office."

"What's going on?" I say.

"We can go into the office if we want. I mean, it's not like he's going to stop us," Angela explains. "But he would prefer that we didn't make a mess; he just cleaned it."

I give him a wry smile.

"Tell him we intend to leave everything exactly the way we found it," I say to Angela.

"If he tells anyone we were in Turner's office . . ." Michelle adds.

"I know," Angela replies. Then she resumes her conversation with our new acquaintance.

"Es mejor que nadie sepa que estuvimos aquí," she tells him.

Angela's request elicits a knowing smile from the janitor.

"Yo no les digo nada, señorita. No se apure," he says. "Al cabo, esa gente ni caso me hace."

Angela looks at him gratefully.

"Mil gracias, señor."

She turns to Michelle and me.

"We can trust him not to tell, I'm sure of it. I told him it would be better for us if no one knew we'd been here, and he said that Turner and the rest never talk to him, so he has no reason to talk to them."

"Perfect," I say. "Then let's get going."

We step aside to let the janitor roll his cleaning cart past us. He stops when he reaches the outer door, and gives us a conspiratorial look before pushing his cart into the hallway and locking the door behind him.

Michelle, Angela and I walk cautiously into Turner's office, and Angela quietly closes the door behind us.

I take a good look around Marcus Turner's office and nearly burst out laughing. The whole setup is so sumptuous, so perfect, as to be absurd.

On the left side of the room is a huge mahogany desk, with a matching chair. There are two computers on the desk: a laptop and a desktop PC with a docking station. Otherwise the desk is free of clutter, with little else on top but a phone and an ornate lamp, complete with a dark yellow Tiffany shade. The lamp is on, and imparts a golden aura to the whole room.

Across from the desk a pair of heavy curtains cover a huge window that stretches from the ceiling down to the floor. I bet it looks out over the Stanford hills, which must give Turner a spectacular view during the day.

One corner of the office holds a plush reading chair with a standing lamp and a large world globe next to it. Close to the chair is a magazine rack stuffed with back issues of *The Economist*, *Digital Business*, and *Red Herring*. Another wall is nothing but floor to ceiling bookshelves, containing everything from computer manuals to Japanese/English dictionaries. A few of the shelves hold various mementos from Turner's life, including exotic items from his world travels and memorabilia from some of the companies he's funded.

The wall facing the bookshelves is adorned with a large print of M.C. Escher's lithograph "Hand with Reflecting Globe." Next to the artwork is a picture gallery with an array of framed photographs of Turner with other power players. In the center is a color photo of him posing with the President. Other photos show Turner with Hollywood agents, studio executives, professional athletes, and various Silicon Valley entrepreneurs.

Angela makes a beeline for Turner's desk. She's reaching to boot up the PC when Michelle stops her.

"Wait!" my wife whispers harshly. "Our systems record the last time they were used. Besides, you need special passwords to access anything useful."

"Where's Dan Guerra when we need him," Angela says, disappointed.

"We'll just have to snoop the old-fashioned way," I say. "Let's take a look in these cabinets over here. I bet he backs up a lot of his files with hard copies."

Ironically, the file cabinets are not locked. We each pull open a drawer and start thumbing through its contents. After a couple of minutes, however, it's clear that the files on the startups are pretty sparse.

"I haven't found anything on Hays Software yet," Michelle says, looking up from the file drawer she's been inspecting. "It's his hottest project these days, so he may be keeping those files in his briefcase. In which case, they're home with him right now."

"We don't have access to his briefcase," I say. "Keep looking and maybe we'll get lucky."

Another five minutes pass. It seems longer, probably because I half-expect Turner to come barging into the office.

Finally, though, I come across something interesting.

"Aha!" I say, like the proverbial detective. "Turner doesn't have all the Hays files with him."

At the back of one of the drawers, I've located a drop-file labeled "Hays SW–Stock." Like the other company files, it's thin, but at least it's something.

I take the file over to a round conference table and turn on the green-shaded lamp suspended above it. Michelle and Angela follow me to the table, eager to see what I've found. I place the file on the desk, and open it up to reveal a single document.

"Bingo!" Michelle immediately exclaims, grabbing the document and flipping through it.

"What is it?" Angela asks.

"An initial draft of a stock prospectus," Michelle explains without looking up. "It looks like Hays Software is getting ready to go public. And soon."

"I already knew that," I say, disappointed.

Michelle doesn't respond; something else has caught her interest.

"This is funny," she says.

"What is?" I ask.

"I'm looking at the list of investment partners," she explains. "There's a couple of individual investors listed, but they're not named. They're simply called Angel One and Angel Two. That's odd."

"But angel investors prefer a low profile," I say.

"Yeah, they do," Michelle agrees. "But I've never seen this before. Usually by this stage the private investors have all been named. I guess these guys want to keep their names out of it until the last draft, so they can remain anonymous as long as possible."

"How much did they put in?" Angela asks.

Michelle runs her finger down a column of numbers.

"It looks like Angel One put in $50,000. That's a fairly typical passive investment," she tells us. "And Angel Two has invested . . . $5 million!" Michelle looks up at us, confounded. "It's got to be a typo. Otherwise, it's as much as the combined investment of Grimshaw Turner and the corporate partners."

"Is it that unusual?" Angela asks. "There are plenty of filthy rich people around here."

"There are, but I've never heard of an individual risking this kind of money on a startup," Michelle tells us. "It's a huge stake. This company must be really hot."

"Angela and I tested Cheetah the other day," I tell her. "It's years ahead of what's out there. If Angel Two's investment pays off the way I think it will, he'll have enough money to support a small country."

"And I'm sure that's just what he'll do with it," Angela says sarcastically.

"Whatever," Michelle says. She goes back to skimming through the prospectus.

"The underwriting is a little unusual," she says after a moment, "but nothing I haven't seen before. Nothing else here stands out." She looks at me. "Well, dear, does this help?"

"I'm not sure," I say. "But let's make a copy just in case."

I'm reaching for the document when I hear a jangle of keys outside.

"Security!" Michelle whispers hoarsely. "They must be making their rounds."

"Everybody under the table," I order.

"But the lights," Angela says.

"No time!" I snap back.

We scramble to the floor and do our best to squeeze in between the two wide legs that support the table. It's not an easy fit. Michelle lands on my lap, and I instinctively put my arms around her. Angela has just barely managed to wedge herself in between the table leg and my back when we hear the door to Turner's office open.

From my position I can see the bottom of the door swing open and a pair of size 16 shoes enter the room. It must be Grant. He walks to the center of the office and stops. Then he turns and approaches our table determinedly. I tense, expecting to hear him order us out with our hands up. Instead he walks right up to the edge of the table, and I hear the lamp switch off above us. Then he walks over to Turner's desk, and shuts off the Tiffany lamp. Finally, he goes to the door and closes it behind him, leaving us in complete darkness.

We wait until we hear him lock the door of the outer office, and then disentangle ourselves from each other and get out from under the table. I grope around blindly in the dark for a few seconds until I find the switch for the table lamp and turn on the light.

"That was too close," Angela says, rubbing her left shoulder gingerly. "I'm glad that's over."

"It's not," Michelle says nervously. "Security always starts their rounds on Partner's Row, and then works their way over to the associates' offices. We've got to get to my office before Grant does, or we'll be in a load of trouble."

"Then we'll have to work fast," I say, picking up the prospectus and handing it to Michelle. "Make a copy of this. I'll keep an eye on Grant."

We run to the outer office. Michelle slides the document into the copier and starts the machine. Angela stands next to her, holding the open file folder. I take up a post at the window, pulling back the venetian blinds just enough to peer through. I'm just in time to see Grant walking into an office at the end of the corridor. He's there for no more than fifteen seconds, and then I see him walk out of the room, check to make sure the door is locked, and walk to the office directly opposite.

"He's already working his way back down the hall," I whisper urgently to Michelle.

"Almost finished," she says.

The next ten seconds are agonizingly slow.

"Got it!" Michelle says excitedly as the machine spits out the last page. She scoops up the original and hands it to Angela, who sticks it in the file and hurries back to Turner's office to put it away.

I look out from my vantage point and see Grant walking into the last office on the hallway. We have less than fifteen seconds to get out of here.

"We've got to go now!" I call out.

Michelle has turned off the copier and joined me at the door. I see the lights go off in Turner's office and a second later Angela hurries out, softly closing his door behind her. I don't even bother to check if the hallway is clear before opening the outer door and pushing Michelle and Angela out of the room.

"Run!" I tell them.

They take off, quickly but quietly, as I fumble with the door's lock. It takes a couple of seconds to figure out how to work it. Finally, I hear it click. I hastily close the door, then bolt down the passageway, without ever looking back.

I get to the end and turn onto the floor's main corridor. I race down it a few feet and then take a sharp left onto another hallway. I can see Angela and Michelle in front of Michelle's office. It looks like they just got there.

I catch up to them just as Michelle is sliding her spare key into the office door. She tries turning the lock, but it seems stuck.

"What's wrong?" Angela whispers anxiously. "Why won't it work?"

"I don't know," Michelle says, nearly in tears. "It must not be a good copy. It won't turn."

"Let me," I say.

I take the key out and shove it in again as hard as I can, then twist with all my might. The key sticks initially, then suddenly turns in one rapid motion. I open the door and we practically fall into the office, relieved to have made it.

Somebody behind me turns on the overhead light, which is overwhelmingly bright after all the time we've spent in semi-darkness. It takes a few seconds for our eyes to adjust.

Michelle is the first to speak.

"Those bastards!" she says, looking around the room. "Look at this place!"

The office Michelle left intact just a few hours ago is unrecognizable. There are boxes strewn on the floor, filled with books and files. The bookshelves are completely empty, as are the file cabinets and the desk drawers. Even the plants are gone.

"They must be moving someone else in here right away," Michelle says with fire in her eyes. "I can't believe it."

"It looks like they're planning to mail you your personal items," Angela says from one corner of the office. "There's a box full of your things over here."

I look over to where Angela is standing. On top of a pile of books, files, and mugs in an open box, I can see a framed picture of Chloe in her softball uniform.

"I'm sorry, honey," I say.

"I know," she replies, walking over to the corner and angrily picking up the box. "Let's just get the hell out of here."

"Ms. Trudeau?" a voice says from the open doorway.

I turn around and see Grant walking into the room, a confused expression on his boyish face.

"What happened to your office?" he asks.

Michelle sighs.

"I didn't want to tell anyone," she says honestly. "But I got fired today."

"Oh, I'm real sorry to hear that," Grant says sincerely. "Real sorry."

"Me too," she replies, "Anyway, I just came to pick up a few of my things."

"Let me carry that for you," he says, reaching for the box she's holding. He lifts it in one hand, as if it were a carton of tissue paper.

We follow Grant out of the office, and walk leisurely down the stairs. The security guard doesn't say anything, but there's an awfully sad expression on his face. When we get to the main lobby I take the box from him.

"Thanks for the help," I say.

"You're welcome," he replies, barely aware of me. Then he turns to my wife, a disconsolate expression still on his face. "I wish you the best of luck. It won't be the same without you."

"That's nice of you to say," she replies.

We exit the building and Grant locks up behind us. I can't help feeling that he's watching us walk away, no doubt pining over the loss of Michelle's company.

"You never mentioned that Grant had a crush on you," I say lightly.

"Yeah, I guess he does. It's pretty sweet," she says. "Too bad he didn't have a say in whether or not I kept my job."

The drive back home is a sullen one. Michelle is stone silent in the passenger seat next to me, a depressed look fixed on her face. Angela is almost as quiet. If it weren't for the drumming of her fingers on the handrest, I could almost forget she was in the car.

It's after eleven when I pull into our driveway. Michelle has her door open before I've even stopped the car.

"Thanks for all your help," Angela says from the back seat.

Michelle pauses.

"You're welcome," she says, and then gets out and walks hastily to the front door.

I park the car in the garage, and Angela gets out.

"What time should I come by tomorrow?" she asks me.

It takes me a couple of seconds to remember what she's talking about.

"Right, the trip to the bus station. Let's do it first thing in the morning. Can you be here by seven?"

"See you then."

Angela walks out to her car and gets in. I wait until I hear her start the engine before closing the garage door and going into the house.

I find Lois in the family room, but Michelle is nowhere to be seen.

"How did it go?" Lois asks me. "Michelle seems kind of upset."

"I think this is hard for her," I reply vaguely.

"I bet. Need any help carrying anything in?"

"No thanks. I thought we'd just leave it in the car for now, and deal with it tomorrow. But thanks for the offer."

"You're very welcome," Lois replies.

Her pale brown eyes have a sharp look to them.

"And where did your cousin go? I assumed she'd be coming back with you."

"She did," I say, trying not to let my annoyance show. "But she had to go home. It's pretty late, you know."

I can tell that Lois would love to ask a few more questions, but I don't have the time or the patience for it. I scoop up her sweater and drape it around her shoulders as I nudge her gently towards the door.

"Here, let me walk you home," I say in my most neighborly voice.

"That's very kind of you."

I get her out of the house and rush her across the street.

"Thanks so much for helping us out. We owe you one," I say when we arrive at her doorstep.

"Oh, it was no trouble at all. Anytime I can help, you just let me know," she says as I'm walking away.

# Chapter Eighteen

I'm awakened by the sound of someone banging on the front door.

"What's going on?" Michelle says sleepily.

I look at the clock.

"It must be Angela," I say, getting up. "I asked her to be here at seven."

"Why can't she be late like everybody else?"

I lean over and kiss Michelle.

"It's time to get up anyway."

"Maybe for you," she replies, rolling over and looking at me. "But I am no longer employed. Remember?"

"Oh, so you're going to lie in bed all day?"

"The thought had occurred to me," she replies. "But you know, I think I want to go somewhere outdoors. Maybe I'll take Chloe to Point Reyes. She can afford to miss one day of school. And it's supposed to be beautiful today."

"Good idea."

I can hear the door bell ringing now.

"I'd better let Angela in."

I put on my robe, make my way downstairs, and open the front door just as Angela is about to begin knocking again.

"I was wondering what happened to you," she says, walking in.

"I forgot to set the alarm last night," I say, turning around to walk back upstairs. "Just give me ten minutes."

By the time I get out of the shower, Michelle and Chloe have started getting ready for their excursion. I can hear them chatting in Chloe's bedroom about visiting the lighthouse at Point Reyes and hiking along Drake's Bay.

I dress rapidly, then stop by Chloe's room to say goodbye before heading downstairs.

"That was quick," Angela says to me as I enter the living room. "Do you have the access code with you?"

"I've got it. Do we have any idea where we're going?"

"I looked it up. The Greyhound station is located on Almaden Avenue," she informs me. "I'm familiar with the area."

"Let's get started then."

We move out the door and towards the driveway. Angela walks over to her car.

"Are you volunteering to drive?" I ask her.

"Sure am." She opens the driver's side door and gets in. "My car is much more fun than yours."

"Whatever makes you happy," I reply, getting into the passenger seat next to her.

She revs the engine a couple of times, and then backs out. In less than ten minutes we're cruising down the freeway.

Despite the cool breeze this morning, Angela has the top down on her Mustang. The cold wind is bracing, and it helps me think. I try to analyze what we learned last night. Does any of it have a connection to Leticia's death? I can't see any. It seems that every time I dig up more on Hays Software, all I do is confirm that the company is legitimate and that Hays and his investors stand to make a lot of money off it. Except for Patrick Nagel's suspicions about Cheetah, Hays Software looks like your classic Internet success story.

"Hey, I want to ask you something," Angela says, interrupting my thoughts. "You haven't told me what you found out from that executive in Marin."

I give her the rundown on my conversation with Hank Pilsbury, and then go on to tell her about Patrick Nagel. Angela seems particularly intrigued by Nagel's stories about Hays' temper.

"Arthur Hays is a nut case," she says.

"I think Patrick Nagel would agree with you."

Angela shakes her head, and then glances over at me.

"Boy, you've been busy. I'll have to tell Tina not to send me to any more boring trade shows until Hays is behind bars."

"I'll be sure to let you know the next time I set up a clandestine meeting with someone," I tell her jokingly.

"You do that."

We lapse into silence. I stare at the brown hills along the freeway, glad for the peace and quiet of the drive. But I can't quite relax, because Angela keeps glancing my way, like she's sizing me up, or trying to get up the nerve to say something.

"There's something I've been meaning to say to you," she finally blurts out.

"What's that?"

"I'm getting to know you pretty well, and I've noticed . . ." She stops, looking at the road ahead and searching for words. "I don't know how to put this, so I'll just say it." She looks over at me. "It's not your fault," she states simply.

It takes a few seconds for me to realize what she means. When I do, it's my turn to stare at the road in front of us.

"If I hadn't pushed Leticia for that information . . ."

"She'd still be dead," Angela interrupts. "Look, I'm sure Leticia didn't get to the top of her profession by being a wimp. She went digging for that data because she wanted the publicity as much as you wanted the cover story."

"Maybe," I say, unconvinced.

"Maybe nothing," Angela retorts. "Leticia didn't strike me as a pushover. In fact, I figured you two were such good friends because you're both driven as hell. I mean, you're the only person I know who . . ."

Angela's voice trails off. She's staring at the rearview mirror.

"What's wrong?" I ask.

"Probably nothing. But just to make sure, what kind of car did those goons who beat you up have?"

"I think it was a BMW. Why do you ask?"

"There's a black BMW behind us," Angela says, looking again at the rearview mirror. "It's been right behind us for awhile, but I didn't think much of it until it followed us onto 87 just now."

I glance quickly over my shoulder.

"It looks like the same car," I say. "But there's only one way to be sure. How fast is your car?"

"My brother souped it up when he first got it. It's supposed to be able to keep up with the best of them."

"Good. Let's hit it, and see what this guy does."

Angela punches the accelerator; the muffler rumbles for a second and then the Mustang takes off. Angela's hair blows straight back, as if being held by wires.

"We're past 90, now up to 100," she says glancing at the speedometer.

Angela darts from one lane to the next, making her way past several cars.

I look over my shoulder again.

"He's staying with us," I tell her, shouting over the sound of the wind. "We're definitely being tailed."

"What should we do?"

The wind whips away her words. I can barely hear her.

"We're going to have to exit someplace and try to lose him on side streets," I yell back.

"No way," she shouts.

"Do you have a better idea? We can't drive at this speed forever. Here's an exit, let's take it."

Angela waits until the last second and then exits hard on to Santa Clara Street, tires squealing. I look back and see the BMW swerve to follow. As he jerks on to the exit he almost hits a Volkswagen bug. The VW driver honks his horn and flips him off. The BMW barrels past the little car, halfway in the emergency lane, and pulls in right behind us again.

"Quick; make a right at this first street," I say as we come on to Santa Clara. Angela jerks the steering wheel hard to the right and the car fishtails before straightening out again. The BMW does the same.

"Make another right here," I say as we approach the first cross street.

Angela complies, and we cross over a small bridge and go past a park.

"Make a left at the stop sign."

Angela starts to slow down.

"Just run it!"

She wavers momentarily, then hits the accelerator. The BMW also runs the stop sign, then speeds up to follow as we enter the curve.

"We're getting close to San Jose State," Angela says. "Maybe we can lose him there."

"Go for it."

Angela makes another left, then a right. The BMW is on our tail the whole way. We're coming up on 4th Street, and we still haven't lost him.

"Make a left here," I say.

Angela turns.

"It's a one way street!" she shouts. "We're going the wrong way!"

Angela moves over to the right lane to avoid a minivan coming at us head on. People are honking their horns and yelling at us. I can hear a lot of tires squealing as drivers try to get out of our way. Angela is weaving and dodging, doing her best to avoid the oncoming traffic. Incredibly, the BMW is still behind us.

Suddenly a car pulls out of a parking structure on our right and comes straight at us. Angela hits her horn and swerves to the left. The BMW follows our move.

We're finally at a cross street.

"Go left here," I shout, looking over my shoulder. I watch the BMW follow us tightly around the corner.

"He's still with us!" I yell to Angela. "Punch it!"

Angela slams her foot hard on the accelerator and we immediately pick up speed. I look back and see the BMW drop behind. I think we surprised him this time.

"A red light . . ." Angela says as we run it.

As we race through the intersection, I hear the screech of tires and a deep horn blaring. I look to my right and see a panel truck coming right at us. This is it, I think to myself, and brace for the impact.

But somehow we make it through the intersection without colliding. Behind us, I hear more screeching tires, then a crash and the sound of shattering glass.

Angela slams on the brakes and we both turn to look behind. For a couple of seconds, everything is quiet. Then all of a sudden, the BMW emerges from the other side of the truck and speeds off down the street, burning rubber. The passenger side of the car is all dented and the window is blown out.

"Looks like he's out of here," I say as the car whips around a corner and disappears from sight. "Let's get going."

We drive another block. I look over at Angela, and notice her hands are trembling on the steering wheel.

"Make a right here at Market."

Angela turns without saying a word. She drives a little further and then pulls into the parking lot of the art museum.

For a moment, neither of us says anything. The adrenaline is flowing and my heart is pounding.

Angela takes a deep breath.

"Okay, let's go home," she says. "I've had all I can take for one day."

"We can't go yet. We haven't gotten into that locker."

"I don't care," she says, giving me an angry look. "We can come back tomorrow. We almost got killed back there, and right now, all I want to do is go home, take a hot bath, and drink a case of wine."

"But tomorrow will be too late. At least now we know those guys aren't following us anymore. There may never be a safer time."

Angela purses her lips and looks like she's about to argue. But she knows I'm right. She shakes her head. I've never seen her this disgusted.

"Alright. But you drive; I've been through enough."

She tosses me the keys, and gets out of the car. I hop over to the driver's side, and Angela takes the seat I've just vacated. She slams the car door closed.

"Let's make this fast," she says.

"Believe me. I have no desire to stick around any longer than I have to."

I put the car in gear and drive slowly across the parking lot. As we approach the exit, I can discern the wail of a police siren. It's growing louder every second.

"Are those police cars?" Angela asks.

"I think so."

I reach the exit and edge out onto the street to check for traffic. Looking to my left, I see three or four squad cars zoom past the cross street just a block down. Angela sees them too.

"They're going to be looking for us," she says apprehensively. "We were driving the wrong way up a one way street; I'm sure someone reported us."

"All the more reason to get what we came for and clear out fast," I say, turning right.

"Fine." Angela crosses her arms. "But you have to pay my bail if we get hauled down to jail."

"Deal."

We manage to make it to the Greyhound bus depot without encountering any police. I park in the back lot, in the far corner next to an old wood-paneled station wagon, which should block the view of the Mustang from any passing police cars. We jump out and walk quickly to the terminal.

There's a bus parked in front of the main door, but the engine is off and no one is boarding it. The sign above the windshield says "Fresno." A few people are sitting around on some outdoor seats, apparently waiting for a different bus to show up.

We enter through the double doors into a large lobby. To the right is another door that leads to a baggage claim area. Farther up on the right is a small bank of public phones, some video game units, and a few vending machines. Directly opposite is the ticket counter.

"Do you see the lockers?" I ask Angela.

"No. I thought they would be right here when we walked in. I'll ask."

Angela darts up to the ticket counter to ask the woman at the desk, and is soon back again.

"They're back in the waiting room over to the left," she tells me.

We head in that direction to a gated area with a turnstile. A sign says "ticketed passengers only," but there's no one there to check for tickets. We walk through the turnstile into a small waiting area that has about thirty mesh metal chairs, most of which are occupied. People look up at us expectantly before returning to their books and conversation, except for some of the men, who continue to stare at Angela.

We look around the room. The walls are plastered with posters. There's another row of phones and a water fountain. Tucked in a corner are the lockers. Instead of the row upon row of lockers I'd expected to find, there are only twelve of them.

"Looks like Leticia was lucky to find an empty one," Angela says as we walk over to the lockers.

I pull my wallet out of my jeans pocket and retrieve the locker receipt.

"Let's see. Locker number ten," I say. "Here it is."

The locker is a gray metal box about two feet tall and a foot wide, with a touchpad on the outside for entering the access code. I punch in the number and try the lock, but it won't budge.

"According to this, we owe money," Angela tells me, pointing to an electronic display that's flashing "$10.00" on and off.

"I don't believe this," I say, reaching for my wallet again.

"I hope you brought a lot of quarters, because the locker doesn't take anything else."

"You've got to be kidding."

I glance around to see where we might get some change. Fortunately there's a change machine nearby that accepts singles and fives.

"Do you have any money?" I ask Angela.

"I think I've got a five."

"Me, too."

We take out our cash and feed it into the change machine. The quarters pour out with a rush and a clatter, like we just hit the jackpot in a Vegas casino. Angela scoops up all forty of them with both hands and we walk back to locker #10. I take a few quarters from Angela's hands and pop them into the coin slot on the locker. As each quarter drops in, we watch the display count down from $10.00 until it reaches zero. It seems to take forever. When the last coin goes in, Angela steps forward and turns the dial handle on the locker. There's a slight click and the door pops open, revealing a large space about three feet deep.

I reach inside and pull out a thin, buff-colored 9" x 12" envelope. There's no writing on the outside. It certainly doesn't look like much. I take a quick look inside the locker, but there's nothing else. I nod to Angela, and she shuts the door.

I start to rip open the envelope, but Angela puts her hand on my arm to stop me.

"We don't have time to stick around," she reminds me.

"Good point."

We walk hurriedly through the turnstile and out of the building. Once outside, we jog to the car. Angela gets in the driver's seat and I toss her the keys. She drives us cautiously away from the bus terminal, using side streets to avoid the police.

"Do you have any idea where you're going?" I ask her as we bump along a beat-up alleyway.

"I have a general idea. We're headed west. Eventually, we should reach a freeway."

We drive furtively through downtown for another fifteen minutes or so, and then we do come upon a freeway; it's Highway 17. Angela takes the entrance heading south.

After a couple of minutes on the highway, I look behind to see if we're being followed. Not a cop car in sight. And no dark sedans either. It looks like we've gotten away.

I'm still holding the envelope Leticia left me. I undo the clasp and tear open the flap. I peer inside and see what looks like a dozen pieces of paper. As I slide out the papers I can see that the top sheet is an e-mail printout. Underneath is more e-mail correspondence, followed by some handwritten notes, and about three pages of programming code. All the pages are on the same type of paper and appear to be photocopies.

I try to read the documents, but with the top down on the car, it's all I can do to keep the wind from ripping the papers out of my hands.

"Well, what does it say?" Angela asks.

"It's too hard to read it here." I put the papers back in the envelope. "Let's pull off and find some place to look at this stuff."

"We're close to Los Gatos; I'll go there."

Angela exits onto Highway 9. Soon we're driving down the little town's main thoroughfare, looking for a suitable side street.

"Try here," I tell Angela. "This street is as good as any."

Angela complies, and then makes another turn into a small parking lot behind a Good Earth restaurant. We park under a tree.

I take the documents out of the envelope, and start reading. Angela leans against me so she can read too.

"It looks like correspondence," she says.

"It is. It's addressed to Arthur Hays, from someone named J. Phillips. He seems to be explaining some technical point to Hays. I can't tell for sure though; I'm no programmer."

"Look at the e-mail address," Angela says, pointing at the page I'm reading. "Whoever this Phillips guy is, he's somehow affiliated with the University of Texas." She pushes her long hair away from her face in one smooth motion. "Isn't that where Hays went after he retired from PCI?"

"It sure is. He taught computer science in Austin for a couple of years, right before he came to California to found his company."

I look at the date on the correspondence.

"The e-mail is a couple of years old, so it must be from Hays' time at UTA. I wonder why he kept it. More than that, I wonder why Leticia thought it was important enough to copy and send to me."

I flip through the other papers. The rest of the correspondence is just as technical.

"Do you understand this stuff?" Angela asks me.

"Can't say I do. I'm no techie." I think for a moment. "But I know someone who is," I continue, looking at Angela.

"You want us to go see Dan," she says.

"He can decipher this lingo for us. Without his help, I don't think we'll be able to figure out the significance of these documents."

"So much for my hot bath," she says with a touch of resignation. She starts the car, and then reaches over to turn up the radio. "At least it's a beautiful day for the drive."

# Chapter Nineteen

We pull in front of Dan's house and get out. As we approach the building we see an old blue jeep parked in the driveway.

"We're in luck," Angela says to me. "Looks like he's back from the beach."

We climb up the stairs and Angela knocks on the door. Dan answers right away and smiles broadly when he sees Angela—I suspect that a visit from her would be welcome any time of the day or night.

Dan ushers us into his apartment, then goes to the kitchen to get a couple of sodas. Angela and I make ourselves comfortable in his living room; I commandeer the beat-up lounge chair, and Angela settles down on one end of the sofa, kicking off her sandals and sitting cross-legged.

Dan comes back with our drinks and joins Angela on the sofa, across from me. He's dressed in his usual work attire: shorts, T-shirt, and no shoes.

"So, whose system do you want to break into now?" he asks facetiously.

"It's nothing like that this time," I tell him. "We have some technical documents that we need help interpreting."

"Let me see them," Dan says, putting out his hand.

But I hesitate to hand him the papers.

"Before you get more involved, I think I should warn you. Our little investigation is getting pretty risky."

"Risky?"

"Somebody roughed me up Monday night, and warned me to back off."

"And then just now, when we went to get these papers, we were chased all over downtown San Jose," Angela adds.

Dan reflects on this.

"Sounds like somebody's getting nervous," he says simply.

"Which is why I understand if you don't want to get more involved," I say.

Dan looks at me and nods his head.

"Now can I see those papers?" he asks.

I smile and hand him the whole stack. He takes it from me and starts looking over the documents.

Angela and I sip our sodas and watch him intently. For his part, Dan is completely absorbed by what he's reading; he seems to have forgotten we're here.

"I think I might know what they're talking about," he murmurs. "Let me look at this code."

Dan seems particularly intrigued by the programming, and is taking forever to look it over. Angela starts drumming her fingers on her Coke can. It's the only sound in the room. I try to keep myself occupied by slouching down in the chair and scrutinizing the ceiling. The spider web is still in its corner, but its occupant is nowhere to be found.

After what seems like an eternity, Dan looks up from the papers.

"This is interesting stuff."

"What is it?" I ask.

"It's hard to tell exactly, but it looks like they're talking about an intelligent agent for the Internet."

Angela looks at me.

"Cheetah," she says.

I nod in agreement.

"What's Cheetah?" Dan asks us.

"It's Hays Software's one and only product," Angela tells him. "It's the only true intelligent search agent we've ever seen."

"It sounds like the program they're talking about in these documents," Dan says. "It's hard to judge with only three pages of code, but it would fit."

"So apparently, Hays didn't write the Cheetah program on his own. He had help," I say, more to Angela than to Dan.

"No, that's not it either," Dan says. "The way Phillips talks about the program, the way he knows all the details—he's got to be the one who wrote it."

"I don't remember any J. Phillips mentioned in the promotional literature for Hays Software," Angela says.

"Neither do I," I say. "And I've read through everything."

"Could he be a silent partner?" she asks me.

"I guess. But that doesn't seem right to me. For one thing, Hays has always taken full credit for creating Cheetah. He's never even hinted that he might have had a collaborator."

"And I've never met a programmer who would keep quiet about being the creator of a breakthrough product," Dan adds. "The recognition is as important as the money."

"Maybe Phillips had no choice," Angela persists. "Maybe he needed Hays' contacts with the venture capital community, and the price was for him to keep quiet."

"No," I tell her. "That's not it. With a product like this, Phillips could have written his business plan on a cocktail napkin and still have gotten funding from all the major VC firms."

I turn to Dan.

"Let's see if we can find out more about this guy. We know he's associated with the University of Texas at Austin. He's probably an assistant professor of computer science, or something along those lines."

"I'm not so sure," Dan says slowly. "I've got a hunch this guy is a grad student. Hays keeps calling him a 'young man' in these messages."

"Okay, let's start with that assumption," I say. "Can you tap into the university's student directory and see if there's a J. Phillips listed?"

"Piece of cake."

We follow Dan into his office. He sits down in front of the Sun workstation and boots up.

Angela and I pull up a couple of chairs. In just a few minutes, we're gazing at a long list of all the graduate students at UTA. The listing is in alphabetical order, so Dan scrolls down to the P section. There are over twenty people named Phillips, including four with the first initial J, all of whom are women. A dead end.

I'm not ready to give up just yet, however.

"What's the date on this list?" I ask Dan.

"It's the current directory."

"For all we know, J. Phillips has graduated," I say. "Why don't you see if you can look up the directory from a couple of years ago?"

Dan turns back to his computer. His fingers fly over the keyboard; but after ten minutes of searching, he comes up empty-handed.

"Apparently, they don't keep old directories on file," he says.

"Try the transcript database," Angela suggests.

Dan gets back to work. I see lines of code race across the screen, none of which make any sense to me.

"Done," he says after a few minutes. "Here's the listing of all the transcripts for graduate students who were enrolled three years ago."

I scan the list. There are five J. Phillips.

"I think we can safely eliminate anyone in the humanities," Angela says.

"Here you go then," Dan says. "Joshua Phillips is your man. He's a doctoral candidate in computer science."

"Great work," I tell him. "Now can we call up his actual transcript?"

"Sure."

Dan rapidly executes a series of commands, and Phillips' university records appear on the screen. I pull my chair closer to the computer and commence reading.

Three years ago, when he was a second year graduate student, Joshua Phillips took two classes with adjunct faculty member Arthur Hays.

"Why doesn't the transcript show anything for the past two years?" Angela asks.

"I don't know," Dan says, shrugging his shoulders. Then he points to the screen. "But here's his address and phone number. Who wants to call him?"

"I will," I say immediately. "I'd love to hear what this guy has to say about Arthur Hays."

I pick up the phone and dial the number. It rings three times before someone picks up.

"Hello," a man answers.

"Hi," I say, in an upbeat friendly voice. "Could I please speak with Joshua Phillips?"

"Who's this?"

"A friend." I'm trying to sound sincere. It doesn't work.

"I don't think so."

I hear a click and know I've been hung up on.

"Apparently that didn't go very well," Angela says.

"Not at all," I reply. "But the guy I talked to knows who Phillips is, I'm sure of it."

"Let me try," Angela volunteers. She turns to Dan. "Where did Phillips get his undergraduate degree?"

Dan looks at the transcript.

"Duke."

She picks up the phone, dials the number, and waits for someone to answer.

"Hi, I'm trying to track down Joshua Phillips. Is he there?" she asks. There's a short pause and then Angela continues in an apologetic voice. "Yeah, that was my brother who just called. He was trying to help me get a hold of Joshua."

Another pause while the guy on the other end of the line says something.

"Please don't hang up," Angela pleads. "I haven't seen Joshua in years and I'd like to get in touch with him."

Another pause.

"We were at Duke together," she says. "I haven't seen him since graduation, but I know he went to UTA for his doctorate. I'm going to be at the business school this fall and I thought I'd see if he were still around."

I'm impressed with Angela's skill in making up this tall tale as she goes along. I just hope it works.

"Oh my God," she says suddenly. "When did it happen?"

Angela looks at me and Dan, her expression serious. I wish I'd thought of listening in on the extension.

"I'm so sorry to hear that," she says to the man on the phone. "That's so sad."

A long pause.

"You did? What a great idea. What's the address?"

Angela stands up abruptly and reaches across the desk for a pencil and pad. She writes down a Web address, then reads it back to her new friend to make sure she got it right.

"Thanks so much. At least now I know."

She hangs up the phone and sits down, a sad expression on her face.

"What happened?" I ask her.

"You're not going to believe this," she says.

"What? What?" Dan asks impatiently.

"Joshua Phillips died about two years ago," Angela tells us. "He was killed in a hit-and-run accident."

"Damn," I say.

Another death. This is weird.

"How exactly was he killed?" Dan asks.

"I'm not sure," she says. "All I know is that he was riding his bike back to his apartment one night, and he got run over by a car. The police investigated, but they never found out who did it."

"This is bad news," I say. "And just a little too coincidental."

"It is, isn't it?" Angela says.

"What's the Web address for?" Dan asks.

"His friends set up a Web site about him," she explains. "Right after the accident, they posted a request for anyone who saw anything to come forward. No one reported anything, but people started to send in their thoughts about Joshua. They've kept the Web site as a memorial to him."

"Let's see what's there," Dan says.

He takes the notepad and turns back to his computer.

"I guess now we know why we've never seen Joshua's name in any of the Hays Software materials," Angela says to me.

I shake my head sorrowfully.

"This was the big scoop Leticia had for me. Hays didn't invent Cheetah; he stole it."

"Yeah," Angela agrees. "With Joshua dead, Hays could just take his ideas and claim them as his own."

Dan looks up from his computer suddenly, like something just occurred to him.

"What I'd like to know is, would Hays kill to get those ideas?" he asks us.

"Yes," I reply with certainty.

Angela nods, but says nothing. I lean back in my chair and cross my arms, thinking about what we've just learned.

"At least now I have a motive for Leticia's death," I say. "She found out that Hays stole Cheetah from Phillips, so he killed her in order to keep his secret from getting out."

"Two murders, and you can't pin either one on him," Dan says. "This guy is slippery."

"He is," I agree. "But I'm not going to let him get away with it. Let me take a look at that Web site."

Joshua Phillips' friends have done a thorough job detailing what happened. What we learn is interesting, and tragic.

A little over two years ago, on a warm April night, Joshua Robert Phillips was biking home from his office on the UTA campus. It was just after 3:00 AM. A few dedicated late night hackers in a nearby building heard the sound of a loud thud, followed by one short cry. Some of them rushed to their windows, but although they could hear a car speeding away, no one saw it.

What they did see, however, was a young man lying very still by the side of the road. His bicycle was about five yards from him; its frame badly twisted. They rushed outside, but it was soon obvious that Joshua Phillips was beyond help.

The local police worked on the case for several weeks. But with only a few paint chips from the car for evidence, they didn't get very far. They checked repair shops to see if anyone had gone in to get a bumper fixed, but they had no luck. Eventually, they gave up.

Joshua had relatives in Austin, an aunt and an uncle. Their house became the headquarters for all the family members who flew in to continue the search for Joshua's killer. They posted a reward for anyone who could describe the car that hit Joshua, or better yet, identify the driver. But no one came forward. After a few months, even Joshua's parents and siblings had to admit defeat, and one by one they flew home.

Now all that remains of the accident and its aftermath is a Web site on the Internet.

"That's not the way I want to go when my time comes," Angela says. "What a shock."

"I'd rather die surfing," Dan says. "Go out like Mark Foo did at Maverick's. How do you want to die, Steven?"

"I'd prefer not to think about that right now. When exactly was Phillips killed?"

"On April 8th," Dan says.

"Hays was still teaching at UTA then," I say. "It was his last semester. He came out to California almost immediately afterwards."

"So, what now?" Angela asks me. "We have a lot of clues pointing to Hays as the killer of not one, but two, people. But we can't *prove* he murdered anyone."

"I know."

I rub my forehead. I'm getting a headache, and my eyes are burning from staring at a computer screen for so long. I don't know how Dan does it.

"We're running out of options," Angela continues. "I think it may be time to visit Kamimoto and see what he can do."

I jerk my head up, ready to protest. But then I think better of it.

"We could use his help," I admit.

"Just don't mention my role in any of this, okay?" Dan asks us.

"Don't worry," I reply. "We're not about to tell the inspector that we've read his e-mail."

I stand up for what seems like the first time in hours. My muscles are sore. I stretch and walk to the bathroom.

On the way back, I overhear Angela and Dan talking in his office.

"This day has been too long," Angela is saying.

"You look like you could use a break," I hear Dan reply. "Why don't you join me for dinner tonight?"

"Works for me," Angela says. She turns to look at me as I enter the office. "Dan's invited us to dinner. Can you make it?"

I don't believe her. How can she not know that Dan's invitation was meant for her alone? Is she that naive?

"Thanks," I say awkwardly to Dan, "but I need to get home."

"Um, some other time then," Dan replies, looking uncomfortable.

We gather our things, thank Dan for his help, and leave the apartment. It's almost six o'clock in the evening.

The drive home is remarkably smooth and quiet. All the traffic is coming the other way, so we cruise easily through all the turns of the freeway. I gaze at the mountain trees along the highway, lost in thought.

"I think there's some candy in the glove box," Angela says after a while. "Could you check for me?"

I open the compartment and rummage around until I find a chocolate bar.

"Here you go," I say, handing it to her.

Angela rips it open and takes a big bite.

"Thanks," she says. "I'm starving."

"You could be having dinner with Dan right now." I'd meant to tease her with the comment, but somehow a note of sarcasm has crept into my voice.

Angela gives me a confused look.

"You said you needed to get home," she reminds me.

"As if Dan even wanted me there." I shift in my seat and look directly at her. For some unknown reason, I feel surprisingly irritated with her. "Angela, don't tell me you don't know how Dan feels about you. Why do you think he's helping us?"

Angela shrugs her shoulders.

"Because he owes me. Or rather, my brother. That's why."

"You go ahead and think that," I say, unconvinced.

Angela drums her fingers on the steering wheel.

"Look," she says after a moment. "Dan was Rafa's best friend, and that's what he'll always be to me. There's no room for anything else."

"I see."

Poor Dan, I think to myself. Then again, he'll get over it.

# Chapter Twenty

"I want to go with you when you see Kamimoto," Angela says to me as we pull into the driveway of my house.

"Of course." I get out of the car and close the passenger door. "You look tired," I say to Angela. "Are you okay to drive home?"

"Don't worry. I've made it home in worse condition," she answers. "Say hi to Michelle and Chloe for me."

I wave to Angela as she backs out of the driveway, then I turn and trudge up the sidewalk, exhausted from the day's events.

As I enter the house I can hear Michelle and Chloe in the kitchen.

"Okay, let's rinse the sand off of these first," Michelle is saying.

I walk into the kitchen and find them washing seashells.

"How did it go?" I ask, managing to smile.

"Fantastic!" Michelle exclaims. "Point Reyes was beautiful."

She looks happy, especially considering that she got fired yesterday. I'm not surprised, though. Michelle has always been able to bounce back quickly from any setback.

"Great Daddy!" Chloe adds. "Look at all the shells I got! I'm taking them to school tomorrow to show everyone."

"Those are very pretty," I say, looking at the shells. "I'm sure your friends will like them."

I walk to Michelle and give her a kiss on the cheek.

"So what's for dinner?" I ask, trying to sound lighthearted. "Oysters? Mussels?"

"As a matter of fact, we did bring home some scallops."

"But we didn't catch them ourselves," Chloe informs me, very serious.

"No, we didn't. They're from the grocery store," Michelle explains. "And Chloe is going to help me prepare them."

"Wonderful," I say, rubbing a sore muscle in my neck. "I think I'll swim a few laps before we eat."

"Okay hon," Michelle says to me. "Then later tonight I want to hear all about your day."

"It was interesting," is all I say.

If there were ever a time I needed a long swim, this is it. Swimming always relaxes me, and it gives me the solitude I need to figure things out.

I don't feel like driving to the local Y, which is where I usually go for serious lap swimming, so instead I improvise in our backyard pool. I swim at a steady pace, trying to clear my head and process all the information we gathered today. It takes a while—now I've got two murders to sort through.

Chloe is already setting the table when I come in from the pool. I dash upstairs to take a five minute shower, and am changing into blue jeans when Michelle calls up to let me know that dinner is ready.

After all the junk food I've had today at Dan's house, it's sheer heaven to sit down to a big plate of scallops on pasta. There's even a bottle of Chardonnay on the table. Michelle is definitely in a good mood.

Chloe and Michelle are both beaming as they fill me in on all the day's events at Point Reyes. They saw pelicans and sea lions, and even caught a glimpse of what they thought might be a whale.

"Sounds like you guys did a lot," I say to Michelle as I help myself to seconds. "When did you get home?"

"A little after four. That reminds me—guess who I heard from today?"

"Who?"

"Helen Farrell. She called to see how I was, and to say again how shocked she was that I got downsized."

"That was nice of her."

"Wasn't it?" Michelle says. "She also shared an interesting little piece of gossip about Arthur Hays."

"And what was that?" I ask, looking up from my plate.

Michelle rests her elbows on the table, and prepares to share her news.

"Well, Monday afternoon he called demanding to talk with Marcus," she begins. "He sounded so angry and upset that Helen walked into Marcus' office so she could warn him."

"And?"

"And then she stuck around the office, supposedly to file some papers, but really so she could listen in—Marcus takes all his calls on speaker phone."

"What did she find out?"

"She was only in there for a couple of minutes, but she heard Hays accuse the firm of leaking proprietary information about Hays Software. He said it was an 'outrageous situation' and was demanding satisfaction from Marcus. Can you imagine?"

Michelle gets up to take a couple of dishes to the sink. I think about what she's just told me. That Arthur Hays would throw a temper tantrum doesn't surprise me at all. But his accusations are uncomfortably familiar.

Michelle continues to relate the story from the kitchen.

"Think about it, no one at Grimshaw Turner would ever divulge information about a portfolio company. And even if someone wanted to, nobody but Turner and maybe a couple of other senior partners know anything about Hays Software."

She walks back in to the dining room, wiping her hands on a dish towel.

"I have to admit, when I first heard what Helen said, I panicked and thought for a minute that they'd discovered our little search of Marcus' files," Michelle says. "Then I remembered that we were there last night, and Hays had his tantrum the day before. So I think we're safe."

Michelle pats me on the shoulder as she says this and goes back into the kitchen.

"Hey," she calls out to me, "it's your night for dishes. I'm happy to help, but I don't want to do it all by myself."

"Be there in a minute."

I'm not looking forward to telling Michelle my suspicion about Hays' outburst.

"Chloe, why don't you go get ready for bed now," I say. "It's getting late."

"I don't feel sleepy," Chloe says simply.

"It doesn't matter; it's time for bed."

"But I don't want to," she says in a whiny, tired voice.

"It's late, you have school tomorrow, and you need to go to bed," I say, losing patience. "Now go get yourself ready."

"I never get to do what I want," she says loudly. "You're mean!"

Chloe pushes herself roughly away from the table. She runs up the stairs, and a moment later I hear the door to her room slam shut.

I walk in to the kitchen and put my dishes on the counter.

"What was that all about?" Michelle asks me.

"Chloe doesn't want to go to bed. Listen, there's something I need to talk to you about."

"What is it?" Michelle asks me, looking up from the dirty pots and pans in the sink.

"I think I know where Hays might have gotten that idea."

"Where?" she asks me, still scrubbing away.

I tell Michelle about my phone call to Hays a couple of days ago.

"You asked him about confidential business partnerships?" she says accusingly.

I nod, but say nothing. Michelle has stopped washing dishes. She's looking at me with her hands on her hips.

"Tell me, does Hays know that you and I are married?"

I balk at answering: I know where this conversation is headed.

"Remember how I talked with Turner and Hays at Grimshaw's birthday party?" I say finally.

"Of course."

"During our conversation, Turner mentioned to Hays that my wife worked at Grimshaw Turner."

Michelle's face turns to stone.

"I guess that now at least I know what happened," she says icily.

"I'm sorry, hon. I never thought Hays would lose it like that."

"Sorry doesn't help me now! Why didn't you think about what you were doing before you called him up? You cost me my job!"

Michelle throws down the dish towel and marches from the room.

I'm left alone in the kitchen. I stare out the window and conclude that without doubt this is one of the worst days of my life.

I swim when I feel awful. Michelle jogs. About five minutes after she storms out, Michelle reappears in the kitchen and announces she's going running. She leaves without waiting for me to reply.

With Michelle gone, all the night-time tasks fall to me. I finish the dishes and go upstairs to check on Chloe. She's fast asleep on her bed, fully dressed and clutching her bag of seashells. I gently remove the bag, and place it on the dresser. Then I put a blanket over her, turn off the light, and quietly close the door.

I go downstairs and turn on the TV. I'm still channel-surfing when Michelle comes home about ten minutes later.

"Hi," she says.

I can tell by her tone that the worst is over.

"Hi," I say back. "How was your run?"

"Not bad. I went around the park a couple of times and then up through Hines Street. I figure I did about three miles."

"Sounds like a good run."

I click off the TV and we look at each other.

"I would never have called Hays if I'd known it would cost you your job," I tell her.

"I know." She sits down in a chair. "It's not really you I'm mad at anyway."

"Then who?"

"The good people at Grimshaw Turner," she says with sarcasm. "Nobody even asked me for my side of the story. I never got a chance to defend myself. That is so unfair."

"You're right." I hadn't even thought of this aspect of her dismissal. "I can't believe they'd take Hays' word over yours."

"Oh, I don't think Marcus believes Hays. I think he figures that Hays is the CEO of a company Grimshaw Turner has invested a lot of money in, and he wants to keep him happy, at least for now. And if Grimshaw Turner has to sacrifice a junior associate in order to placate the great Arthur Hays, so what? They probably figure they can replace me soon."

"You really think that's the way it happened?"

"Yep, I do." She stands up. "Oh well, such is life. I'm going to take a shower."

She jogs up the stairs. I turn the TV back on and find a baseball game in progress. I watch a couple of innings, but nobody's scoring, so I turn off the TV and go upstairs. Michelle is just getting out of the shower when I walk into our room.

"Hey," she says as soon as she sees me. "I forgot to ask you about your day. Did you get the package? What was in it?"

"You're not going to believe what I found out."

I give her a rundown of the day, starting with Leticia's envelope from the bus station, and concluding with our discovery of Joshua Phillips' suspicious death. I skip the part about the car that followed us, and our mad dash through downtown San Jose.

Michelle is intensely curious. She peppers me with questions, asking for details. How did we track down Phillips? Are we sure he was the originator of the Cheetah program? What are we going to do next?

It's almost eleven when Michelle finally winds down her questioning.

"So you're going to talk to Kamimoto tomorrow morning?" she asks.

"That's the plan," I say. "I'll get to work bright and early, then around eight I'll swing by Mitch's office and call Kamimoto to set up an appointment."

"Why go to Mitch's office?" she asks. "Is something wrong with your phone?"

I forgot I haven't told Michelle about the bug. I give her the story, and do my best to downplay the significance of someone eavesdropping on my calls. But Michelle becomes concerned nonetheless. Her eyes grow wide, and by the time I finish, she's pacing nervously back and forth.

"I'm glad you're going to get the police involved," she says. "I'm really getting worried." She walks over to me and hugs me tightly. "Maybe it's time you gave this thing up."

I look at her without replying. Then I raise her face to mine and give her a long, reassuring kiss.

# Chapter Twenty-one

When I walk into the *Digital Business* lobby this morning, I see Catherine standing next to her receptionist's console, dressed even more provocatively than usual. I feel like I've walked into a Hollywood studio. The first thing that confronts me is Catherine's severe cleavage bursting from the top of her blouse. She's wearing a thigh-high skirt, and a pair of very high heels. She's also covered with jewelry, including a glittery diamond anklet. The strong scent of perfume drifts my way.

Catherine smiles broadly when she sees me.

"Steven, how are you today?" she says with her usual lilt.

She blinks at me like a fawn stepping out of a dark forest into a sunny clearing. Maybe it's my imagination, but I could swear she's flirting with me.

"Just fine," I answer.

"Somebody called you already this morning," she informs me. "He didn't want to leave a voicemail, so I took the message. Let me see if I can find it."

Instead of going all the way around the desk, she moves to the side, then inclines toward me as she forages for the note. This has the effect of revealing even more of her abundant bosom.

After much searching, she finds the post-it note with the information.

"Here it is," she says, holding it up for me to see.

I expect her to hand me the little piece of paper, but instead she walks back and stands right next to me. At close range, the perfume is nearly overwhelming.

"From Inspector Komodo," she whispers to me. "He wanted you to call him the moment you got in."

"Thanks," I say, taking the note from her.

"Anytime," she replies in a sultry tone as I move away.

As I walk down the hallway, I look over my shoulder and can see that Catherine is still standing where I left her, her bottom lip curled into a disappointed pout.

I slip into Mitch's office and close the door quietly so as not to attract attention. Then I walk quickly to Mitch's desk and call the number. A receptionist picks up on the third ring and puts me through to the inspector.

"I'm glad you called," he says. "I wanted to see if by chance you or Angela had remembered anything else that might be relevant to Leticia Morgan's death. I know sometimes people don't remember things until a few days or even weeks after they happen."

Kamimoto sounds convincing, but I have a feeling this is just a surreptitious way to ask if we've been holding out on him.

"Actually, we do have something to show you," I say.

"You do?" he replies. "Can you get to my office this morning? Say in about an hour?"

"We'll be there."

As soon as Kamimoto is off the line, I dial Angela's extension and tell her about the appointment with the inspector. As I expected, she's raring to go.

"Just give me a few minutes to reschedule a meeting," she says.

"I'll be in Mitch's office when you're ready," I tell her.

"You know," she continues in an impish voice, "we'd better get Hays soon. I've skipped so many meetings lately, people are starting to wonder if I really work here."

After I finish my call to Angela, I pull out a notepad and pen, and pick up the receiver again. Since I've discovered the bug in my office phone, I've developed the habit of listening to my voicemail messages from different extensions, just in case.

The first message is from Franklin Albright at Van Ness Securities. He's terribly sorry to inform me that a business emergency is causing him to cancel our lunch meeting tomorrow. I'm about to congratulate myself on escaping his boorish company when I hear Franklin volunteering to meet with me at my office tomorrow morning. I decide to forget to call him back.

The next message is from Michelle, and I groan out loud when I hear what she has to say: "Hi, honey. Guess where I am right now—Napa! I called Joan this morning just to say hi, and she told me about this little winery that just went on the market, so I came up to see it."

Not this again. Every time Michelle gets to some big crossroads in life, she fantasizes about buying a winery and settling into the rustic life of a vintner. We went through this when she was trying to decide whether or not to get pregnant, and then again when she was waiting to hear if she'd been accepted to business school.

"Oh sweetheart, you should see this place—Chateau Noblesse—it's just perfect," Michelle gushes. "I was wondering; I know you're busy, but is there any way you could come up here this afternoon to see it? I know you'll love it. I've already called my mom to pick up Chloe, so we can spend the night here if we want. And it would mean so much to me," Michelle adds in a tone of voice that says "Here's your chance to make it up to me for having cost me my job."

I think of all the arguments I could give Michelle to explain why it makes no sense for me to drive up to Napa in the middle of the week to look at a winery we'll never buy. Then I write down the number Michelle left so I can let her know I'll be there by four.

I finish listening to my messages and then return the most pressing calls, including the one to Michelle, who is ecstatic to hear I'll be able to meet her this afternoon. All of this takes longer than I expected, but eventually Angela and I get out of the office for our "breakfast meeting."

"So, I saw Catherine standing awfully close to you this morning. What was that about?" Angela asks me. We're in my car, driving east through the city.

"Nothing really. I think she figures an affair with me will help her move up in the company."

"No, that's not it," Angela says with authority. "My guess is that with all the cops hanging around your office lately, she must think you lead some kind of double life. You know, journalist by day, secret agent by night."

Angela leans in close and whispers with mock allure, "It makes you dangerous and sexy."

We both laugh.

San Francisco's police department has its headquarters on Bryant Street, in the monolithic gray building that houses the Hall of Justice. Bryant is a pretty busy thoroughfare, so I end up having to park three blocks away.

We get out of the car and I remove Leticia's packet of documents from my briefcase. We walk to the fortress-like building, then follow a stream of people up the stairs and through the double doors. Once inside, we join the line to go through the metal detector. Soon we're past the security checkpoint and making our way to the elevators.

"There are a lot more people here in suits than I expected," Angela says.

"Probably lawyers going to court."

"Of course, I forgot there are courtrooms here."

We reach the elevators just in time to catch one going up. We get off at our floor, walk down the hall and into the homicide detail's office, where the first thing we see is a dark-haired woman sitting behind a large desk.

"We're here to see Inspector Kamimoto," I tell her. "He's expecting us."

"I'll give him a ring," the woman says solicitously.

Within a couple of minutes Kamimoto steps into the front office.

"Mr. Cavanaugh, Ms. Madrigal. Come with me."

We follow him through the front office into a bullpen full of old-fashioned wooden desks grouped together in pairs. Kamimoto stops at one of these desks to pick up a binder and some folders.

I take the opportunity to look around. Kamimoto does not work in luxurious surroundings. The floor is linoleum, and the walls are lined with gray metal cabinets and bookshelves. There are black binders everywhere—on all of the shelves, on the desks, and even stacked up on the floor. The decor is limited to a clock and a few wall calendars.

"What are all those binders for?" Angela asks Kamimoto, pointing to a stack near his desk.

"Each one represents a murder investigation."

I survey the room again. There must be over a hundred binders just in plain view.

"Let's talk in here," Kamimoto says, indicating a room to the right.

We walk into the tiny room. It's sparsely furnished: just a plain table with five metal chairs around it. Kamimoto closes the door behind us and we all sit down at the table. He looks at the envelope I'm holding.

"What have you found out?" he asks.

"I think I know who killed Leticia," I tell him.

"Who?"

"Arthur Hays."

"Her boss?" Kamimoto asks. He shakes his head. "It's true his statements aren't entirely consistent. But what's missing is motive. Why would he want her dead?"

"To keep her from telling anyone about these papers," I say, sliding the envelope across the table to him.

Kamimoto opens the package and takes out the contents.

"Where did you get these?" he asks.

I explain about the note from Leticia and the bus station locker. Kamimoto listens to me without comment. When I finish, he spreads the papers in front of him, and spends a few minutes studying them.

"I don't see much here," he says finally. "It's just a bunch of technical mumbo-jumbo."

"But they do make it clear that Hays didn't create Cheetah," Angela says. "Phillips did."

"How can you tell this Phillips guy is the inventor?" Kamimoto asks her.

"We had a programmer I know take a look at the documents," she says discreetly. "He said they make it obvious that J. Phillips is the creator of a search agent for the Internet. It has to be Cheetah."

The inspector shrugs his shoulders, as if to say "who cares?" Kamimoto's beat is homicide, not the arcane area of intellectual property law, so I decide to spell out the implications for him.

"When Hays took Phillips' idea for Cheetah, he robbed him of potentially billions of dollars," I explain.

Kamimoto looks at me, then puts up his hands in a gesture of protest.

"I see where you're going with this," he says. "You think Hays stole Cheetah from Phillips. . . ."

"And then killed Leticia when she found out about it," I say, interrupting him.

"Yes, yes," he says impatiently. "I agree that could be a motive for murder. But there's a big hole in your theory. Namely, if I were Hays, I'd be a lot more concerned about the person I stole from in the first place. I'd be worried about J. Phillips."

"Not if he were dead," I counter.

Kamimoto raises his eyebrows.

"Phillips is dead?"

"When we found out about Joshua Phillips, we tried to track him down," I tell the inspector. "It turns out he was a graduate student at the University of Texas when Hays taught there, and he died in a hit-and-run accident right before Hays came to California and started his company."

Kamimoto is quick on the uptake.

"So now you suspect Arthur Hays of two murders."

"Yes, I do."

The inspector leans back in his chair and considers the evidence.

"I think you guys are starting to see murder everywhere," he says after awhile. "As far as I'm concerned, there's only one homicide here. Hays may very well have had something to do with it, but everything else you've told me is pure speculation."

"We're not just speculating," Angela says defensively.

"There's more," I say. "This past Monday night, somebody tried to get me to stop looking into Leticia's death."

"Who?" Kamimoto immediately asks, bringing his chair closer to the table.

"I wish I knew."

I go on to give the details of the beating. Kamimoto questions me intensively. He seems particularly interested in the men who roughed me up. I do my best to describe them.

"Do you think you could recognize any of them from a photo?" he asks me.

I try to remember their faces.

"I doubt it. It was pretty dark."

Kamimoto looks disappointed.

"We should tell him about what happened yesterday," Angela says.

"Yes, by all means," Kamimoto says, a touch sarcastically, "tell me what happened."

Angela describes our chase through downtown San Jose. She goes into detail, but skips over our wrong way trip up 4th Street, and the red light we ran.

"You've been busy these past few days," Kamimoto says dryly. "But it seems you're right. You must be closer to the truth than I gave you credit for."

"So you'll look into these papers?" I ask him.

"Right away," he promises. "And I'll call Austin and see what they say about Mr. Phillips. But I've got to tell you: most hit-and-runs are just accidents where the driver panics. They're rarely used for premeditated killing, simply because it's too easy to be seen. I bet the accident was just a lucky break for Hays."

"But you do think he killed Leticia, right?" Angela asks.

"I think that *if* Hays is trying to build a company with a stolen product, and *if* Leticia found out about it, then Hays had a motive for killing her. And what's happened this past week shows that someone is pretty worried about being caught. But we're still a long way from proving that Hays is responsible," he says. "Now, was there anything else?"

"No," I tell him.

"I appreciate your coming forward with the new information," he says, standing to leave.

"Can you contact us when you've found out more?" Angela asks the inspector.

"Sure," he replies dismissively.

Angela makes a move to leave, but I remain planted in my seat, staring at Kamimoto. It takes him a moment to realize that I'm not going anywhere.

"I promise to call you as soon as I find out anything," he tells me pointedly. "Okay?"

"Okay," I agree, finally rising from my chair.

Kamimoto escorts us to the front office. He thanks us again, then goes back to his desk.

Angela and I walk to the elevators.

"What do you think?" she asks me. "Will Kamimoto be able to help us?"

"I'm not sure. He's very thorough. I just don't know if it will do us any good. He himself said the evidence is only circumstantial. If he wants to get Hays, he's going to have to take some chances, and he doesn't strike me as a risk-taker."

"So what are we going to do?" Angela asks. "We can't just let Hays go on about his business."

"I know. Let's see what Kamimoto digs up first, and then we'll take it from there."

Because of the lunch hour traffic, the drive back to the office takes awhile. I'm too busy dodging jaywalkers and double-parked trucks to talk much, but Angela has plenty to say, mostly about how she expects Hays to react when we finally prove him guilty of murder.

"I bet he'll laugh hysterically; you know, like a mad scientist," she says. "What do you think?"

I'm slowing for a changing light, so I take the opportunity to turn to her and say something, when suddenly I hear a horn squawk. Someone behind me in a green Acura is flipping me off. I guess he expected me to run the red light.

"Same to you, buddy," I say to the figure in my rearview mirror. I look over at Angela. "I'm glad I'm going to Napa today. I could use a break."

"Napa? Why are you going there?"

"I'm meeting Michelle there this afternoon. She wants me to look at some winery, Chateau something-or-other."

"To do wine tasting?"

"No, to consider buying the winery."

"Buying it? What on earth for?"

"It's Michelle's idea," I say, and then go on to explain how she does this every few years.

"But are you serious about this?" Angela asks me.

"No, I'm not. But Michelle really wants to do this today, and I owe it to her. Besides, I know exactly what will happen. I'll go up there, we'll look at the winery, we'll act like we might buy it for about two weeks, and then it will be forgotten."

We've entered the neighborhood of the *Digital Business* offices. I pull up in front of the building.

"I'm not going to bother going up to the office," I say to Angela. "I'll just drop you off here. See you tomorrow."

"Okay. Good luck."

Angela jumps out and hurries toward the main door.

After a quick glance around, I make a U-turn and head in the direction of the Golden Gate Bridge, my mind far more occupied with Arthur Hays than vintage wines.

# CHAPTER TWENTY-TWO

When I get off the elevator this morning, the first thing I do is look over to the receptionist console, curious to see what kind of outfit Catherine has on today.

It looks like she's not planning to repeat yesterday's performance. The blouse she's wearing is tight, but doesn't show any skin, and she's sporting far less jewelry than before. Even her makeup is more subtle. She looks almost respectable.

I give Catherine a nod and a friendly "Good morning" as I walk by. She responds with a welcoming smile and a sultry "hello."

I've just passed Catherine's desk and am walking towards the main hallway, when suddenly I feel a hand clap me hard on the back. I whirl around, ready to swing, and find myself looking at the startled face of Franklin Albright.

"I'm sorry, I didn't mean to surprise you," he says quickly. "I tried to get your attention when you first walked in, but you were somewhat distracted."

"That's okay," I say, regaining my composure. "Do we have a meeting this morning?"

"In a way," he replies. "Did you get my message yesterday?"

"Oh right," I say, remembering. "Listen Franklin, I've been meaning to call you. My schedule lately has gotten so frantic that . . ."

"I can imagine," Albright interrupts. "I know how busy you journalists are. That's why when I had to back out on lunch today, I figured the only polite thing to do was get here first thing this morning. That way you can still get my interview in on time. I don't want to throw off your editorial calendar."

Or miss out on some career-boosting publicity, I think to myself. Nevertheless, Albright has a point, and until Kamimoto calls, I have nothing better to do anyway.

"Let's talk in my office," I say.

"Great," Albright replies affably. "My flight doesn't leave for a couple of hours. That gives us plenty of time."

I show Albright to my office, offer him a chair, and then proceed to search for my tape recorder and notepad. While I'm rounding up my equipment, the investment banker launches into a brief description of his background. As I suspected, he has all the right credentials—Princeton undergrad, Stanford MBA, joined Van Ness Securities right out of business school and has risen like a rocket. But I don't think hard work or even a top education are the main reasons for his success. It's more basic than that—Franklin Albright has that rare mix of good looks, suave personality, and aggressive nature that are perfect for a business that is half salesmanship and half killer instinct.

Once I have everything ready, I begin the interview by asking Albright to give me a rundown of his bank's current activities. Naturally, he paints a glowing picture. But this isn't what I want to hear. There's been some controversy brewing at Van Ness, focusing on Albright in particular, and I want to know about it. As much as Mitch likes this guy, I have no intention of turning this interview into some kind of puff piece.

"There's no question that Van Ness has been profitable," I say after ten minutes of listening to Albright's practiced spiel. "But I've noticed that the after-market performance of some of the companies you've underwritten hasn't been very good. I'm thinking of Wishbone Multimedia in particular."

Albright briefly loses his boyish grin, and with good reason. Wishbone was one of the first deals he worked on when he joined Van Ness, and it's been in the news a lot lately. The CEO was recently indicted for falsifying sales records and lying to shareholders. In the past few months, the stock price has plummeted from $50 a share to around $2 a share.

"All of the banks have their Wishbones," Albright counters. "It happens. Besides, you know how it is: when the ducks are quacking, you've got to feed them. We don't force anyone to buy stock."

He regains his winning smile, pleased with his quick reply and ready to move on to something else. But I'm just getting started. Other shaky stock deals have come to light, most of them put together by Albright himself. It looks as if Wishbone may be part of a larger pattern.

"It's been said that Van Ness goes beyond the normal boundaries," I assert. "That you push deals out the door just so you can collect your fees and cash out on your stock. Any comment?"

I watch the color drain from Albright's face. This was supposed to be a sympathetic interview from his favorite business magazine, not a segment for *60 Minutes*.

"There are bound to be some turkeys among the companies that soar," he replies weakly.

Albright pauses, looking forlorn. Then suddenly his face relaxes, and he looks happy again.

"Speaking of companies that soar," he says, brightening even more, "I've got one that's going to be the hottest deal in more than a decade."

"What is it?"

"I can't tell you just yet, but you'll hear about it soon enough. We're getting ready to take the company public."

"What market is it targeting?" I ask.

"I can't even tell you that, but I promise that as soon as it's legal for me to talk, I'll let you know everything."

Albright looks at my cassette recorder.

"When this deal comes out," he continues, "Wishbone and all those others won't matter. It's going to turn the high-tech world upside down. It may even be the deal of the century."

Albright has a confident, self-satisfied look on his face. Even so, I know from experience that he might be bluffing, hoping to get me to ignore his past mistakes and shady deals, and focus instead on some phantom hot offering.

"If this deal is so great, how did a boutique bank like Van Ness manage to beat out bulge-bracket operations like Goldman Sachs and Morgan Stanley?" I ask.

Fortunately, Albright doesn't try to bullshit me with platitudes like "superior customer service" and "in-depth technical knowledge."

"My father is friends with the company founder," he says simply.

In his long career as a technology executive, Albright's father, John Albright, got to know many of the players in high tech. And his new profession as a VC has undoubtedly expanded his contacts. The senior Albright is extremely well-connected in the Valley, and it would make sense for him to hand his son a lucrative business opportunity like this one.

Franklin Albright could be telling the truth. There's only one way to find out.

"You know, this deal of yours does make for more compelling news than another Wishbone story," I say to him casually, "but without details, I'm forced to go with what I can verify."

Albright gives me an appraising look, then laughs smugly.

"I understand you," he replies, "or more precisely, I appreciate your tactics. In fact, I've used them myself when necessary."

I'm not sure how to respond. Somehow, I feel like I've been insulted.

"This will have to be off the record, for now," Albright adds in a confidential tone.

But before he can continue, there's an urgent knocking on the door. I look up just as Angela bursts into my office.

"We heard from Kamimoto," she says. "He wants us to get down to his office right away."

The deal of the century vanishes from my thoughts.

"Let's go," I say, standing up.

"What about the interview?" Albright asks, confused.

"We can finish it when you get back from your trip," I tell him. "By then you might be able to go on record about that deal."

I walk out the door with Angela, and leave Albright sitting in my office, a bewildered look on his face.

When we arrive at the homicide office, the receptionist recognizes us from our previous visit, and rings Kamimoto's desk without waiting for us to ask. A few minutes later, Inspector Morrison comes out and leads us to the same little room we were in yesterday.

Kamimoto is already there, waiting for us. He has the papers from Leticia spread out in front of him, covering the desk. He greets us cordially, asks us to take a seat, and then jumps right in.

"I had the computer guys review these documents," Kamimoto tells us. "They came to the same conclusion as your friend."

"Great," I say.

"We also did some checking on Mr. Joshua Robert Phillips," he continues. "You'll be happy to know that the police in Austin agree with you. They don't think his death was an accident. There were no skid marks at the accident site. Whoever hit Phillips never even tried to slow down."

"I knew it," Angela says triumphantly.

"So can we—I mean, you—arrest Hays?" I ask.

"No. It's a compelling coincidence, but it's not enough to justify an arrest. There are no witnesses in either case, and our evidence is shaky."

"What about searching his office for more evidence?" I ask.

"I might be able to get a warrant for that," Kamimoto says, "but Hays may have cleaned out his files after Leticia went through them, just to prevent anyone else from doing it again. In that case, we'd find nothing, and we'd tip him off that he's a suspect."

"This is so frustrating," Angela says. "We know he did it. And we're just going to sit here and let him get away with it?"

"That's not exactly what we had in mind," Morrison says reprovingly.

"There might be a way to get to him," Kamimoto adds.

"What would that be?" I ask him.

"If Hays is as rash as you make him out to be, then he might admit some of this to you, if he didn't think anyone else was listening."

It takes me a few seconds to realize what Kamimoto is asking.

"You want me to meet with Hays and tape the conversation," I reply. "Sure I'll do it."

"Don't be so quick to volunteer," Kamimoto responds. "There is some risk."

I think for a moment. No way am I backing down now.

"If you've got a phone handy, I'll call him right now and set it up," I reply.

Kamimoto looks at me thoughtfully.

"Good," he says. He walks out of the room and returns with a phone, which he places on the table. Morrison plugs the phone cord into a wall jack; then Kamimoto picks up the receiver and dials a four-digit number.

"Yes, I need this call to go on an outside line," he says. "Just a minute."

Kamimoto flips through a notepad, finds the number for Arthur Hays' office and reads it off to the police operator. A few seconds later he hands me the receiver.

"You're on," he says.

The phone seems to ring forever before someone picks up.

"Arthur Hays' office," the assistant says. Her voice comes through faintly on the phone's speaker, just loud enough for everyone in the room to make out what she's saying.

"This is Steven Cavanaugh calling from *Digital Business* I'd like to speak to Arthur."

"He may have left for lunch already," she says haltingly. "But I'll check. May I say what this is about?"

"I need to ask some more questions about Cheetah."

There's a long wait before his assistant gets back on the line.

"Mr. Hays can't talk with you now."

I'm not surprised. After our unpleasant exchange the last time we talked, I figured I was now on his list of people to ignore.

"Tell him that I have some information about Cheetah from UT Austin, and I'd like to ask him about it."

This time there's only a short delay.

"This is Arthur Hays."

I feel the adrenaline flowing, but I manage to calmly respond, "Hi Arthur, Steven Cavanaugh here."

No reply.

"I'd like your comment on something," I continue. "I understand that at least one graduate student was involved in developing Cheetah. Is that true?"

"What the . . . ?" Hays starts to respond, but then stops.

For several seconds, there's nothing but dead silence on the other end of the phone.

"Hello?" I say finally.

"Yes, I'm here," Hays answers reluctantly.

"Anyway, I want to talk with you about the origins of Cheetah; you know, to set the record straight," I tell him. "And the sooner the better, because I'm on deadline."

I can hear Hays breathing heavily on the other end, laboring to get oxygen.

"I'm really busy today," he says at last. "But I suppose I could meet with you tonight to discuss this."

"What time?"

"Can you be here at nine?" he asks.

"I'll see you then."

I hang up the phone, relieved. So far, so good.

"You handled that well," Kamimoto says to me. He turns to Morrison. "Talk to Jensen in surveillance. Tell him we need a team for tonight. And I want experienced people this time."

"I'll get Hopkins and Washington," Morrison says as he leaves the room.

"We'll be at your house by seven tonight," Kamimoto tells me. "That should give us enough time to set up the wire and test it."

I nod my understanding.

"Is there anything I can do?" Angela asks Kamimoto.

"Yes," he says. "Leave everything to us."

Angela crosses her arms petulantly, disappointed by his answer. But Kamimoto doesn't notice. He's hurriedly gathering up the papers on the table, impatient to get back to his desk so he can begin coordinating tonight's activities.

He finishes putting the files in order and stands up.

"Let me walk you out," he offers.

Kamimoto accompanies us to the reception area, and gives us a perfunctory, distracted goodbye before turning abruptly on his heel and marching back to his desk.

As I walk back to the car with Angela, I think about what I've just promised to do. I have no idea how I'll explain this to Michelle.

# CHAPTER TWENTY-THREE

"I'm really proud of you," Angela says to me. "I think it's great that you're going to confront Hays, face to face."

We're in my car, driving back to the office.

"Just be careful," she adds softly.

I look over at her, touched by her concern.

"Don't worry," I say. "I will."

I pull in front of the office building and park the car.

"You're coming in?" Angela asks.

"I want my jacket," I explain.

Both the lobby and the elevator are full of people, so Angela and I ride up to our floor without exchanging a word.

"You are one lucky girl," Catherine says to Angela as soon as the elevator doors open.

"What do you mean?" Angela asks.

"Go check your office," she replies coolly.

I walk with Angela past the lobby and into the bullpen. As we approach her cubicle, I notice a big bouquet of roses on her desk. It looks like Dan is stepping up the offense.

Angela goes up to the vase and sniffs a rose, a puzzled—but pleased—expression on her face. She searches for the card, and extracts it from the thorny stems. But when she opens the little envelope and begins to read, her countenance changes quickly to one of disgust.

"¡Qué pegajoso!" she exclaims. "That stupid horndog will not leave me alone."

"Are you talking about Dan?" I ask, surprised by the vehemence of her reaction.

"The flowers aren't from Dan," she replies. "They're from Matt."

"Matt?" I say. "I didn't know he was that romantic."

"Romance has nothing to do with it," Angela replies curtly. She waves the card at me. "He just invited me to go with him to Vegas this weekend."

"Oh."

Angela tosses the card on her desk in a gesture of annoyance.

"I can not figure out how to get rid of this guy. I've tried telling him 'no' in a gentle way, but he just won't get the hint."

"Subtlety doesn't work with Matt," I tell her.

"Then I'll just have to stop being so polite. In fact . . ."

"Hi Angela," Matt says brightly, popping into the cubicle as if on cue. Judging from the goofy grin on his face, he hasn't heard any of our discussion.

"I see you got my roses," he says to Angela, seating himself on her desk and crumpling her appointment book in the process. "What do you think?"

Angela picks up the flowers with both hands. Before Matt can utter the question forming on his lips, she shoves the vase of roses into his chest. Some of the water sloshes onto his silk shirt and designer tie. He stands up, gripping the vase. Little droplets of water are dripping from his tie onto the floor.

"What the hell is this?!" he exclaims loudly. "What is wrong with you?"

"You are," Angela says, completely exasperated. "Can't you take a hint? I don't want to sleep with you again!"

From my vantage point, I can see heads popping up from their cubicles all over the place. Both Matt and Angela have voices that carry. I'm sure everyone here knows what's being said.

"Then just say so," Matt replies loudly. "So I'll know to stop wasting my time with you." Matt draws himself up, and tries to recover some of his dignity. "There are plenty of other women who would appreciate the invitation."

"I'm sure there are," Angela says. Her initial anger has worn off, and now she's trying to strike a conciliatory tone. "I'm just not interested in being with anyone right now."

"Fine with me," Matt says haughtily. He turns his back on Angela and walks briskly out of the cubicle, still holding his roses.

"Must be that time of the month," I hear him mutter under his breath.

Angela and I watch him walk down the hall towards his office. One by one, our co-workers' heads disappear into their cubicles, but nobody's returned to work. I can hear low whispers all around us, punctuated by an occasional giggle.

"Well, isn't this just wonderful. Now everyone knows I slept with Matt," Angela says, sitting down wearily. "At least it's over."

"Are you okay?" I ask her.

"Yeah, I'll be fine. I'm just going to focus on my work."

"Good idea," I say, patting her on the shoulder.

I start to leave her office, but she grabs my arm.

"Wait," she says. "I just wanted to be sure to wish you good luck tonight."

She jumps up and gives me a kiss on the cheek.

"I'll be thinking of you," she adds.

I smile at her.

"Thanks."

When I walk into my office, Tina Davis is there, leaving me a note on my desk.

"Good, you're here," she says. "I'm glad. It's better to talk in person."

"Look Tina," I say, snatching my jacket off my chair and preparing to leave. "I'm sure whatever it is you have to tell me is very important, but believe me, I have something even bigger going on today. Let's talk about this Monday."

"I'm pulling the Hays story," she says bluntly. "I came here to get your files."

I stare at Tina in disbelief. I've never had a story taken from me. Never.

"I'm sorry to do this, Steven," she continues. "But you seem to have stopped working on anything anymore. And that piece you turned in on Yogi—an intern could have written it."

She walks a little closer to me.

"I don't know what's going on," she says. "But you are out of control. Now I need that Hays interview for the September cover, and you're not getting it done. So I'm going to turn it over to Matt."

Tina's gaze meets mine without wavering. I can tell by the tilt of her head, and the way she holds her hands, that she's expecting a fight. And my first impulse is to give her one.

But then it dawns on me. I've tracked Hays down. I don't need the story anymore. Now, it's just an article.

"Of course," I say.

I open a desk drawer, and pull out three files and a cassette tape. Then I walk over to Tina and hand them to her.

"This is everything I have on Hays Software," I tell her. "Angela has a couple of other files, and she can help Matt with any questions he might have. Although to be honest, I don't think he'll be wanting her help just now."

Tina takes the items from me slowly. She looks confused.

"Thanks," she says blankly.

She starts walking towards the door, but then stops and turns around to face me.

"What just happened here?" she demands. "You just gave up a feature—a cover story, of all things—without so much as a peep. This is not like you. Now I know something is seriously wrong."

"Nothing I can't handle," I tell her.

"I hope so," she says, a concerned look on her face. She takes a deep breath before continuing. "Look Steven, maybe it would be best for everyone if you took a break from your responsibilities here."

"A break?"

"I just think you should consider taking some time off before . . ." She falters, searching for words.

"Before I lose my job," I say, completing the sentence for her.

"Just think about it," she replies.

I watch her walk out of the room, and turn left down the hallway, towards Matt's office.

"Maybe I will," I say to no one.

# Chapter Twenty-four

When I get home, Michelle is in the kitchen sweeping up shards of glass.

"What happened?" I ask, stepping carefully past a few outlying fragments.

Michelle gives me a frustrated look and then goes back to her sweeping.

"Chloe was helping me empty the dishwasher and she tried to carry three glasses at once. Before I could stop her, they were all over the floor. Can you get me the dustpan?"

I go to the laundry room and pluck the dustpan from its hook on the wall. When I come back, Michelle is finishing up. She takes the dustpan from me.

"Where's Chloe?" I ask her.

"I got mad and sent her to her room. I don't know, maybe I could have handled it better. But I've told her a thousand times not to carry more than two glasses at a time, and she just doesn't listen. Here, could you put this stuff back?"

She hands me the broom and dustpan, and I take my time returning them to the laundry room. I'm in no hurry to tell Michelle what's on tonight's agenda.

"I have something important to discuss with you," I say when I walk back into the kitchen.

Michelle is slicing tomatoes. She looks up from the cutting board, a worried expression on her face.

"What is it?"

"I'm meeting Arthur Hays tonight."

"Whatever for?" she asks, gripping the knife tighter.

"To ask him about Joshua Phillips, for starters."

Michelle's face changes from concerned to angry.

"Are you nuts!? You can't tell him you know about that. Who knows what he might do!"

She slams down the knife.

"I have to face him," I tell her. "It's the only way I can get him to admit the truth."

She walks up to me, hands on her hips.

"And then what?" she asks. "You'll know what you already know right now, and you'll still have no way to prove it. Why risk your life just to hear him admit he's guilty?"

"No, that's not it. The whole reason I'm meeting Hays tonight is so that I can get the proof I need. I'm going to record the entire conversation."

Michelle looks at me, dumbfounded.

"Kamimoto and his team will be here soon to wire me with a mike," I continue.

"You have really done it this time," she says, obviously hurt. "Thanks for including me in your decision."

She walks out of the kitchen without another word.

I follow her to the living room where I find her sitting on the sofa, crying. I sit down and put my arms around her, which makes her sob even harder.

"I'm sorry," is all I can think of to say.

"You have no right to make me a widow," she says between sobs.

"I have no intention of making you a widow." I hold her face gently and make her look at me. "I'll be fine," I tell her. "This is Arthur Hays we're talking about, not a linebacker for the 49ers."

"You are so damn sure of yourself," she says angrily. "How do you know he doesn't have a gun?"

"I don't," I reply honestly, "But the police will be listening to every word tonight. If things start to sound dangerous, they'll come get me."

Michelle dries her tears on her shirtsleeve.

"You could always change your mind, you know. Kamimoto has no right to expect you to do this."

"It's too late. I've already told Hays I know about Phillips. Now I have to see this thing through."

"Oh, hon," she says, leaning against me. "This is like a nightmare."

"We'll get through it," I reassure her. And I mean it.

Kamimoto shows up a little before seven. He has Inspector Morrison with him, along with a woman I've never met.

"This is Inspector Hopkins from surveillance," Kamimoto says by way of introduction. "She'll be wiring your mike."

Hopkins shakes hands with me and Michelle, and then opens up a small suitcase and starts removing its contents.

"I think I'll go check on Chloe," Michelle says, excusing herself.

"Could you take off your shirt?" Hopkins asks me.

I comply. Hopkins works quickly. She starts by taping a small microphone to my chest. Then she threads the mike's wire around my ribcage and down my back. I feel a patch of something fuzzy against my lower back, just above my pants.

"What's that?"

"A piece of moleskin," she says. "It will keep the transmitter from burning your skin."

Hopkins tapes the transmitter on me, then steps back to look at her work. She makes a couple of adjustments.

"I think we're ready," she says to Kamimoto as she sits down and puts on a pair of earphones.

"Okay, let's test it," Kamimoto says, looking at me. "Say something."

"What do I say?"

"Did they get that?" he asks Hopkins.

"Loud and clear," she replies.

"Who's 'they'?" I ask.

"The guys in the van," Hopkins informs me. "You can get dressed now."

I put my shirt back on.

"There are a few things you need to know about this mike," Hopkins tells me as I'm buttoning up. "First of all, don't talk too much. If you and the suspect are both speaking at the same time, we're not going to hear much. Second, don't fold your arms across your chest or move around a lot; it can block the mike. Also, you'll need to keep away from metal structures like filing cabinets; they might disrupt the signal. And above all, act natural."

"Right," I say, trying not to sound facetious.

"That should do it," Kamimoto says once I'm finished dressing. "We'll follow you to Hays Software. You won't see us or the van anywhere, but we'll be close by, believe me."

I slip on a jacket and go upstairs to Chloe's room. She and Michelle are reading a story.

"I came to say goodbye," I announce when I walk in.

"Where are you going Daddy?"

Michelle's face is like stone. She won't look at me.

"I'm going to help the police with a special project."

"What is it?" my daughter asks me.

"That's enough, Chloe," Michelle says. "Daddy will tell you more about it tomorrow. You'd better let him go now or he'll be late."

"Okay. See you later, Daddy."

"See you later," I say. "I love you both."

Michelle still won't look at me. I back out of the room and move quickly to the front door. Outside, I see a nondescript van across the street with its engine running. I look at my watch. My meeting starts in less than an hour.

# Chapter Twenty-Five

The drive to Hays Software is shorter than I remembered. Before I know it, I'm exiting the freeway and getting on to the expressway that leads to the startup. I check the rearview mirror several times, but I don't see any sign of Kamimoto's van.

The technology park is so dimly lit, I almost miss it. The unoccupied buildings have no lights out front, which makes the whole complex look even more abandoned at night. I pull into the parking lot and park right in front of Hays Software. There are about a dozen cars scattered throughout the lot. Most are older models and probably belong to Hays programmers, who despite the late hour are still slaving away at their computers. There's still no sign of the SFPD van anywhere; I can only assume Kamimoto and his colleagues are at their post. I do see a red Ferrari parked near the front door; no doubt it belongs to Arthur Hays.

I try opening one of the tall glass doors, but it's locked. I peer through the glass and can see a security guard sitting at the reception desk. He's got his feet propped up on the console and is watching TV. I knock on the door, but the guard doesn't hear me; he's too busy laughing at something on the tube. So I try again, banging loudly on the door with my fist this time. The guard looks up, squints at me, and then swings his feet on to the floor behind the desk. I motion to him to come over. He gets up, walks languidly in my direction, and then stands close to the door without opening it.

"Yeah?" he says, eyeing me warily through the glass.

The man in charge of protecting Hays Software tonight is tall, thin and young. His blond hair has been cut very short, except for one small discreet braid in the back. He looks like he's barely out of high school.

"I'm here to see Arthur Hays."

The guard raises his index finger, indicating I should wait. He turns and walks back to the desk, where he picks up the phone receiver. He's back in just a few seconds to unlock the door and let me in.

"Mr. Hays is expecting you. I'll have to escort you."

He locks the front door again and checks it twice.

"This way," he says.

We cross the lobby and pass through the same door I went in the day we interviewed Hays. As we walk through the programmers' bullpen, I feel a strange sense of déjà vu. Many of the same programmers are in their cubicles, banging out code and drinking sodas. It's like they're frozen in time, oblivious to whether it's day or night out. No one even notices me when I walk by.

I half expect us to head into the conference room where I interviewed Hays. But instead we climb a flight of stairs to the second floor. We make a left and walk down a long corridor towards an office at the very end. There we stop at the door, and the guard knocks.

"Yes?"

I recognize Hays' voice.

"Your appointment to see you sir," the guard answers.

"Yes, thanks," Hays says from inside the office. "I'll be out in a moment, you can leave him here. It's okay."

"Yes sir."

The guard hurries off, probably hoping to catch the beginning of the next sitcom.

The door opens sharply. Hays is standing in front of me, looking pale and rumpled. He's probably putting in a lot of overtime these days, getting Cheetah ready for release and preparing for the road show. An initial stock offering is sure to bring in a lot of cash, especially if Cheetah is the hit I think it will be. Hays must feel that he's on the verge of becoming the rich and famous techno-wizard he's always wanted to be.

And now here I am trying to spoil the fun.

"Come in," he says, not really looking at me.

I walk in and look around. Hays' office is huge, and just as plush as the conference room downstairs. But aside from the wood paneling and expensive carpet, the office is sparsely decorated. There's a bookshelf against every wall, and a couple of file cabinets. In the middle of the office is a large mahogany desk, cluttered with piles of paper, a computer, and various desk accessories.

"Mind if I sit down?" I ask, spying a chair near his desk.

"Go ahead," he says, closing the door.

I pull the chair closer to his desk and sit down. Hays moves nearer, but remains standing behind me. I feel myself tense up, but resist the urge to jump up and face him. Finally, Hays moves toward his desk. But he doesn't take a seat; instead he stands right behind his chair, and looks down upon me imperiously.

"When you called earlier, you said something about the University of Texas," he says with disdain.

"Yes."

I want him to do most of the talking. Hays, however, isn't cooperating. He stands silently before me, glaring at me over his glasses. About thirty seconds pass this way before I decide to move things along.

"I understand that you were at UTA for a couple of years before you came out here and founded Hays Software," I continue.

"Just about every journalist in Silicon Valley knows that," Hays says sarcastically. Then he seems to catch himself. His face softens and he says in a voice that's almost friendly, "I was an adjunct professor of computer science. It was a very fruitful experience; I was able to do some important research there. I'd be happy to tell you more about it."

Hays pulls out his chair and sits down. He's switched tactics. He must be hoping that all I want is more benign background information.

"Tell me about Joshua Phillips," I say.

Hays gives a slight start, but regains his composure quickly. He's quiet for a moment, no doubt thinking about how to respond.

"Joshua Phillips," he says slowly. "Yes, of course, I remember him. He was in the computer science program. Smart boy, good researcher."

"Did you ever work with him?" I ask.

"Oh my, no," Hays replies. "He did come to me from time to time to ask my opinion, naturally. As an industry veteran I was able to give him a business perspective on certain issues. That's part of what adjunct faculty are supposed to offer—real-world advice. We are not, however, advisers or collaborators in the usual sense."

"Is that so?" I respond. "And yet the two of you discussed Cheetah extensively."

"That's impossible," Hays responds forcefully. "We never worked together."

"In other words," I say, "Phillips created Cheetah all by himself."

"That's a damn lie!" Hays shouts. He slams an open palm on the desk, sending a couple of post-it notes fluttering to the floor. He clenches his fist, and I sit up straight in my chair, ready to take action. But then Hays relaxes his hand. For now at least, he's content to scowl at me.

"It's no lie," I continue calmly. "And I have the papers to prove it."

For the first time, Hays looks panicked. He opens and closes his right hand repeatedly, in an unaware, nervous gesture.

"How did you get these documents you think are so incriminating?" he says finally, trying to regain his composure.

"Leticia gave them to me."

"I was afraid of that," he mutters to himself. Then he looks at me and smiles. His face looks almost friendly, but his eyes dart from side to side, like a trapped animal's.

"Now that I think of it, I did get some input from Phillips regarding Cheetah, when I was refining my ideas. What of it? That hardly means he invented it."

Hays is calmer now, but he's still edgy. He picks up a rubber band and starts playing with it nervously, stretching it out into an odd sort of cat's cradle, then letting it snap back. It occurs to me that I have no idea what's in the desk drawers; I watch his hands closely.

"I also have copies of programming code and handwritten notes," I say to him. "They make it clear that Phillips was the genius behind Cheetah, not you."

Those were the magic words. Hays pounds the desk angrily with his fist. Then he jumps up from his seat, leans over, and glares down at me.

"How dare you!" he shouts at me. "How dare you insult me this way!"

His eyes are wild now, and he's shouting so hard that his voice is raspy. If I'm ever going to find out the truth behind this mess, now is the time. I stand up, and stare back at him. Our faces are only inches apart. Every nerve in my body is on alert.

"I also know that Joshua Phillips was run down on campus right before you left the university and came here to found this company," I say, keeping my voice level.

Hays stares at me. His mouth is contorting, like he's trying to say something, but has lost control of his vocal cords. I'd love to be able to keep an eye on his hands, just to make sure he doesn't reach for a weapon, but for some reason, I can't break eye contact.

"Augh!" Hays shouts. It's a loud, low guttural sound, like the noise of an animal. At the same time, he pushes hard against me. The abrupt move catches me off guard; I fall back over the chair and land on the floor. The wind is completely knocked out of me, and it takes me a few seconds to fill my lungs with air again. For a brief moment I'm completely helpless. Fortunately, Hays doesn't seem to notice me right now. He's too angry to see anyone.

"That little twit!" he grunts. "Without my pioneering work at PCI, that punk would never have been able to come up with an application like Cheetah."

Hays is walking back and forth behind his desk, talking more to himself than to me.

"He was nothing but a pygmy, standing on the shoulders of a giant," he declares.

I grab the edge of the desk and pull myself up. It hurts to breathe, but at least I'm upright again. I hope the microphone is still working.

"So you admit that Cheetah was Phillips' creation?" I say between deep breaths of air. "That you stole his intellectual property?"

Hays whirls around to face me. He's completely disheveled—his shirt is half out of his pants, and his hair is sticking up in patches.

"What property?" he bellows. "He didn't own it. I could see when he first showed me the code that it was predicated on my life's work; the years I'd spent at PCI, waiting for the technology to catch up with my ideas!"

"Is that why you killed him?"

"You should have seen him." Hays is off in his own world now. "Every time he walked into my office, he'd have some new piece of code to show me." Hays looks at me. "He was mocking me, you know. Oh, it was subtle. I'm sure he thought that the old man wouldn't notice. But I did. I could tell what he was thinking: that I was over the hill, past my prime. But I showed him; I showed everybody."

"You killed him."

"Of course I killed him," Hays says to me, like I'm stupid for needing the obvious pointed out. "I couldn't just let him take over my life's work. Cheetah was supposed to be my idea. I did the real research years ago. Phillips just happened to stumble onto the application first."

Got him! I think to myself. I have what I came for, at least part of it. Now all I've got to do is ask about Leticia. But first, I have to satisfy my curiosity on one point.

"If Phillips did base some of his ideas on your original research, then why didn't you offer to partner with him? Why didn't you two team up and found a company together?"

Hays blushes red.

"Impossible. Why should I share the glory with a mere imitator? And anyway, he was planning to form his own company. He was already shopping around for venture capital in Austin when he died." Hays gives me a look of complete disgust before continuing. "The little jerk came to my office one night all excited about the company *he* was going to build. He had the nerve to act like I should be happy for him. But I knew he was just taunting me; rubbing my nose in the fact that he'd beaten me to Cheetah. That's when I decided to stop him."

"That was the night you ran him down in your car."

"What of it," Hays replies icily. "Disposing of him was a minor transgression compared to his crime."

"His crime?" I ask. "What was that?"

"Taking what should have been my idea, of course," Hays says arrogantly.

I've heard enough. I'm sick of this man, and now I just want to get this over with. I'm ready to hit him with the final blow and ask about Leticia, but Hays has apparently had enough conversation.

"You're a smart man, Cavanaugh," he says, backing away from the desk. "I really hate that it's come to this."

His intent is obvious; he must have a gun here somewhere. I circle around the desk rapidly, set on tackling Hays. But before I even get close, he picks up a brass lamp from a nearby bookshelf and yanks it hard. It sparks briefly and then dies as the cord is wrenched from the wall socket. He begins walking deliberately towards me.

I don't believe it. He's going to try to kill me with a light fixture. I'm so relieved, I burst out laughing.

"You've got to be kidding," I say to him.

As if to assure me otherwise, Hays takes a swipe at me with the lamp. His aim is unexpectedly accurate, and I have to jump out of the way to avoid being hit. Instead of connecting with its intended target—my head—the lamp comes down on a laptop computer perched on a corner of the desk. It crumples and breaks into several pieces as it falls to the floor.

Now I'm mad.

I rush at Hays and reach him just as he's raising the lamp for another swing. I grab his arm and push back until he lets go of the lamp, which drops to the floor with a thud. Then I twist his arm around his back and put him in a choke hold. His free hand claws frantically at me, but he can't break my grip. Hays struggles briefly, but after a few attempts to escape, all the while shouting profanities, he finally exhausts himself.

"I don't have all the answers I came for," I tell him. "Why kill Leticia?"

Hays doesn't respond. I tighten my grip momentarily, until I feel him strain for air, then loosen my hold again.

"I asked you a question," I say.

"I didn't want her to die," he says, gasping. "If only she hadn't meddled."

"Meddled?"

"She went through my files," he elaborates. "She should never have gone through my files. I always kept them locked, but I made the mistake of keeping the key in my desk."

Hays makes a weak attempt to break free, then gives up.

"I figured out what happened the day she resigned," he continues. "I found her letter of resignation when I got into the office, and then later that morning, I was going through one of my files and noticed that the papers were out of order. Worse than that, one of my originals was missing; it had been replaced by a photocopy. It wasn't hard to figure out who did it."

He takes a deep breath of air.

"I never thought anyone but me would want to see those files," he moans.

"I asked her to get me more information about Cheetah," I say to him. "If you'll recall, you weren't very forthcoming."

"Then you're just as guilty of killing her as I am."

His words cut like a knife. I hurl him away from me angrily. He stumbles a few feet and lands sprawled on the carpet.

I'm moving towards him when I'm stopped by a familiar voice: "We'll take it from here, Mr. Cavanaugh."

# Chapter Twenty-six

I look in the direction of the voice, but Kamimoto and Morrison are already in motion. I'm amazed at how fast the two inspectors can move. They have Hays up off the floor in no time. While Morrison handcuffs Hays, Kamimoto joins me near the desk.

"Did you get everything? Is the mike still working?" I ask him anxiously.

"Yes, we've heard everything."

"He's wearing a mike?" Hays asks Kamimoto in a plaintive voice.

"Yes he is."

"Oh."

Hays hangs his head, defeated.

"Sorry it took us so long," Kamimoto says. He sits down in Hays leather swivel chair and reclines comfortably. "The security guard told us you were on the third floor."

"But this is the second floor."

"Right, you may want to point that out to him."

On the other side of the room, Inspector Morrison is trying to read Hays his rights, but the industry legend seems to have regained some of his old spirit.

"This is entrapment!" he protests. "Entrapment, pure and simple. You have nothing on me. I was making it all up."

"You can tell us all about it at the station, sir," Morrison tells Hays as he leads him out of the office.

"Shall we?" Kamimoto says to me, standing up and gesturing in the direction of the door.

"Let's get the hell out of here."

I walk out of Arthur Hays' office with Kamimoto close behind. Everything looks different somehow. I feel better than I have in days; I actually feel physically lighter, like the pull of gravity is somehow less than it was before. It's starting to register that it's finally over. Hays confessed, and I have it all on tape. It's done; I've got him.

There's a couple of uniformed officers in the hallway. They give me a funny look when they see me, and I realize that I'm grinning from ear to ear. I must look like the village idiot. But I don't care. I finally nailed Hays, and I'm enjoying the moment.

Kamimoto orders one of the officers to stay put and guard Hays' office. The other one joins our group as we head downstairs.

"I need to speak to my lawyer," Hays bellows to Morrison.

"You can call your lawyer from the station."

"You're damn right I will!"

Hays is pretty feisty, and he has a booming voice. He's still going on about police abuse and false arrest as we approach the bullpen where all the programmers are.

The normally industrious atmosphere of the bullpen has been replaced by one of confusion. Apparently the sight of armed police running past their cubicles a few minutes ago was enough to get most of the workers away from their computers. Only a few of the die-hard programmers are still hacking away. The rest have gathered in small groups, sipping sodas and eating pastry and whispering among themselves, no doubt trying to figure out what's going on.

Hays is still protesting his arrest as we enter the bullpen. The voice of the company CEO grabs everybody's attention, and even the die-hards look up from their monitors to see what's going on. I see eyes widen and more than one jaw drop at the sight of their fearless leader being led away in handcuffs. Nobody says anything, however. The only one speaking is Hays; other than that, our audience is deathly still.

All that changes once we leave the bullpen. The minute we walk past the last cubicle, the whole floor erupts in conversation. I can hear questions and declarations of astonishment behind me. They fade gradually as we move beyond the programmers and into the main lobby.

The security guard is still at his post when we reach the lobby, probably because he wasn't sure what else to do. The TV is on, but he's not watching it. He sees us come in and stands up at his desk. He looks like he might ask a question, but Morrison walks right past him with Hays, who's finally finished his tirade against law enforcement.

Like Morrison, I pass by the guard without a word. Kamimoto and the uniformed officer follow behind. I can hear Kamimoto giving the officer instructions about dealing with questions from the building's late-night workers. I guess he's planning to post the patrolman here.

Inspector Morrison opens the glass door for Hays and follows him closely, still holding him by the elbow. I'm right behind them, eager to get out of the building. I step outside and take a deep breath of fresh air.

All of a sudden I hear a hissing sound, and see Hays slump in front of me. I'm watching him drop to the ground when someone pushes hard against me. I hear the hissing once again, and feel something brush past my cheek.

"Down! Down!" Kamimoto yells at me as he shoves me to the ground.

It takes me a couple of seconds to realize we've been shot at.

Kamimoto and I crawl as fast as we can back through the door, and then help Morrison pull Hays into the lobby. The patrol officer is on the floor near the door, weapon drawn, trying to see the sniper. But that's impossible. With most of the buildings in this complex still unoccupied, there's not much light to see by.

"Follow me," Kamimoto whispers hoarsely, "and stay close."

We crawl on our bellies to a corner away from the line of fire, dragging Hays along with us. When we finally reach our refuge, I pause to look at the fallen entrepreneur. He's been hit, but I can't tell where the bullet got him because his blood seems to be everywhere.

My God, I think, and look away.

"Were you hit anywhere else?" Kamimoto asks me, drawing his gun from his holster and looking around the room.

"What do you mean?" I ask him.

"Here, hold this against your cheek," Kamimoto says by way of explanation. He hands me a handkerchief. For the first time, I notice that my right cheek is throbbing with pain. I put my hand up to touch it, and it comes away with blood.

"It's just a flesh wound," Kamimoto says. "Keep the cloth pressed against your face. That will stop the bleeding."

Kamimoto looks over at the police officer, who has taken up a position not far from the receptionist desk, the security guard cowering next to him.

"Did you call in?" he asks the officer.

"Yes sir," the policeman responds. "They're on the way."

With our sanctuary at least temporarily secured, Kamimoto finally turns his attention to Arthur Hays.

"How is he?" he asks Morrison, who's bent over the CEO, checking for a heartbeat.

Morrison shakes his head.

"I'm not getting a pulse; he's dead."

"Then leave him. I need you with me."

Morrison's movements are efficient, but thoughtful. I watch him place the dead man's hands on his torso and close the staring eyes. Then he draws his gun and joins his partner. The two men watch the open front door, trying to peer into the darkness outside.

"Do you see anything?" Kamimoto asks Morrison after a few moments.

"It's too dark out there," the younger man replies.

"I know." Kamimoto sneers in disgust. "Damn it! I should have had more backup. Now the sniper is going to get away."

"You had it set up right," Morrison says. "How could you have known that someone would be shooting at us?"

"I should have expected some sort of trouble."

"Hey, what's going on?" somebody shouts. We look over to the right, and see a group of programmers clustered around the entrance to the bullpen.

"Get back and close the door!" Kamimoto yells, waving his gun for emphasis. The young men scatter like geese, and someone slams the door shut.

We sit in silence, motionless. It's so quiet, I can hear the low buzz of the fluorescent lights. It seems to me that we should be doing something, but I'm not sure what.

"What do we do now?" I ask Kamimoto.

He gives me a weary look.

"We sit, and we wait."

It seems like we've been waiting for hours when I finally hear the sound of an approaching siren. In reality, it's probably been less than ten minutes since the ordeal began.

The siren gets louder, and it's joined by others. Now I can hear the whir of a helicopter flying overhead, and I see its searchlight sweeping the ground outside.

Two officers enter by a side door.

"Over here," Kamimoto shouts as soon as they run in. They race over to us and arrive just as we're standing up.

"We have a sniper out there," Morrison tells them.

"Yes, we know that sir," the officer replies. "We're looking for him."

"You won't find him," Kamimoto tells them. "He was a pro. He knows better than to stick around."

Kamimoto holsters his gun and walks to the front door.

If the coast is clear, then I want out too. I hurry to the exit, leaving Morrison and the officers to keep vigil over Hays' corpse.

I step outside just as a couple of ambulances arrive. They park with a jerk, and the paramedics leap from them. I watch two young men pull a gurney from their ambulance and make their way into the lobby with it.

Someone taps me on the shoulder and I turn my head. It's another paramedic.

"Let me take a look at that," he says, moving my face so he can see the gunshot wound. "I thought so. Come with me."

I go with him to an ambulance, where I climb inside and sit down. The paramedic jumps in after me, and right away starts to work, removing the blood from around the wound and cleaning it with antiseptic.

"Actually, this isn't as bad as it looks," he tells me without taking his eyes off his work. "The bullet just grazed you. I bet it smarts though."

"It does."

The wound is throbbing in time with my pulse.

"That's better," he says a few moments later. "But you should see a plastic surgeon right away. Otherwise you'll end up with a pretty noticeable scar."

The paramedic reaches into a nearby case for a bandage, and is taping it over the wound when Kamimoto pokes his head in the door.

"How are you doing?" the inspector asks me.

"Okay."

"I'd like to talk to you if you're finished."

I look at the paramedic, who's putting away his supplies.

"I've done all I can here," he tells me. "Like I said, you need to get to a hospital and have a doctor take a look at your face."

"I'll do that."

I get up to leave the ambulance and then stop.

"Can you get this mike off me?" I ask the paramedic.

"Sure."

I take off my shirt. The paramedic peels away the tape that's holding the microphone and the transmitter and removes the whole unit from my body. He puts everything into a plastic bag and hands it to me.

"Thanks," I say, taking the bag. I jump out of the back of the ambulance.

The front of the building is swarming with people. Uniformed officers are everywhere, and all the programmers seem to be milling around aimlessly outside, dumbfounded by the situation.

"Let's get away from this commotion," Kamimoto says to me.

We start walking down the road, away from Hays Software. I hand him the plastic bag with the microphone in it.

"Thanks," he says. We walk in silence for another fifty feet before Kamimoto asks me: "So, do you have any idea who might have been shooting at us?"

"No, of course not." I'm surprised by the question. "What makes you think I would?"

Kamimoto stops and reaches into his jacket. He pulls out a pack of sugar-free gum and offers me some. I decline. He takes out a stick, carefully unwraps it and puts it in his mouth. I wish he'd tell me what he's thinking.

"Why do you think I should know who shot us?" I ask impatiently.

"I'm not saying you should," he tells me. "But I thought you might have a clue. At least I wish you did. See, there's a couple of things that worry me about what happened."

"I should think so. We were almost killed, and we don't even know why."

"That's not exactly right," he counters. "*We* weren't all being shot at. Only two shots were fired, at least that's all I heard, even though it took us a few seconds to make our way back inside. During those few seconds, we were easy targets, but the sniper didn't bother to fire again. So I have to ask myself, why?"

I shake my head; I have no idea.

"Because he figured his job was done," Kamimoto says. "He saw Hays drop, and he saw you go down too. Maybe he figured he'd nailed you. He almost did. If I hadn't pushed you, you'd be dead right now, just like Hays."

I think of Hays' body, now on its way to the morgue, and I feel my neck muscles tighten involuntarily. I knew I'd been shot at, but I'd assumed it was because I happened to be in the wrong place at the wrong time. Now I find out I was targeted.

"More likely," Kamimoto continues, "he knows he missed you. But I was blocking his shot, so he gave up. For now."

I don't know what to say. I thought this nightmare was over, but it's only getting worse. My body feels heavy, and completely numb. The ground is slowly turning in circles around me.

Kamimoto puts his hand on my shoulder.

"Are you all right?" he asks. "You look a little green."

"Leave me alone," I say, and stumble to the curb. I sit down and rest my head on my hands.

Kamimoto comes over and sits next to me.

"I'd like to have a couple of officers stay with you," he says. "At least until we can figure out what happened here tonight."

I raise my head and look at him. Then I start to laugh, loudly and sarcastically.

"And how long will that take?" I ask. "You have no idea who's behind this. What am I supposed to do? Spend the rest of my life glued to a couple of bodyguards? And what about my family?"

Kamimoto gives me a concerned look.

"I'll get to the bottom of it," he promises.

I stand up and look down at him.

"*This* was supposed to be the bottom of it!" I yell at him as I motion to all the activity around us. "We have Hays. Case closed. Only now, someone is trying to kill me!"

My shouting is attracting attention. A couple of the patrolmen closest to us look over. Kamimoto stands up.

"Just stick with me for a while longer. We'll figure this out."

"No," I tell him, this time in a calm voice. "If it were just me, maybe I'd do it. But I have a family to think about. You might be able to post a couple of policemen, but you can't guarantee my family's safety, can you?"

Kamimoto says nothing.

I turn around abruptly and start walking towards my car. I expect Kamimoto to come running after me, but he doesn't. Maybe he knows me well enough by now to realize that I won't be stopped once I've made up my mind.

I get in my car and maneuver around the emergency vehicles and on to the main road. Soon I've reached highway 280. It's a clear night, and at this hour, the freeway is deserted. I step on the gas and race recklessly towards my house, desperate to get home.

# Chapter Twenty-seven

The lights are on when I arrive at my house. Michelle waited up for me; I figured she would.

I park the car in the garage, and go in through the kitchen door. I can hear the TV on in the family room. When I enter the room, I see Michelle lying propped up on the couch, a book in her hands. She's not reading it though, neither is she watching TV; she's staring absentmindedly at the fireplace. There's no wood burning in the hearth; Michelle is looking at the cold ashes of a fire we lit days ago.

"Hi," I say softly, coming around to the front of the sofa.

"Thank God!" she says, jumping up and throwing her arms around me. We hug for a long time. She squeezes me tightly, pressing hard against my chest. I kiss the top of her head and bury my face in her hair. I don't want to ever let go.

She finally pushes back from me and looks at my face.

"What happened to you?"

"It's nothing, just a flesh wound."

"A flesh wound? Were you shot? How bad is it?"

"I'm fine," I begin.

"Did Hays try to kill you?" she interrupts.

"Sort of," I say, "He came after me when I accused him of killing Leticia and the graduate student at UTA. He admitted everything."

"He admitted it? That's great!" Michelle says happily. "Now it's over. So they arrested Hays?"

I sit down on the sofa without saying anything.

"He *is* in custody, isn't he?" she asks again.

"No. He's dead."

"Dead?! What do you mean 'dead'? What happened there tonight?" she asks, sitting down next to me. She takes my hand and looks at me intently.

The story tumbles out of me in a rush. I tell her how I confronted Hays, got him to admit to the murders, and how we got shot on the way out of the building.

Michelle is clenching my hand tightly now. She's scared; I can hear it in her voice.

"Why would anyone want to kill you?" she asks pleadingly.

"I don't know, and I don't have time to think about it right now. You and Chloe are at risk. We have to get you out of here right away."

"But what about you? You're the one in the most danger. You should come with us."

"No."

I take Michelle by the shoulders, as if I could drive home what I have to say just by touching her.

"Kamimoto thinks that Hays was nailed by a professional assassin. A guy like that will track me down wherever I go. My only chance is to find out who hired him and why. And that means I have to stay here. Besides, you and Chloe will be safer if I'm not with you."

"But Steven . . ." Michelle says, starting to object.

"No arguments," I say tersely, and then more softly I add, "I'm sorry, Michelle."

"And just where are we supposed to go?"

"I've already thought about that." I pick up the phone and hand it to Michelle. "Call your cousin Valerie and tell her you're coming to Paris. I'll check the flight schedules. One of the airlines must have a red-eye going out tonight."

"This is ridiculous!" Michelle protests.

"I'm sorry honey, it's our only option. After we call Valerie and book the flights, we need to start packing."

I head to my PC to check airline schedules. It turns out there's a 1:30 AM flight to New York, and fortunately, it's far from full. After a brief layover at Kennedy Airport, Michelle and Chloe will be able to pick up a connecting flight for Paris. But we'll have to dash to catch the plane.

I run to our walk-in closet and begin hauling luggage off the top shelf. Michelle joins me a few minutes later.

"I left Valerie a message to let her know we're coming. But I'm still not sure about this." She opens a dresser drawer, and stares at her clothes without moving.

"I don't know where to begin," she says with a lost voice.

"Just the basics," I tell her, handing her a handful of lingerie. "And hurry. We've got to get you on that flight. I'll go wake up Chloe and get her started."

---

The drive to the airport is like a hazy dream. As we speed north on the freeway, I glance periodically into the rearview mirror, looking for cops, or worse, any car that might be following us. Michelle is staring out the window, apparently lost in thought. After the initial hubbub of getting everyone packed and into the car, Chloe has nodded off in the back seat and is already in dreamland again.

Michelle breaks the silence.

"I still don't see why you can't come with us."

"We've been over this already," I say, clenching my teeth. "Kamimoto hasn't come through the way I'd hoped, but I believe him when he says the killer is a pro. I don't want him tracking us all down."

"Damn it! Damn it!" Michelle suddenly yells. She hits the dashboard with the palm of her hand. "I hate this!"

Chloe stirs in the back seat, but doesn't wake.

"I know you do, but we're out of options," I say. "You don't want Chloe to be in danger, do you?"

"Of course not," Michelle says quietly.

We make the rest of the drive without exchanging another word.

We arrive at the airport and follow the signs for departing flights. I jerk to a halt at the curb, waking Chloe, who yawns and opens her eyes sleepily.

"Here we are," I say, trying to seem upbeat.

I jump out of the car, open the trunk, and lift out the bags. Michelle gets out of the car and opens the back door for Chloe. I look around and spy an abandoned luggage cart on the sidewalk. I run over and wheel it toward the car, and then throw all the luggage on it.

"Michelle, you push this, I'll carry Chloe. We're going to have to go directly to the gate. It's number 74."

I pick up Chloe and she rests her head on my right shoulder. I feel her relax and go back to sleep.

"Let's go," I say. "We have to hustle."

Michelle pushes the cart briskly and I hurry alongside, almost jogging. When we reach the gate, the passengers are already boarding the plane. We rush up to the check-in podium.

"We have two to board," I say. "The name is Cavanaugh."

The desk attendant calls up the reservation on her computer and issues the boarding passes. She leans over the podium to look at the luggage.

"You'll have to check those," she informs us.

"Fine, fine," I say.

The attendant tags the bags and hands us the boarding passes.

The plane is now only minutes from takeoff. We hasten to the boarding tunnel. I put Chloe down next to Michelle, and give them both a strong hug. I kiss Michelle one last time, and take a deep breath of her perfume before I let her go. She walks into the tunnel a few feet and then stops to look at me. Chloe waves goodbye sleepily. Then they turn to get on the plane. I watch them walk a bit farther, and then round a corner and disappear.

I wonder if I'll ever see them again.

When I get back outside, I find a parking ticket on the car. I snatch it off the windshield, crumple it up in my hand, and throw it on the ground.

I get in the car and drive away from the terminal. I'm not sure where to go next. There's no way I can return to the house—that's the first place my stalker will look for me. I drive down the road and approach the entrance to highway 101. I hesitate for a moment, and then take the freeway north, simply because it's in the opposite direction of my house.

I try to think things through, but my mind has turned to mush. So I continue driving north, with no particular destination in mind. As I get closer to downtown San Francisco, however, I realize that I need a sounding board; someone who can help me think about what happened and figure out a plan of action. I decide to go to Angela's apartment.

I open my wallet and dig out her address. Angela lives in Noe Valley, in an apartment off 24th Street. I take the Army Street exit off the freeway and head west. Ten minutes later I'm parking my car.

I climb the stairs to the second floor. Angela lives in a converted Victorian house, and the owner hasn't bothered to mark the apartments. Fortunately, there are only four of them. I take my best guess, and approach the door nearest me on my left. I ring the doorbell. Nothing happens. I wait a few seconds and ring again, this time longer.

"Alright, alright. Who's there?"

It's Angela's sleepy voice on the other side. Lucky me, I guessed right.

"It's Steven."

Angela opens the door a crack. She still has the safety chain on.

"It is you," she says "What's the matter?"

"Everything."

"Everything? What do you mean? Are you okay?"

"I'm still alive and kicking."

"Wait a minute."

She closes the door, unlocks the chain, and then opens the door all the way.

"Come on in," she says as she takes my arm and leads me in.

She guides me to a sofa and has me sit down.

"You look awful," she tells me. "What happened to your face?"

"I got shot."

"Shot? Are you kidding?" she says, shocked.

"I wish I were."

"Tell me what happened," she says.

"It's a long story."

"I've got time."

She goes to sit down in a stuffed chair, but changes her mind.

"Hold on, let me get you something first."

Angela walks from the living room to the kitchen. A tile countertop is the only thing separating the two rooms, so I can watch her movements without getting up from the sofa. She opens a cabinet and pulls out a couple of snifters. Then she gets a bottle of brandy from another cabinet and pours us both a drink.

Angela hands me a glass, and I take it from her gratefully. I take a sip, and feel the warmth of the liquor fill my throat and spread gradually through my chest. Usually I hate this stuff, but tonight it tastes like nectar.

Angela settles into the stuffed chair and draws her legs up under her. She's in her pajamas—a large T-shirt and a pair of boxer shorts.

"Did Hays do this to you?" she asks me. "I knew that guy was a nut case. You're lucky to be alive."

"Yeah, I am, but Hays didn't do this."

"Then who did?"

"I wish I knew."

Angela raises her eyebrows and gives me puzzled look. I explain the events of the past few hours to her, with a lot more detail than I was able to give Michelle. Angela listens without asking me any questions, but her intense gaze and constant nodding make it clear that she's hanging on every word. Halfway through my narrative I finish my brandy and Angela refills my glass. This time she leaves the bottle on the coffee table.

"Who in the world would want to kill you?" she asks when I've finished my story.

"I have no idea," I say, yawning. "And I'm in no shape to think about it right now. I'm exhausted."

"Of course you are." Angela stands up. "Come on. Let's get you to bed." She takes my hand and helps me up.

"Help me lower the futon," she asks. "I'll take this side. You take the other. Just pull out that peg you see there."

I follow her directions and we have the sofa converted into a bed in less than thirty seconds.

"You can sleep here tonight. It's pretty comfortable, at least that's what my guests have told me. I'll go get you some sheets and a pillow."

In less than a minute, Angela is back with the linens. She sets to work making the bed, and refuses my offer of help, insisting that I rest instead. I give in to her admonitions, and find myself dozing off in her chair.

"That should do it," she says at last, plumping the pillow to her satisfaction. She pats my arm. "Sleep well."

I raise my head to look at her. "Believe me, I will."

"Uh-oh," she says. "That doesn't look good."

"What?"

"You're bleeding again; that bandage is soaked." She bends down to examine it further. "We need to take care of it right now. Wait here," she adds, as if I had anyplace else to go.

When Angela returns she's carrying scissors, tape, antibiotic, and some packaged gauze pads. She drops them on the futon, and gestures for me to join her there.

"You're certainly well-stocked with medical supplies," I say as I sit down on the bed, facing her.

She leans over and begins removing the bandage. "Yeah I know," she says. "Fortunately for you, I actually take earthquake-preparedness seriously." With one quick motion, she rips the rest of the dressing off my face.

"Hey!" I say, "you could've warned me."

"That would have hurt even more," she answers unapologetically. She gently tilts my chin so she can better examine the wound. "This isn't as bad as I expected," she tells me.

She takes a gauze pad, puts a little clear liquid from a bottle on it, and raises it to my face. "This won't hurt," she tells me. "I promise." She dabs at the wound carefully, softly. She's right, it doesn't hurt at all.

"I don't know what the hell Kamimoto was thinking sending you in alone," she says when she's finished removing all the old blood from my face. She opens up another pad and places it over the wound. "You know you could have been killed," she chides. "And then what?"

"What do you mean?" I ask her.

Angela doesn't answer immediately, but instead continues bandaging the cut. I watch her, not sure what to make of the expression on her face. When she places the last piece of tape on the dressing, she smoothes it on gently, her fingers lingering on my cheek.

"I just don't know what I'd do if . . ." her voice trails off.

"If what?" I ask her, gazing into her eyes with intense curiosity.

But Angela doesn't answer my question. Instead she leans close, and leaves a tender kiss on my lips.

Despite my surprise, my response is immediate, automatic. I pull her close to me, kissing her forcefully. Angela returns my passion, and after a long initial kiss, I feel her lips move slowly across my face, caressing first my cheek, then my neck, behind my ear. Now my hands, as if they had a mind of their own, let go of the thick, silky tresses they've been holding, and travel down Angela's back to her waist, where they reach under her shirt, and then move back up.

I've succumbed completely to the moment, intoxicated by Angela, the warmth of her next to me, the softness of her skin, the feel of her seductive lips on me.

But then something happens. As I'm kissing Angela's shoulder, lost in the sensation of her body against mine, a quiet, seemingly innocuous thought snakes its way into my mind: only one other woman has ever made me feel like this.

The thought of Michelle is like a splash of cold water. I pull back from Angela, slowly but deliberately, and disentangle myself from her. Then I stare at the floor, rub my forehead, and do my best to think; it feels like trying to swim against the tide.

"I can't do this." I say the words out loud, but I'm talking to myself.

"I know," I hear Angela say. I look up, and see a pair of beautiful sad eyes before me. Angela stands up. "I should go," she says.

But before she can leave, I grab her hand.

"I have to tell you," I begin, looking up at her earnestly, "I've never been so . . . I'm sorry."

I let go of her hand and Angela moves away from me without a word. She picks up the brandy bottle and the snifters from the coffee table, then walks to the kitchen counter and quietly sets down the glassware.

"You know what's so ironic about this?" she says, facing me. "The thing about you that I find most compelling is your integrity." A faint smile crosses her face. "Go figure."

She walks out of the room, flipping off the light as she leaves.

I watch her turn to go down the hallway. A moment later, her door closes, leaving me alone in the darkness. I lie down on the futon, and stare futilely into the night. In spite of my exhaustion, it takes me hours to fall asleep.

# Chapter Twenty-eight

I slowly open my eyes. I forget where I am for a moment, then the memories of last night come flooding back to me, and I close my eyes again. I'm not ready to deal with Angela yet. I don't know exactly what to expect from her, but I'm sure that at the very least, it will be awkward.

I give myself a few more moments of peace, and then decide it's time to face the day. I roll over on my side and open my eyes again. It must be late in the morning; the sun is streaming in through the living room window and hitting me right in the face. I have to blink a few times to get used to it.

Behind me, I hear someone moving around in the kitchen. I prop myself up on my elbows, and am immediately greeted by the smell of bacon and eggs cooking. Suddenly I realize how hungry I am.

Angela leans over the tile countertop to check on me.

"Hey you. How are you doing?" Her voice is light and friendly, as if last night didn't happen.

"Okay," I answer cautiously. "What time is it?"

"Nearly ten," she replies cheerfully.

Angela strolls out of the kitchen into the living room. She's in an old pair of faded blue jeans, an olive green V-neck T-shirt, and blue canvas sneakers. Except for her watch and a pair of dangling earrings, she's wearing no jewelry. Her jet black hair is wet and brushed back. Even dressed down she looks great.

"So what's for breakfast?" I ask.

"One of my specialties," she answers. "Breakfast like my grandmother used to make. You'll love it."

"It sounds wonderful," I say. "When do we eat?"

"Soon. You have time to shower first if you want. It's down the hall, to the right," she says, motioning with the spatula in her hand. "I left a bath towel out for you."

"I appreciate that," I reply, grateful that she's spared us both from a painful dissection of what happened last night.

I get out of bed and walk to the bathroom. Like the rest of the apartment, it's tiny. There's a shower stall—no tub—a sink, a toilet, and a medicine chest. That's it. There's not even enough room for two people to stand in here at the same time.

I undress, turn the shower water on full blast, and step in. The warm rushing water is invigorating. I feel my muscles loosen, and the dull ache in my head gradually fade away.

By the end of my shower, I'm feeling better, even relaxed, and have turned my attention back to the more pressing problem of Hays Software. I towel off rapidly and pull on my clothes, all the while trying to make sense of my meeting with Hays. I still can't see why someone would want me dead.

As soon as I'm dressed I open the medicine chest to look for a bandage. No luck, but I find Angela's first aid kit under the sink. I take out a large band-aid and put the kit back. Then I straighten up and look in the mirror to apply the fresh dressing. The gesture brings back a vivid memory of Angela, and I stop in mid-motion. But almost immediately I push the thought from my head, and quickly cover my cut. If Angela can forget about last night so thoroughly and completely, then so can I—it's what I want, after all.

"Something smells great," I say as I walk into the kitchen.

"Thanks," Angela replies. "Take a seat and I'll get you a plate."

I sit down at the small round table and take a sip of the coffee waiting for me there. Angela prepares a couple of plates and brings them to the table.

I look down at the food Angela sets before me. She certainly doesn't skimp on portions. The dish is piled high with eggs, potatoes, bacon, and mashed beans. It looks really good. I dig in, famished.

Angela seats herself across from me and picks up a flour tortilla from a basket on the table. She tears off a piece and uses it to expertly pick up some eggs and beans, and then pops the concoction into her mouth. I watch her repeat the process a couple of times, impressed that she can eat that way without ever dropping any food.

"You look like you're doing better this morning" she says to me.

"I am," I reply between bites of bacon. "I just wish I knew who wanted me dead."

"I've been thinking about that all morning," Angela says. "For starters, the killer—or whoever hired him—has to be someone who knew you would be there last night. It must be someone Hays knew."

"And someone who has a big stake in keeping the rip-off of Cheetah a secret," I reply. Suddenly it dawns on me. "Like the biggest investors in Hays Software."

Angela stops eating.

"What?"

"Think about it," I say. "If the truth about Cheetah comes out, then Hays Software folds like a house of cards, and everybody involved loses their investment."

"Are you trying to tell me that venture capital firms are now hiring assassins to protect their interests?" she asks.

"No, I was thinking more about the angel investors. Especially the one who put in $5 million. That's a lot of incentive."

Angela tilts her head, contemplating what I just said.

"Then lets find out who the $5 million angel is," she suggests. "That info should be in the latest prospectus, right?"

"It should be by now," I answer.

"Then there's our solution. The investment banks underwriting the stock sale have copies of the prospectus on computer. The lead underwriter is guaranteed to have the latest version. Let's see if Dan can crack their system and get us a copy."

"That should work," I say. I think hard for a moment. "Damn! I don't know who the banks are. But that information has to be in the papers we copied at Turner's office, I'm sure of it." I sigh heavily. "There's only one problem. I've been keeping that file at home."

Angela's response is immediate.

"You can't go back there. It's not safe."

"I don't have any choice," I say. "I'm dead in the water without those papers."

Angela gazes at me thoughtfully.

"If you really want to do this, then I'm right behind you," she tells me.

"I knew I could count on you," I say.

She reaches over and squeezes my hand, warmly but quickly, and then gets up and begins clearing away dishes. I wolf down the rest of my breakfast and take my plate to the counter.

"I'll be ready in a minute," she says to me.

Angela hurries to her bedroom and returns right away, with a black sweater wrapped around her waist. She grabs her car keys from the kitchen counter.

"I think I should drive," she says. "They might be looking for your car."

"Good point. We'll go in yours."

Angela's apartment may be small, but at least she has her own parking space, a premium commodity in San Francisco. We descend the stairs rapidly and jump in her car. In less then twenty minutes, we've left the city behind.

# Chapter Twenty-nine

As we get closer to my neighborhood, I find myself looking over my shoulder, checking to see if any cars are following us. Angela asks for few directions as she drives; I guess she's already learned the way to my house.

Soon we're approaching my street.

"Isn't that it?" she asks.

"Yeah, but keep going. Take a left at the next street, and then park in front of the fourth house, down on the left. That's the place directly behind mine."

I figure I can go through my neighbor's backyard, hop the fence on to my property, and enter through the back door. That way if anyone's staked out my place, at least they won't see me coming.

"How are you going to explain what you're doing to your neighbors?" Angela asks.

"I'll think of something."

As soon as Angela stops the car, I leap out and dash up the walkway to the front door. I ring the bell, wait a few seconds, and then try again. No answer. I peek in the living room window; it's completely dark inside. The Randalls must be gone.

I glance across the street to make sure no one is watching, and then cut across the grass to the side yard gate. I reach over the redwood fence and undo the latch. The gate swings open, and then slams shut behind me before I can stop it. I move quickly down the sidewalk toward the back.

"Brad? Janet?" someone calls from next door.

It's the Randalls' neighbor. He must have heard the gate shut and figures they've come home. Fortunately, the two backyards are separated by a tall fence overgrown with foliage. I'm sure he can't see me through all the greenery.

"No, it's the pool man," I say.

"Oh, I didn't know you came on weekends."

Why is my neighborhood so full of busybodies?

"The Randalls requested some special maintenance while they were gone, so I'm making an extra visit this week," I say, trying to sound professional.

"I see."

A second later I'm relieved to hear the sound of hedge clippers—the nosy neighbor has gone back to his gardening.

I jog to the back yard. Once there, I pick an open spot, get a running start, and then scramble up and over the fence.

I hurry to my house, open the back door and go directly to the front hallway so I can disable the alarm. But when I get there, it's already off. I spin around, expecting to find someone behind me. But the house is quiet, and seemingly empty. I must have forgotten to set the alarm last night.

I walk to my home office and go straight to my desk. There I take a seat, open the bottom drawer, and pull out the strong box that Michelle and I use to store our wills and other important papers. The box makes a loud scraping sound as I place it on the desktop. I catch my breath and listen for a moment, but I don't hear anything unusual.

I sort through the keys on my chain, and find the diminutive key that opens the box. I raise the lid slowly, half expecting the box to be empty. But no, everything is still there, including the file I need. I take it out and close the lid. Then I lock up the strong box and put it back in my desk. Time to go.

I start back towards the front hall. But as I'm passing by the staircase, it occurs to me how good it would feel to change into something clean and comfortable. I hesitate, then decide to risk it. If there were any assassins in the house, I'd be dead by now.

I race upstairs and into my bedroom. The room is still messy from last night's frantic packing effort. Michelle's clothes are all over the bed and on the floor, and most of the bureau's drawers are still open. I step over the piles of clothes to my side of the bureau and pull out my favorite pair of jeans and a polo shirt. It takes me all of two minutes to change. Once I'm dressed, I walk into our closet and exchange yesterday's loafers for a pair of lightweight hiking boots. Now I'm set.

I hurry down the stairs and set the alarm. Then I exit the house quickly and quietly, and backtrack to the fence. Once there, I shove the folder inside the back of my pants so I can have both hands free. On this side of the fence I can use a low hanging branch of the Chinese Elm to pull myself up. I get on top of the fence and balance there precariously.

Unfortunately, there are several large rose bushes at this end of the Randalls' yard. I jump hard and manage to clear them, but my aim isn't perfect. My footing slips and I fall on my butt into the mud. Damn! That's all I need. I get up, and rescue the folder from my pants. It's splattered with specks of mud, but the papers inside are okay.

I jog back to the front gate, hoping I won't hear anything more from the Randalls' inquisitive neighbor. Peeking over the fence, I can see Angela waiting in her convertible. She must be feeling nervous; the car's engine is still running, and I notice that for once she's left the top up.

I move soundlessly through the gate, and dash to the car.

"Did you find the stuff?" she queries.

"Yes." I open the door and get in.

"What happened?" she asks, noticing the dirt on my rear. "Did you get hurt?"

"No, I slipped when I jumped the fence."

Despite the circumstances, Angela can't suppress a giggle.

"Joke's over," I say as we're driving away. I'm not really annoyed though; it's good to know Angela and I can still kid around.

She drives us out of the neighborhood and on to the main road. Soon we're heading south on 280, on our way to Santa Cruz. I pull out the Hays file and begin reading.

Angela is listening to the radio and seems more relaxed now that we're on the move again.

"Did you find the names of the investment banks?" she asks after a few minutes.

"I'm still looking," I say, flipping through the papers from Grimshaw Turner. "Here they are."

I scan the pages quickly.

"The lead underwriter is Van Ness Securities," I say, surprised. "That's interesting."

"Why?"

"Because Franklin Albright is at Van Ness," I explain to Angela. "I just met with him yesterday. He's been under fire lately for doing some flaky deals, but now he has some hot offering in the works that he's convinced will make up for all his past screwups. But he never got a chance to tell me which company it was."

"And you think it's Hays Software," Angela says.

"It has to be. Albright said this new company was the deal of the century."

I stare at the papers in front of me.

"Would Albright kill to save the Hays deal?" I wonder out loud.

Angela laughs.

"You don't really think he would, do you? A banker?"

"I wouldn't put it past him," I reply seriously. "His career could go either way right now. If the Hays offering goes through, he's an investment god. But if it fails, he's finished."

"I don't know. It's hard to believe someone would commit murder just to hold on to his job."

"That's not all," I say, remembering more of yesterday's conversation. "Albright told me he found out about Hays Software through his dad. Now John Albright is a rich man. He could very well be the $5 million angel."

"So now you think his father murdered Hays?" she asks me.

"He might have. And maybe Leticia too."

"Leticia? I thought Hays did that."

"So did I, at first. But I've been thinking, and now I'm not so sure. Something Hays said to me: 'You're just as guilty of killing her as I am.' Maybe he was right."

"You're not responsible for what happened to Leticia," Angela vehemently asserts.

"Not directly," I reply. "And maybe Hays wasn't either. I don't think he ordered the hit."

"But he admitted it."

"He admitted killing Phillips," I say. "He never said he was responsible for Leticia, I just assumed he was. But he used a car to kill Phillips—pretty clumsy. Leticia, on the other hand, was killed by a pro, the same way Hays was. I'm willing to bet it was the same hit man, hired by the same person."

The more I think about it, the more it makes sense.

"Yeah, Hays killed Phillips and stole Cheetah," I continue, "but once he got to California, someone else started running the show."

Angela drums her fingers on the steering wheel, thinking.

"The question is, was it Albright Senior, or his son?" she asks.

"Or both."

Angela looks disgusted.

"A father-son venture. How nice," she says sarcastically. "We'd better hope that Dan can find a way to access the Van Ness database."

# CHAPTER THIRTY

When we pull in front of Dan's house, the driveway is empty.

"I don't see his car," Angela says.

"Let's check anyway, just in case."

"I'll do it," she volunteers. She gets out and jogs across the front yard, into the driveway and up the stairs to Dan's apartment. She rings the doorbell and knocks vigorously.

Finally she gives up and comes back to the car, looking disappointed. She walks up to the passenger side and crouches down to talk to me through the open window.

"He's not home," she tells me.

"I see that."

"Now what do we do? It could be hours until he gets back." She stands up and leans against the car, apparently resigned to a long wait.

Maybe she has the patience to stay here, but I don't.

"I'm not about to stick around and do nothing," I tell her, craning my head out the window so she can hear me. "It makes me feel like a sitting duck. Come on, get in the car. I have an idea."

Angela circles around to the driver's side and gets in.

"What's your plan?"

"The way I see it, Dan is probably surfing around here somewhere," I say. "Let's go find him."

Angela gives me a skeptical look.

"Isn't that like looking for a needle in a haystack? He could be anywhere."

"It beats waiting. Besides, I don't plan to search at random. We'll start with the surf shops on 41st. Maybe someone there knows how he likes to spend his Saturdays."

We drive along the coast, head east past the Boardwalk, then across town in the direction of the shops.

After a few miles, we turn on to 41st Avenue. It's buzzing with traffic. The sidewalks are full of pedestrians—tourists with cameras mixed in with locals on skateboards. I'm starting to wonder myself how much luck we'll have finding Dan in all of this.

"There's a surf shop over there," I say, pointing to the left. "Let's try it."

We turn at the next street, then make a left into a wide alley that runs behind the shop. There we squeeze into a small parking spot between a jeep and a pickup truck.

We enter through the shop's rear entrance and find ourselves in a cramped hallway filled with racks of wetsuits on one side and a row of surfboards on the other. Beyond the hall is an open area, where a couple of guys in swim trunks and T-shirts are standing behind some glass cases that surround a cash register. One of them is talking on the phone. We approach the other guy.

"We're looking for Dan Guerra, do you know him?" I ask.

"Sure do," he says, flipping his blond hair out of his eyes. "I saw him out at Steamer's Lane this morning."

"Do you know where he might be now?" Angela asks him.

The guy puts his hands in his pockets and looks pensive.

"He likes to eat lunch at Pollo Grande, down the street. You could try there. Or he might be Frisbee-golfing up at De Laveaga Park."

"Which way to Pollo Grande?" I ask.

"Go out the front door and make a left. You'll see it right away."

We walk rapidly up the street, past a thrift shop and a bookstore. Soon we come to a bright yellow stucco building with a huge sign that reads "Pollo Grande."

As we move toward the front entrance, we scan the people sitting at the small white tables outside the restaurant. No sign of Dan. We walk inside and go past a line of customers waiting to order. The place is packed with people, but Dan is nowhere to be seen.

"Let's try out back," Angela says. "There may be more seating on the patio."

We go out the back door and right away see Dan at a table in a far corner. He's eating a burrito and reading the newspaper. I lead the way over to his table.

"What happened to you?" he asks as soon as he sees me.

"It's complicated," I reply.

"We need your help again," Angela says urgently.

"Somehow, I'm not surprised," he replies.

Dan rolls the half-eaten burrito in its foil wrap and quickly downs the rest of his soft drink.

"Let's go."

The three of us walk briskly out of the restaurant.

"We'll meet you at your house in fifteen minutes," Angela says to Dan. "We know the way."

"Excellent. See you there."

By the time we pull into our familiar spot in front of the house, Dan has already parked his jeep in the driveway and gone inside.

We climb the stairs and enter through the open door, closing it behind us. Dan is in his office, booting up the workstation.

Angela walks to the other side of the office, moves a surfboard out of the way, and takes the chair it was leaning against. She pulls the chair over to Dan's desk and sits down next to him. I appropriate a nearby stool and join her.

"We wouldn't ask for your help again if it weren't an emergency," Angela says softly to Dan. "Steven is in big trouble."

Dan looks at me.

"What's happened now?"

"Someone tried to kill me last night. That's how I got this," I say, pointing to the bandage on my face.

"What! How?"

Angela jumps in and tells Dan my story. She describes the trip to Hays' office, our fight, Kamimoto's arrival, and the shooting at the building's entrance. I'm impressed by how many details she remembers. I must have been more coherent last night than I thought.

When Angela finishes talking, Dan shakes his head in disbelief.

"That's awful," he says. "Of course I'll do whatever I can. What's your plan?"

"Whoever killed Hays must have some involvement in his company," I say.

"That makes sense," he agrees.

"One of the angel investors put in $5 million, which is highly unusual," I continue. "He might be our killer. We need to find out his name."

"And how do we do that?"

"The lead underwriter for the Hays IPO has the latest prospectus, which by now should include the names of the angels," I say to him. "We need you to tap into their network."

"I can do that. Which bank is it?"

"Van Ness Securities."

"Van Ness?" Dan asks with concern.

"Right," Angela and I say at the same time.

He looks thoughtful.

"This should be a challenge."

"How so?" Angela asks.

Dan leans back in his chair and runs his hands through his abundant black hair.

"Remember how I used to work at NetGuard?" he asks her.

"The computer security firm. Yeah, I know. What about it?"

"A few months before I left, Van Ness hired NetGuard to do an analysis of its network security and to plug any holes that we found. It was a complete workup—intrusion tests, penetration analysis, that kind of stuff."

"But if you upgraded their network, then don't you know your way around it?" Angela asks him.

"I would, if I'd been the one doing the analysis, but I didn't work on that project. Diane Sumter did it, and believe me, she's good."

"Are you saying you can't crack their system?" I ask anxiously.

Dan laughs.

"I'm not worried about getting in," he says. "It's just going to take longer than usual. Like I said, Diane is good."

"So their system isn't perfect," I say, relaxing.

"Far from it," Dan replies. "Diane recommended that they air-wall their network, but they insisted on keeping their Internet links so it'd be easy to communicate with their clients. No matter how good their security is, if they're hooked up to the Net, I'll find a way to get in."

"Great!" Angela says, patting his arm. "So what are you going to do first?"

"I'll start by spoofing the system for an IP address with access to their network. That'll get me past their firewall."

I have no idea what Dan is talking about, but it doesn't matter.

"Go for it," I say.

Dan turns eagerly back to his keyboard. This may be risky, but I can tell that he loves the challenge of breaking into a system. In two minutes, he's forgotten about me, Angela and the rest of the world. He's completely absorbed by the task at hand.

Angela draws her chair up closer so that she can watch what he's doing.

"Will this take long?" she asks Dan.

"It depends on what Diane's done here. I've got some automated tools I usually use for this, but I'm sure I'll have to tweak them to get past her defenses."

Angela nods her head and falls silent, letting Dan concentrate on his work. I stand up and go to the living room to take my usual place on the sofa. It feels good to stretch out. I look for the corner spider web I've grown so accustomed to seeing, but it's gone. Dan must have done some housecleaning recently.

I roll over and do my best to unwind, but I can't push the events of the past twenty-four hours out of my mind. Whenever I close my eyes, all I see is Hays dropping before me, Michelle and Chloe waving goodbye, and Angela . . .

"We're in!" I hear Angela yell. "Steven, come here, Dan just got into the Van Ness network."

I rub my eyes wearily, glad for once to have someone interrupt my thoughts. Then I get up and return to Dan's office.

"Congratulations," I say to him as I sit down. "So now can we start searching for the information we need?"

"No, it's not that easy. We're in, but we don't have access to a whole lot."

"Oh," I say, disappointed. "What happens now?"

"Now I use a sniffer program to gather user names and passwords. What we're looking for is the master password of the network administrator. That will give us access to the entire system and all its files."

"Wait a minute," Angela says, looking worried. "I've heard of sniffer programs. Don't you have to wait for someone to log on before you can capture their password?"

"Right," he tells her, not understanding her concern.

"But today is Saturday. No one's at work."

Dan smiles at her naiveté.

"Every network administrator I know puts in at least a few hours on the weekend," he says. "In fact, I'm not at all worried about when he'll get on. I'm worried about when he'll get off. It's too risky to pretend to be him while he's on the system, and if he works all weekend, we might be stuck."

"You mean it could take us *days* to get access to the files we need?" I ask him.

"It's possible," he says casually.

"I don't have that kind of time," I say heatedly. "I have someone looking for me, trying to put a bullet in my head."

I stand up and glare down at him. All the fear and rage I've been keeping down for the past two days is about to come out, like a boiling pot getting ready to explode.

"This isn't just some game!" I yell at him. "This is for real. My life is at stake!"

Dan stares back at me, stunned and angry.

"Hey, I'm doing the best I can! If you think you can do better, feel free to try."

"We don't want anyone else," Angela says to Dan, getting up. "You're the best hacker I know. If anyone can get us those files, you can."

Angela looks at me reprovingly.

"Let's go into the living room, Steven."

She walks over and puts her arm around me. I shake it off, but I do walk with her out of the office, only because I know that if I stay I'll probably take a swing at Dan.

"Why don't you have a seat?" she says to me.

"I don't want to sit down."

"What do you want?" she asks, clearly aggravated.

"You know what I want?" I say bitterly. "I want to hit someone. No, better yet, I want to kill someone. I want to choke the life out of whoever is out there, trying to hunt me down."

Angela crosses her arms.

"And since you can't get hold of your enemy, you take it out on Dan instead."

"Don't lecture me."

We stand there, scowling at each other in silence.

"You're not in this alone, you know," she says to me finally, her expression softening as she speaks. "If you don't know by now that you can count on me, well . . . And Dan, he's over there, putting himself on the line for you."

"You know why he's helping," I respond harshly.

"That's beside the point," she retorts. "It doesn't make what he's doing any less noble, and you know that."

"Yeah, I do," I concede. Suddenly I'm tired again, and in no mood to argue. I take a seat on the sofa, and gaze for a moment at Dan's office. Then I turn my eyes to the beautiful young woman in front of me.

"He's a good man, Angela."

Her response is immediate.

"Don't," she says sharply. "Don't do that."

"Don't what?"

"Look," she says, coming closer. "I can accept how our relationship is, how it has to be. But don't insult me by offering me some . . . some damn consolation prize. I don't want it."

The force of Angela's reaction catches me off guard.

"I just want you to be happy," I tell her truthfully.

Angela sighs and joins me on the couch.

"I know," she says to me. "Just let me figure it out myself, okay?"

"Excuse me," someone says.

I look in the direction of the voice and see Dan standing at the threshold of the living room. I wonder how much of our conversation he heard.

"I've been monitoring the Van Ness system," he continues. "Only one person logged on, and it turned out to be a pretty low-level password. I don't think it would get you the files you want."

"What do you recommend we do?" I ask solicitously. I regret the way I took out my anger on Dan just a few minutes ago.

"It's about time for dinner," he says. "You guys might want to go grab a bite to eat."

"Why don't we all go?" I say. "You don't need to be here for your computer to pick up the passwords, do you?"

"No, it's an automatic procedure."

He hesitates, not sure whether to accept my olive branch.

"Come with us, Dan," Angela says, entreating him. "I think we all need to stick together."

He looks at Angela, and I can tell by his face what his answer will be.

"Dinner sounds good," he says. "There's a great little Chinese place within walking distance. I'd go there."

"Then it's decided," I say. "It'll be my treat."

# CHAPTER THIRTY-ONE

When Dan called the restaurant we were going to "a little place," he wasn't exaggerating. The Plum Tree is about thirty feet deep, and about as wide as my college dorm room. A few tables run along the right wall, but it seems most people take their food to go; there's a steady stream of customers coming by to pick up neatly wrapped boxes of dinner.

An attractive young woman with an armful of menus comes up to us. She's wearing a T-shirt from UC Santa Cruz, complete with a picture of the school mascot—a banana slug.

"Hi Dan," she says warmly, setting the menus down next to the cash register.

I figured Dan was probably a regular here. Good food at a cheap price, and close to home. What more could any hacker want?

"Hi Mei Mei," Dan says to the waitress. "How does it look tonight? Do you have anything open?"

"There's a couple of tables getting ready to turn. It shouldn't be more than five minutes," she replies before leaving to take an order.

Near the cash register is an aquarium with some tropical fish in it. I watch a big fish, striped with bright yellow and black ribbons, dart into a sunken castle at the bottom of the tank. I wait for him to come out, but he seems content to stay in his sanctuary.

I look up and see Mei Mei heading towards us.

"Right this way," she says.

We follow her to a table next to the back wall. The table is made of metal and fake wood, and the chairs remind me of my parents' dinette set when I was a kid. It takes a bit of maneuvering, but we manage to squeeze into the limited spaces allotted us. Instinctively, I sit on the side facing the door, with my back to the wall. Dan and Angela take their seats opposite me.

"What's good here?" she asks him.

"Everything," he replies. "They don't have a lot to choose from, but it's all top-notch."

"Then why don't you order for the three of us," I say. I don't care what I eat.

"Sure, why not?" Angela echoes my sentiments. "As long as we get mushu chicken. I love mushu chicken."

Dan signals to Mei Mei, and when she comes by, he rattles off his requests without even looking at a menu.

"I have something for you," Mei Mei says to Dan as she takes our menus from him. She reaches into her pants pocket and pulls out a piece of paper. But before she hands it to Dan, she glances around the restaurant to make sure no one is watching.

Dan takes the paper from his friend and unfolds it.

"I can't believe you got this," he says, obviously pleased. "I thought you said your Mom never writes down her recipes."

"She doesn't," Mei Mei tells him. "I watched her make it the other day, and wrote down what I saw."

Dan skims the paper.

"Tabasco sauce?" he asks. "That's hardly traditional for sweet and sour pork, is it?"

"Mom likes to experiment," Mei Mei says.

"No wonder I could never get it to come out the same," he says as he slips the paper into his pocket. "Thanks for the recipe. I'll have to try it out soon."

"Let me know when you do," Mei Mei replies. "I'll want to taste it. Oh, and whatever you do, don't tell anyone where you got that recipe. If my Mom finds out I gave away one of her culinary secrets, I'll never hear the end of it."

"I promise to keep my mouth shut," Dan assures her. Mei Mei smiles at him affectionately and hurries off to seat another customer.

Meanwhile, Angela has been watching the interchange between Dan and Mei Mei with amused curiosity.

"I didn't know you could cook," she says to Dan once Mei Mei has left.

"There's a lot about me you don't know," he answers. He draws his words out slowly, as if he were extending an invitation, or a challenge, perhaps.

"I guess we've both changed a lot since the old neighborhood," Angela says contemplatively, as if the notion has just occurred to her.

"Yeah, you're not the same kid who locked herself in the trunk of my car and had to be rescued," Dan says teasingly.

"Hey, if you and Rafa had just agreed to take me to the movies with you, I wouldn't have been forced to try and sneak in."

This leads to a discussion of childhood pranks and mishaps, interrupted only by the arrival of our food. We must all be equally famished, because all conversation is suspended for fully ten minutes while we dig in to the feast before us. Dan was right about one thing, the food here is delicious.

A half hour later, I'm feeling better. With a full stomach and a couple of imported beers, I begin to relax a bit. I look around the restaurant at nothing in particular, and think of Michelle and Chloe. Dan and Angela have resumed their trip down memory lane, and are lost in each other's company.

A teenage waiter with a streak of purple in his close-cropped black hair deposits the bill on our table and rushes away.

"Don't you think it's about time we got back to check the sniffer program?" I say to Dan.

He looks at his skin diver's watch, which glows a faint green in the darkened restaurant.

"Yeah, I guess we've been here for awhile. Maybe our friend has been online by now."

"Let's check our fortunes first," Angela says, passing out the cookies that came with the check.

We each open a fortune cookie and pull out the small slip of paper. I crumple mine up and drop it on my plate as soon as I've read it: "A new romance is about to begin in your life."

"So Dan, what does yours say?" Angela asks.

"It says, 'You are rich with friends,'" he replies. "What about yours?"

"'A wise man knows his own ignorance,'" she answers. "I rather like that one. What's your fortune, Steven?"

"Nothing interesting."

"Oh, come on," she says playfully, swiping the paper from my plate before I can stop her. But as soon as she reads the fortune, her smile vanishes and her cheeks turn a dark red.

"What's it say?" Dan asks her.

"Nothing," she says hurriedly. "We'd better get back to your computer."

Dan gives me a questioning look, but I pretend not to notice. Instead, I pull out my wallet and lay down a credit card.

The walk back is anything but leisurely. The streets of Santa Cruz are filled with Saturday night revelers, mostly college students, with a few older tourists thrown in. We have to dodge and weave through the crowded sidewalks to make our way back to Dan's duplex.

As we approach the stairs in front of Dan's place, I feel a rush of anticipation.

We burst through the front door, all of us curious to know if we've caught our fish. Dan goes straight to his computer terminal. A click of the mouse activates the screen and he's able to read his network log.

"The sniffer has captured something," he announces. "Let's see what we've got."

Dan studies the captured data intently.

"Hmm, there's been a lot of activity for a Saturday evening. Mostly people connecting remotely."

"Any sign of the master password?" I ask.

Dan continues checking his data. After a couple of minutes he gives a low whistle.

"The gods must be with us tonight," he says triumphantly. "Here it is."

"Yes!" I say excitedly. I may get out of this alive after all. "Now let's see what it gets us."

Dan types a couple of commands, and then gets a prompt. He enters the password.

"We're in. And I don't see any sign of the system administrator." Dan looks at me and Angela. "So, where do you want to go today?"

"We need to look for a file on private companies that are about to go public, or maybe even a file specifically on Hays Software," I tell him.

"Let me try a search for Hays Software."

Dan's fingers fly across the keyboard.

"Bingo!" he says. "And now we need to look for a stock prospectus, right?"

"Yeah," I say. "They might call it a red herring."

Dan scrolls through a list of file names.

"Let's try this one," he says, picking a file and bringing it up on the screen. "Is this what you need?"

I scan the document quickly. It's the Hays prospectus alright, and it looks like it was updated just this past Thursday. Most of the informational gaps have been filled in, suggesting that Van Ness was getting ready to announce the stock sale very soon, perhaps even this coming week. Of course, now that Arthur Hays is dead, the sale will be postponed for awhile.

"This is exactly what I need," I say, elated.

Two hours ago I wanted to punch Dan. Now I'm so happy I could kiss the guy. Instead I slap him on the back. Dan shrugs, as if the whole process has been child's play.

"Let's do a word search for 'angel' and see if it turns up our silent investor," I say to him.

Angela and I peer over Dan's shoulders as he does the search. It speeds by, and soon we're at the heart of the prospectus, which lists the primary investors, along with the amounts they've put in.

"Here's Angel One," Dan says, pointing to the screen.

"I see it," Angela replies. "There's the amount—$50K—and here's the name."

She slides a finger across the screen, then looks at me with a surprised expression.

"John Albright," I say slowly.

"You sound disappointed," Dan says to me.

"Not exactly," I reply. "But I was sure that Albright had put in the $5 million. $50,000 isn't that much money to a guy like him. Not enough to kill for."

"If it's not Albright, then who's the $5 million man?" Angela asks, turning her attention back to the screen. "Who's Angel Two?"

Dan continues scrolling the document.

"Stop, stop," I say. "This is it."

"Oh, my God," Angela says, reading over Dan's shoulder. "Angel Two is . . ."

" . . . Marcus Turner," I say, just as stunned as Angela.

I stand up and walk away from the computer, trying to absorb what we've just learned. Angela goes over to the window, opens it, and breathes deeply of the sea air. Meanwhile, Dan starts printing out the prospectus. He looks over each sheet of paper as it comes off the printer, as if to confirm that the hard copy says the same thing as his computer screen.

After a few moments, Angela turns away from the window and is the first to speak.

"This means that Marcus Turner is responsible for one, maybe two, murders."

"We've got to let Kamimoto know right away," I say abruptly.

I walk over to Dan's desk and pick up the phone. I've dialed the area code and the prefix when the line suddenly goes dead. I fiddle with the phone, trying to get a dial tone, but without success.

"Hey, your phone's dead," I say to Dan.

He looks up from his stack of papers.

"It happens sometimes. Try again in a couple of minutes."

"I don't like this," Angela says nervously.

"I don't either," I reply. "Do you have your cell phone with you?"

She shakes her head.

"I forgot it."

I head to the kitchen, planning to try the other phone. All of a sudden, however, I hear the light sound of footsteps on the stairs.

"Are you expecting anyone?" I ask Dan.

"No, no one."

"Lock the door!" I yell.

Angela springs to the door, banging loudly against it. She hit it hard, but seems unfazed by the blow. She's reaching for the deadbolt when the door is suddenly pushed open with such force that she ends up pinned against the wall. A nondescript man in sports jacket and dark trousers appears in the open doorway. He's holding a gun, and he looks familiar.

The man closes the door halfway, and then grabs Angela by the arm and pushes her back into the office, where she takes refuge against the wall. Then he motions at Dan with his gun, indicating he should move away from his computer. Dan complies, makes his way over to Angela, and puts his arm protectively around her waist.

"You," he says to me. "Over next to your friends."

I walk slowly over to Angela and Dan, never taking my eyes from the weapon.

The gunman opens the door wider.

"It's all clear," he yells into the darkness.

Once again, there's the sound of footsteps on the stairs. Then the door opens all the way, and in walks Marcus Turner himself.

I clench my fists involuntarily. Angela gasps, and Turner looks over at her.

"I guess you know then," he says placidly as he closes the door behind him.

None of us says anything. For twenty seconds, the room is in complete silence. I stare at the revolver. I don't know much about guns, but I think I recognize a silencer on the end of this one.

"Come, come," Turner says at last. "There's no use denying it. I can tell by the look on your faces. You know I killed Hays."

# Chapter Thirty-two

Turner adjusts the cuffs on his shirt. He's wearing one of his trademark Italian suits, impeccably pressed. He walks over to the computer desk, unbuttons his jacket nonchalantly, and sits downs in Dan's chair.

"Although to be absolutely accurate," he continues, "I didn't kill Hays. Roger did."

Turner nods at the dull-looking man with the gun, and then adds, "He would have killed you too, Cavanaugh, if Detective Kamimoto had been just a bit slower."

Turner yawns, and politely raises his hand to cover his mouth.

"But these things happen," he says. "No matter, it's nothing that can't be fixed."

Angela and I exchange glances. I can see the fear in her eyes. I glare at Turner, then look over at the man he calls Roger. Suddenly it clicks. I know where I've seen Turner's henchman before—in the parking lot outside my office last week. He was the goon who took so much pleasure in kicking my guts. I bet he was also driving the car that chased us through San Jose the other day. Roger looks back at me and gives me a sick smile. He can't wait to kill us.

I turn my attention back to Turner.

"As long as you intend to kill me," I say to him, "I'd at least like to get some answers first."

Turner raises an eyebrow aristocratically, studying me.

"You're a reasonably intelligent man, Cavanaugh. I suppose I owe you that much. It's the intellectual equivalent of a last meal."

"Humph," grunts Roger. He's clearly disappointed by the delay. Turner glances at him, but says nothing.

"Have a seat. I insist," Turner says to me. He looks at Angela and smiles. "And we mustn't leave the lady standing," he adds, gesturing to a chair.

With Turner sitting down, there are only two seats free. Dan leans up against the wall, next to the surfboard. As Angela and I settle cautiously into our chairs, Turner swivels around and studies the computer screen.

"How clever!" he exclaims, turning back around to face us. "So that's how you tracked me down. You just looked to see who had the most invested in Hays Software, and figured that must be the killer. It's a bit of a stretch, but in this case, you happen to be right. I knew you were smart." He pauses. "It's kind of ironic, isn't it?"

I decide to play along.

"What is?"

"If you were stupid, you'd stay alive. Rather contradicts Darwin's theory, doesn't it?"

Turner must find the thought highly amusing, because it elicits a wry chuckle from him. I hate his sense of humor.

"But I digress," he says, looking serious once again. "I promised to answer your questions. Go ahead."

"Why Leticia?"

"You mean why kill her?"

I nod.

"It wasn't my plan originally," Turner says. "All I wanted at first was for Roger here to scare her into telling us where she'd put the documents she'd copied. But then Roger rightly pointed out that as long as Leticia was alive, Hays' little secret was vulnerable to exposure, and I couldn't have that."

I look over at Roger. His face is expressionless, but somehow I have no doubt that he enjoyed killing Leticia. It's hard to decide who I hate more.

"Anything else?" Turner says. "I'm in a bit of a hurry. I have an important meeting in New York tomorrow morning."

"Why kill Hays?" I ask him. I already know the reason, but I need time to find a way to get us out of here alive.

"Isn't it obvious?" Turner answers haughtily. "He was starting to crack from the pressure. Surely you must have noticed. It got to where I couldn't trust him to keep his mouth shut." Turner's expression is one of supreme annoyance. "And you," he continues, spitting out the words, "you've been a thorn in my side for far too long. So when Hays called me yesterday to tell me he'd been stupid enough to set up a meeting with you, I saw a golden opportunity to eliminate you both."

"How efficient," I reply sardonically.

"Isn't it, though?" the VC replies.

Dan has his hands in his pockets, and looks contemplative despite the situation.

"I don't get it," he says.

"What don't you understand, young man?" Turner says, sounding almost benevolent.

"How can you run Hays Software without Arthur Hays?" he asks. "It's his company."

Turner laughs.

"You programmers don't know anything about business, do you?" he says condescendingly. He crosses his arms and prepares to lecture. "Like all successful venture capital firms, Grimshaw Turner has a system set up to cultivate CEOs for our startups."

"The executive-in-residence program," I add dryly.

"Right you are, Cavanaugh," Turner says. "We know that most technical geniuses aren't any good at running the companies they found, so we maintain a pool of executive replacements. That way, whenever we need a new CEO, we have several candidates to choose from."

Turner examines his manicured nails before continuing.

"Arthur Hays was just one more entrepreneur who had to be replaced, that's all."

"You won't get away with it," Angela says bravely. "The police have Leticia's documents."

"But they won't have them for long," Turner replies. "It's costing me a bundle, but I've already arranged for those papers to disappear."

Turner smiles at me.

"You see, I know about your involvement with the police. I've been keeping tabs on you since Jason Grimshaw's party."

"Is that when you decided to bug my phone?"

The smile on Turner's face vanishes.

"You know about that?" he replies, caught off guard for once. "That would explain the exceedingly boring conversations I've been privy to this past week. I knew I should have sent Roger back to finish wiring your office. But I didn't want to risk it. Unfortunately, Roger is not as skilled in surveillance as he is in assassination."

Roger snorts from his corner of the room, but makes no other response to the insult.

"That's not the only mistake you made," I say. "The police recorded my conversation with Hays. They know all about Cheetah."

"You're lying," Turner says simply.

"No he's not," Angela says defiantly. "Why do you think the police were there last night?"

Turner gives us an appraising look.

"It doesn't matter," he says finally. "I can make the tape disappear as well."

He uncrosses his legs and shifts in his seat.

"That means the only loose ends left are you three."

Turner's last remark is followed by a deathly silence. I've calculated the distance to every exit in the house, and decided that the front door is probably our best way out. But I don't see how we can get out without at least one of us getting shot.

"Three people dead already, and you're planning to kill another three," I say, once again stalling for time. "What could possibly be worth that?"

Turner gives me a look of utter contempt.

"You could never understand," he sneers at me. "Your kind just doesn't get it. You're content to make your small respectable salary and wield the very limited power of the press. That's not enough for me."

Turner stands up so he can look down on us.

"You've seen Cheetah," he continues. "You know what a breakthrough it is. I've been waiting years to back a product like this. Not just for the money I'll make, and I'll make billions, but for the sheer power of owning the biggest piece of the biggest pie."

He puts his hands on his hips, and stares off into space. "I'm going to make Bill Gates look like the corner grocer."

Angela, Dan, and I stare at Turner. He's standing there in front of us, posing like a statue, and feeling completely justified in what he's about to do. He's crazy. It's a calm, cold, measured dementia, but he's insane nonetheless.

"In any case, I hope that answers all your questions," he says, returning to the present. "Because I need to get going. My jet's warming up at SFO."

He walks to the door and opens it.

"Are you sure you can handle this alone?" he asks Roger. "I can't have you screwing up again."

"It'll be easy, but stick around and watch if you want to make sure I do it right," Roger says gruffly.

Turner gets a disgusted look on his face. He may have no problem ordering our deaths, but he doesn't want to see them.

"Just come down when it's over."

Turner exits, closing the door behind him.

Roger moves closer to us, and I can see his hand tighten on the gun. I tense up, and get ready to spring. I'm not going down without a fight.

Suddenly I see a white blur to my left, and then hear a muffled shot. The force of the blast throws Dan against the wall, still clutching the surfboard he used to hit Roger.

"No!" Angela screams. She bolts towards Dan, who's now collapsed on the floor, bleeding from a chest wound. But I lunge forward at the same time and grab her by the waist. Dan's blow knocked Roger down, but the hit man still has hold of the gun. I can see Roger struggling to hoist himself up from the floor.

I hold Angela tightly and drag her to the door.

"Let me go!" she yells.

"You'll be killed."

As if to punctuate my words, a bullet whizzes past and lodges in the wall behind us. I open the door and practically push Angela down the stairs. We stumble down to the bottom. She hesitates one last time, and then springs forward with me. We pass a white Lamborghini parked in the driveway, and I hear a stream of profanity issuing from inside it. Turner has been disappointed by Roger once again.

I hear footsteps coming down the stairs. There's no time to waste; we have to get out of here. At the end of the walkway we make a hard left on to the main sidewalk and pick up the pace. Angela doesn't need to be encouraged now. She's pumping hard, and together we race down the block at top speed. But I can feel my left knee starting to twitch. I don't know how long I'll be able to keep up this pace, and I don't want to slow down Angela.

We sprint for another hundred yards and then stop at an intersection.

"We'd better split up," I say. "It'll be harder for them to keep up with us if we go in different directions."

"But . . ."

"Just trust me," I say. "There's no time to lose. Now go."

Angela wavers momentarily, then nods grimly and pivots to the left. She takes off like a shot, and disappears into the nighttime shadows. I look in the opposite direction. The street is better lit than I'd like, but it still has enough shadows, trees, and bushes for me to make my way without being in the open the whole time. I start running as hard as I can, trying to avoid the streetlights and keep hidden in the darkness.

As I run along the sidewalk in front of a long row of houses, I see what looks like a boardinghouse up ahead. There's an alley between it and the house next to it. I need to get away from the main street, so I head for this narrow road, hoping it will lead me to another street where Turner and his goon are less likely to look for me.

I make a sharp right into the alley and run past the boardinghouse, underneath a string of darkened windows. The gravel crunches under my feet as I run. After about twenty yards, I hear quick footsteps behind me. They're getting closer—it must be Roger. Despite the growing pain in my knee, I quicken my pace. But the footsteps are relentless, and sounding nearer all the time. Just then I come to a dead end. Damn! There's a high adobe wall blocking my way. But instead of slowing down, I sprint even harder. If I can build up enough momentum, I might be able to boost myself up and over.

"Stop!" someone yells at me threateningly. I race even faster, adrenaline pumping.

I approach the wall at full speed and jump up to grab the top ledge with both hands. I pull myself up, and feel my feet leave the earth.

I'm just about to swing my legs over the wall when someone grabs me by the ankles and pulls hard. I lose my grip and fall backwards to the ground, knocking my pursuer down in the process. Recovering my balance quickly, I stand up and peer into the darkness. I can see the shadowy figure of a man getting to his feet.

"Alright you bastard, that's it!" I say as I swing at him with a roundhouse right hook. My fist finds his face; his head snaps back and he drops to the ground. I can tell by the feel of the blow that I've probably broken his nose. I pounce on him, and try to wrestle away his gun.

"Wait, wait," the man shouts.

The voice doesn't belong to Roger or his boss. But it is familiar.

I stop trying to beat the guy up and look at him more closely. It's Inspector Morrison!

I scramble to my feet, and offer Morrison a hand. He takes it, but gives me a dirty look just the same. I don't blame him; it looks like I really banged him up. Blood is streaming from his nose on to his black turtleneck, and he has a bruise over one eye.

Morrison pulls out a handkerchief and holds it up to his nose in an effort to stop the bleeding.

"It's better if you lie down to do that," I tell him.

"Thanks so much for your help," he says sarcastically through his handkerchief, sounding as if he had nothing but a common cold.

"Sorry about hitting you, but I thought you were Turner's gunman. What are you doing here?"

"We've been tracking you since Hays got shot. After you went by your house today, we saw someone else following you. So we started tailing him, and ended up here in Santa Cruz with the rest of you. Unfortunately, we didn't count on that other guy showing up. They got into your friend's house before we had a chance to intercept them."

"So you were just going to hang around and let them kill us?" I ask angrily.

"Of course not." Morrison looks insulted. "We were working our way in through the back of the house when you and Angela bolted. Kamimoto sent me after you, and the rest of the team took control of the situation."

"So where's Turner now?" I ask. "The guy in the suit."

"He should be under arrest. I'm sure we got his flunky too."

"And Dan Guerra?"

"I don't know about him," the inspector says.

Morrison starts walking back down the alley, still pinching his nose with his handkerchief. I go with him.

"There should be a squad car waiting for us on the street. They weren't far behind when I followed you in here," Morrison informs me.

As we pass the boardinghouse, a light flickers on in one of the rooms and shines out into the alleyway, illuminating Morrison's face. I can't help but feel sorry for him—he looks pretty forlorn.

When we get to the street I see a young cop standing next to a police car parked under a tree. The officer gapes at Morrison when he sees him, but doesn't say anything. He must know better.

"Get us back to the scene, Kingston," Morrison says to the officer as he climbs into the passenger seat up front. I get in the back seat, and Kingston starts the car. Soon we're driving the quiet streets back to Dan's house.

We haven't even gone two blocks when the police radio in the car squawks to life. It seems to be a general call to all cars in the area. I can't make out a whole lot through the static, but the announcer clearly says something about a "suspect last seen going north on Olive Street."

A suspect. I wonder if it's Turner, or Roger. Apparently, Morrison was wrong to assume that everything was under control back at Dan's house.

"Olive Street, where's that from here, do you know?" Morrison asks Kingston.

"I think it's just a block or two ahead."

"Then get us there," Morrison says, still holding his nose.

Morrison picks up the microphone and announces that we're headed to the suspect's last reported location. We arrive at Olive Street, and Kingston turns right. Morrison orders him to slow down. We cruise slowly up the street, peering at every shadow.

Suddenly, I glimpse a figure moving out of the darkness just a block ahead. It quickly turns a corner and disappears.

"Hey!" I shout.

"I see him. Take a right up here," Morrison orders Kingston.

When we turn the corner, the street looks deserted. Not far up the street, however, one of the darkened restaurants has a door hanging open.

"There, over there," Morrison says. He grabs the microphone, declares his intention to enter the restaurant, and requests backup.

Kingston parks down the block from the restaurant. It's a large two-story place, set back several yards from the street. From where I sit, all I can make out is the facade—it looks like a converted house.

"Okay," Morrison says, "You take the front, and I'll go around the back. Give me a two-minute head start before you go in."

"But sir," Officer Kingston protests, "Shouldn't we wait for backup?"

"There's no time," Morrison replies, opening the door, "I'm not about to let him slip out the back way."

Morrison gets out of the car, and soon disappears behind the building.

"Is there anything I can do to help?" I ask from the back seat.

"Yeah, stay put," Kingston replies. He gets out of the vehicle, crouches down, and makes his way quickly to the front of the restaurant. He looks around a couple of times, and then goes in through the front door. Soon I can see the flicker of a flashlight as Kingston begins his search.

I sit in the squad car, feeling restless. My mind is racing. I wonder where their backup is, if the suspect is armed, and especially, who the hell the suspect is.

All of a sudden I'm jolted by the sound of gunfire coming from the restaurant. I instinctively drop to the floor of the car. I stay crouched for a moment, my heart pounding. Slowly, I bring my head up just high enough to look out the window. It's pitch black in the restaurant; Kingston's flashlight seems to have disappeared.

I'm still staring out the window when the restaurant door swings open wider, and I see Officer Kingston stumble out. He barely makes it through the door before falling against the building.

I open the car door and listen intently. The street is completely quiet. Hopefully, the gunman has gone back into hiding.

I get out of the car and run quickly to where Kingston is slumped against the wall. He looks worse close up. His face is pale and his arm is bleeding profusely from a bullet wound.

"He came out of nowhere," Kingston says, wincing in pain. "Some short guy."

It must be Roger.

"We've got to get you back to the car," I say to Kingston.

"No, it's too dangerous out in the open."

"It's more dangerous here. You're a sitting duck."

I lean Kingston forward and grab him from behind under the arms. Then I stand up and pull with all my might. Kingston is not a small man, so it takes a while to make it to the street. For ten agonizing seconds, I brace myself for the impact of a bullet. But today I'm lucky; I make it to the squad car in one piece.

I lay Kingston on the back seat. Then I roll up his jacket and place it under his head. That's when I notice that Kingston still has his gun. He's clenching it in his right hand.

I pry the gun from his grasp.

"What are you doing with that?" Kingston says, trying to lift his head.

"I'm not sure yet."

I put my hand around the handle of the gun. It feels heavier than I thought it would, and instead of being cool to the touch, it's still warm from Kingston's viselike grip.

"Stay here," I say as I back out of the car.

"What are you doing?!" he whispers hoarsely. "You can't go in there."

"Feel free to report me," I reply as I close the car door.

I crouch low and race across the lawn to the front door. I pause at the entrance and then step noiselessly over the threshold. Soon I'm moving cautiously down a hallway. It's dark in here, but not as dark as I expected. The full moon shining through the windows gives me enough light to make out large objects fairly easily.

I come to a staircase and stop to listen. The building is completely silent. I decide to press on. I pass a couple of small dining rooms, and investigate each one to make sure there's no one hiding in there. I'm ready to make my way to the kitchen when I hear a creak above me. I freeze, and listen closely. A couple of seconds later, there's another creak. Someone is upstairs. I backtrack to the stairs and begin climbing them as quietly as I can. Halfway up, I step on a stair that squeaks loudly. I stop and stand motionless, straining to hear in the darkness. Nothing.

I'm just beginning to relax when suddenly there's a loud commotion ahead of me. I hear a gun go off, and the voices of two men shouting. I race up the rest of the stairs and into a narrow hallway.

Now I hear loud crashing noises, and more yelling. I run down the hallway and into a large office. There in front of me, I see Morrison and Roger engaged in hand to hand combat. Roger has a gun and is trying to use it, but Morrison has hold of his wrist and is keeping the gun pointed up in the air. The two men move back and forth across the room as they take turns shoving each other in an effort to gain control. For now, Morrison is holding his own, but thanks to me he was already injured when he came into this fight. How long can he last?

I tighten my grip on the gun in my hand, and make a decision. I raise the weapon, ready to shoot. I point it at Roger, but he immediately moves from my line of sight and is replaced by Morrison. That's when I realize they're too close to each other; there's no way I can fire.

Just then Roger manages to free his other hand from Morrison's grip. He punches the inspector deep in the stomach. Morrison doubles over, and Roger pushes him roughly into a desk. Morrison hits the desk, bounces off and lands on the floor. He's not moving.

Roger doesn't see me standing in the doorway. He's too busy laughing, thrilled by the opportunity to kill someone else. I point my gun at him and pull the trigger. The shot echoes loudly in the room. I stare at Roger, expecting him to drop. But my aim was off, and the bullet just misses him.

He immediately whirls toward me and fires. I dive for the floor as the bullets fly over me. On the way down, my hand hits the corner of a table and I lose my grip on the gun. It skids across the floor and into the shadows.

I roll into a corner of the room away from the windows and take refuge in the dark. I've managed to save my skin, but I've lost my gun in the process. I watch Roger stoop down and feel around for my lost weapon, all the while looking about the room for me. He doesn't find the gun.

Roger stands up and takes a couple of steps.

"Come out, come out, wherever you are," he says mockingly. He takes a random shot in my direction, but misses me by several feet.

I peer out of the darkness, and I can tell by the look on Roger's face that he can't see me. Next to me is a metal waste basket. I put my hand on it, and wait for my chance.

Roger moves slowly towards my corner. He's got both hands on his gun, ready to shoot, and he's squinting his eyes, trying to see me.

Just a little closer, I think to myself.

Finally, Roger gets near enough for me to risk it. I grab the waste basket off the floor as I rise up. Roger hears the sound and turns to fire just as I swing the trash can straight into his face.

He staggers back and falls heavily against the desk. The force of the impact sends the gun flying out of his hand. I leap to retrieve it, and am about to pick it up when I'm pushed to the ground by a strong blow. I look up to see Roger reaching for the gun and manage to use my legs to trip him. He goes down, kicking the revolver farther away in the process. I flip over and scurry on my belly towards the weapon. A hand grabs my leg, but I kick hard into a soft face, and the hand releases.

I seize the gun and stand up.

"Don't move," I shout hoarsely, pointing the gun at him.

Roger stares up at me, blood trickling from a cut over his eye. There's a blank expression on his face.

"Okay, okay," he says. "Just don't shoot."

"Why shouldn't I?" I ask, taking a step closer. My breath is coming in heavy gasps. "Give me one good reason why I shouldn't kill you."

Roger doesn't say anything. He just looks at me. My hand tightens on the gun. It would be so easy. Just pull the trigger, and I can finally nail the bastard who murdered my friend, and tried to kill me.

I take another step towards him. Roger continues to gaze at me, emotionless.

"You know," I say. "I can't think of any reason not to shoot you."

"I can," comes a voice from the doorway.

I glance to my right in time to see Kamimoto step into the moonlight.

"Put down the gun, Steven," he says quietly.

"No," I say. "I finally have him right where I want him."

"Yes, you do," Kamimoto says. "So what are you going to do about it?"

"I should execute him. He doesn't deserve to live."

The inspector walks slowly towards me.

"It's not your job to decide that," he says.

"I don't care. You know what he did. Why shouldn't I kill him?"

Kamimoto is just a couple of feet from me now.

"Because you're not like him," he says, putting his hand on my shoulder.

He reaches for the gun in my hand, and I let him take it.

# Chapter Thirty-three

The street in front of Dan's house is lit up like a Christmas tree. It looks like a replay of the scene outside of Hays Software—was it just a day and a half ago? It seems like I've lived a lifetime since then.

I step out of the police car and survey the activity all around me. The commotion has brought the neighbors on to their porches, front lawns, and even into the street to see what's happening. I see officers instructing them to go back to their homes. A policeman is interviewing Dan's landlady, and officers and other official-looking people are traipsing up and down the stairs to Dan's apartment. A medic closes the door to an ambulance, and jumps into the passenger seat. It pulls away from the curb, lights flashing. Dan must be in there. I hope he's okay.

Kamimoto has gotten out of the car as well, and is standing next to me, getting an update from one of the officers.

"How's Dan?" I ask anxiously, interrupting their conversation.

"He's going to be fine. The bullet didn't hit any vital organs," Kamimoto says good-naturedly. He dismisses the officer with a nod, and then continues. "That little stunt he pulled with his surfboard probably saved your lives. Fortunately for him, Roger was so desperate to get at you that he didn't check to see whether your friend was dead or alive."

We walk slowly down the street together.

"So what happens now?" I ask.

"We'll get Roger to cop a plea and finger his employer; that will give us a case against Turner."

Kamimoto looks directly at me.

"Good thing Roger didn't get killed back there. Without him to testify, I doubt we'd ever nail Turner."

I let his remark pass without a reply.

We've come up alongside a police car. Marcus Turner is in the back seat, handcuffed. The window is down and he's glaring at us.

"Detective, get me my lawyer, now!" Turner demands.

"It's 'Inspector,'" Kamimoto replies. "And I'm not your secretary. You can call your lawyer from the station."

The look on Turner's face gets even nastier. He's about to shout something else when the squad car he's in pulls away from the curb with a jerk, and Turner is thrown against the back of the seat.

I watch the car drive away and feel a profound sense of relief. This time it's really over.

Kamimoto has pulled a stick of gum from his coat pocket, which he unwraps and pops in his mouth. He seems very relaxed, and in no hurry to get back to the station.

A couple of blocks away, a police car turns the corner and heads down our street. It moves cautiously through the mass of people and cars in front of Dan's house, and stops right in front of us. The passenger door opens and Angela jumps out.

"Steven!" she yells. "You're okay!" She runs up to me and gives me a bear hug that almost knocks me over.

"Yeah, I'm fine," I say, laughing at her exuberance.

She breaks the hug to look at me.

"How's Dan?"

"He's in stable condition," Kamimoto tells her. "They've taken him to Dominican Hospital."

"Great, let's go," she says, taking me by the hand. "I'll go get my car keys."

But Kamimoto blocks her path.

"Wait a minute. I need statements from both of you first."

"Later," Angela says, making a move to leave.

The inspector doesn't budge.

"Mr. Guerra is in surgery," he says. "There's no way you can see him now anyway."

"I can if I want to," is Angela's determined reply. Her change in attitude is almost palpable—Dan isn't just a consolation prize anymore. And all he had to do was take a bullet for her.

"I think Inspector Kamimoto is right," I tell her. "Even after Dan gets out of surgery, he'll be asleep for hours."

Angela lets go of my hand.

"I guess you're right," she says, recognizing the reality of the situation. "I can wait till we're done here."

"It won't take long," Kamimoto promises.

"Good," I say, rubbing my eyes and feeling more weary than ever. "But let's sit down for this. How about that bench over there?"

"That would be fine."

We walk across the street and settle down on the bench, which sits atop a low cliff overlooking the beach. The tide is crashing on the shore, in regular and deliberate intervals. It's a pleasant night; cool, but not chilly. A full moon shines overhead, and in the distance I see a couple walking hand-in-hand along the sand.

Kamimoto pulls out a notepad and a pen.

"Let's start with you, Steven. What can you tell me that I don't already know?"

It takes quite a while to recap the night's events: our conversation with Turner, Dan's shooting, our escape, the fight with Roger.

Angela interrupts my narrative only once, near the end.

"Don't forget about the spy in the police department."

"What spy?" Kamimoto asks abruptly.

"Turner bribed someone to steal the documents I gave you last week," I tell him.

"Are you sure?"

"That's what he said."

Without another word, Kamimoto jumps up and jogs to his car. He's back in less than five minutes.

"Everything is still there," he informs us. "And I've alerted the department. If anyone tries to remove those items, we'll get them."

Kamimoto returns to the business at hand, and asks Angela for her story of what happened. Her version is different from mine: she focuses on details I'd missed, and argues with me about the precise order of events. It's funny how two people can be in the same place at the same time, even go through the same experience, and walk away with different memories. On the main points, however, there's no disagreement.

Kamimoto plies us with a few more questions, and then closes his notepad.

"Hey!" I hear someone call out behind us.

I turn around to see Inspector Morrison moving hurriedly towards us, limping noticeably as he walks. There's a big bandage covering his nose, and he has dark circles under his eyes.

"Wow," Angela says, looking at his bandaged face. "Roger really knocked you around, didn't he?"

Morrison glances at me.

"Yeah," he says quickly.

Morrison immediately turns his attention to Kamimoto. Apparently, Turner has arrived at the police station and is already starting to make all kinds of noise. Kamimoto's boss wants to talk with him.

"So, it's begun," Kamimoto says. "Let's get going."

I extend my hand to him before he leaves.

"I want to thank you," I say awkwardly, "for everything you did."

"You're welcome," he replies simply as we shake hands.

He says goodbye to Angela and walks away with Morrison. I can hear them planning their next steps. For them, catching Turner is just the beginning. For me, thank God, it's the end.

Angela seems to feel the same way. I haven't seen her this tranquil in days. She has her legs drawn up under her chin, and is resting her head on her knees, gazing at the full moon hanging low over the ocean.

"It's beautiful, isn't it?" she says. "It's just so beautiful."

I can tell by her voice that she's crying. I put my arm around her.

"It sure is."

# Epilogue

I should probably mow the lawn today, maybe pull a few weeds too. But not now. I'm too comfortable, sitting in my favorite lounge chair and watching the breeze blow through the Chinese Elm.

This is my favorite time of the day, mid-morning, when it's warm but not too hot. So for the past couple of weeks I've indulged myself, coming out here after a late breakfast to finish my coffee and let my mind wander. I've been thinking about all the possible writing projects I could do—a novel, a biography, a work of history—any one of these would be interesting.

The ringing of the doorbell breaks my reverie. This is a rare event during the day. Occasionally a courier brings by a package, but mostly my solitude is undisturbed. I put on my sandals and go answer the door. I open it and am immediately embraced in a warm hug. I look down into a beautiful, smiling face.

"Angela! It's great to see you. Come on in."

She steps inside, and I close the door behind her.

"Can I get you something to drink?"

"Orange juice, if you've got it," she says, settling down on the sofa.

"Coming right up."

I go to the kitchen, pour a couple of glasses of juice, and carry them to the living room.

"You'll never believe who called me last week," I say to Angela as I hand her a glass.

"Who?"

"Joshua Phillips' parents."

"You're kidding. Why did they call?"

"They wanted to personally thank me for catching their son's killer."

"Of course," Angela says pensively. "Now that they know who killed Joshua and why, they can finally put him to rest."

"That's exactly what they said," I tell her.

She just nods.

"So what's going to happen to Cheetah?" she asks, switching to an easier topic.

"Joshua's parents have hired a lawyer. Once they prove that Cheetah belonged to Joshua, and therefore now belongs to them, they'll probably license it to some of the big software companies."

Angela looks surprised.

"What is there to prove? It's obvious Joshua invented the product."

"Nothing is obvious when billions of dollars are at stake. But I think the Phillips' will win this one. It's just going to take time."

Angela shakes her head.

"Joshua. Leticia. It's so sad."

We sit in silence, a quiet tribute to the dead.

But I'm not inclined to dwell on the past. I quickly move to another subject.

"How's the office these days?"

"Same as always," she answers, snapping out of her melancholy musings. "Except for one new bit of gossip. We've hired a new staff writer, and she spends a lot of time with Mitch in his office."

"Same old Mitch," I say with a grin. "Speaking of lust, is Matt still giving you trouble?"

"No, not since he started dating Catherine."

"Matt and Catherine?" I ask, laughing at the pairing. "Actually, they're perfect for each other."

"I couldn't agree more."

Angela proceeds to fill me in on all the doings at the office since I've been gone: who's new, who's gone, who's been promoted, etc. But ten minutes into our conversation, she pauses. She leans forward on the couch, a concerned look on her face.

"I talked with Mitch the other day," she says. "He asked me if I had any idea when you were planning to come back to work. I think he's getting impatient. I'm afraid if you don't get back soon, you may be out of a job. It's been almost two months, you know."

"Yeah, I know. Mitch called here last night, and gave me a polite ultimatum. He asked if he should start looking for someone to 'pick up the slack.'"

"What did you say?"

"You know, it's funny, if Mitch had called me two weeks ago, I would have promised to go back the next day. But that was before my trip up to Napa last week."

Angela gives me a sly look.

"You bought a winery, didn't you?" she asks.

"A vineyard, not a winery. But we plan to add a winery as soon as we've learned enough about making wine."

Angela reclines against the couch, a teasing sparkle in her eyes.

"So you're going to be a country squire, ruling over your own little estate in Napa," she says facetiously.

"Something like that."

"But I thought the winery was Michelle's idea. What are you going to do all day while your wife is out tending the vines?"

"I plan to get back to some long-neglected writing projects," I say simply.

Angela's face lights up.

"That's wonderful!" she says. "I can't wait to see what you write. I know it will be brilliant."

"I don't know about that, but at least I'll be doing what I really want."

"Well, I'm happy for you. What made you finally decide to take the plunge?"

"It just seemed like the right time," I respond. "Everything that happened—Leticia—the whole hellish experience—just got me to thinking. Life is short, why wait?"

"That's exactly what I think. In fact, that's why I came here today. I wanted to say goodbye."

I raise my eyebrows questioningly.

"I'm heading to Mexico for a while," Angela explains. "Dan has some relatives there he's always wanted to meet. He asked me along to translate."

"He doesn't speak Spanish?"

"Not a word. That's why he wants me to come."

"I think your translation skills are a secondary consideration."

Angela gives me a half-smile.

"I think you're right," she says.

"How's he feeling these days?" I ask. "I haven't seen him since your birthday party."

"He's healing fast. He's bummed because the doctors won't let him get any exercise yet, but he should be surfing again in another month."

"That's good to hear," I tell her. I stretch out in my chair. "How long are you going to be gone?"

"A few months, probably. But we'll be back for the trial. I promised Kamimoto I'd check in with him periodically."

"That long?" I ask. "What about your job?"

"I quit. I don't think *Digital Business*is really for me. Too dangerous," she says jokingly. And then she adds on a more serious note, "I need some time to figure out what I want to do with my life."

I nod in understanding.

"It sounds like we won't see each other for a while," I say, feeling sadder than I would have expected.

"No, I guess not," she replies quietly.

We look at each other for a moment, then Angela glances at her watch.

"I wish I could stay longer, but I've got to go," she says. "I left Dan waiting for me in his car."

"There's no reason for that. You should have brought him in with you."

"No, I asked him to wait there. I wanted to say goodbye alone."

I smile at her.

"I understand."

We stand up and walk to the entryway. I open the door and we step outside on to the front porch. I can see Dan, sitting in his jeep outside. He's reclining in his seat, his head tilted back on the headrest. I can't tell if he's asleep or listening to music. Angela has parked her red Mustang right behind the jeep.

"One last thing," she says to me. "I have a favor to ask of you."

"What's that?"

She pulls a set of keys from her purse.

"Take care of my car for me while I'm gone, will you?" she asks, dropping the keys into the palm of my hand. "You know, take it on long drives; don't let the engine sit idle for too long."

I look at the keys in my hand.

"Your brother's car," I say. "Are you sure?"

"I can't take it with me," she replies. "And you're the only one I trust with it."

She stands on her tiptoes and kisses me lightly on the cheek. "Take care."

"I will," I promise. "You too."

She nods silently, her eyes misting. Abruptly, she turns around and bounds down the front steps, and into Dan's jeep. They both wave and drive off.

I stand on the porch, transfixed, and watch them drive a couple of blocks and then turn a corner and disappear. I look down at the keys I'm holding.

What the hell.

I make my way quickly to the Mustang, slide the key in and open the door. I've been in this car a dozen times, but this is the first time I've been in a frame of mind to really notice it. The only word I can think of to describe it is . . . fun.

I put the key in the ignition and bring the engine to life. The gas tank is full. Nice touch, Angela.

Fifteen minutes later I'm heading south on the freeway. I've got the top down and the radio on. Turner's in jail, and no one is trying to kill me anymore. Life is good.

# About The Authors

Michael C. Perkins is the co-author of the best-selling book, *The Internet Bubble* He is also a founding editor of *Red Herring* the world's top technology business magazine.

Celia Núñez is a veteran of several Silicon Valley companies, including Apple computer. Her writing has appeared in *Red Herring, PC World,* and other national publications.

9 780595 097340

9 780595 097340